FICTION RIVER

UNNATURAL WORLDS

FICTION RIVER

Year One

Unnatural Worlds
Edited by Dean Wesley Smith & Kristine Kathryn Rusch

How to Save the World
Edited by John Helfers

Time Streams
Edited by Dean Wesley Smith

Christmas Ghosts
Edited by Kristine Grayson

Hex in the City
Edited by Kerrie L. Hughes

Moonscapes
Edited by Dean Wesley Smith

Crime (Special Edition)
Edited by Kristine Kathryn Rusch

FICTION RIVER

UNNATURAL WORLDS

Edited by

DEAN WESLEY SMITH & KRISTINE KATHRYN RUSCH

Fiction River: Unnatural Worlds

Copyright © 2013 by WMG Publishing
Published by WMG Publishing
www.wmgpublishing.com
Cover art © copyright 2013 by Rashevskaya/Dreamstime
Book and cover design copyright © 2013 by WMG Publishing
Cover design by Allyson Longueira/WMG Publishing
ISBN-13: 978-0-615-78350-5
ISBN-10: 0-615-78350-3

Contents

The Return to Publishing

Dean Wesley Smith

Twenty-six years ago, Kristine Kathryn Rusch and I started Pulp-house Publishing over my kitchen table in a small apartment in Eugene, Oregon. We had no idea what we were getting into. We decided we would be happy if we sold a few copies of the first issue of *Pulphouse: The Hardback Magazine*. We sold out.

After that, we embarked on a massive learning curve. We figured out how to publish an anthology series and start a publishing company all at the same time. We did it on the wages of a part-time bartender and part-time secretary, supplemented by our writing. We never really caught up.

When we finally shut Pulphouse down nine years later, we had a lot of debt and the knowledge that our little company had changed the science fiction and fantasy field. We had gone from that kitchen table to the ninth largest sf publisher in the nation.

We paid back the debt with our writing income, and vowed never to start a publishing company again. Actually, Kris vowed that. I continued to talk annually about starting a magazine, or editing an anthology, or starting another company.

Kris didn't agree until publishing changed. With the rise of e-books and print-on-demand, publishing became easy. Make that easier. It's still hard. We're established writers now, not beginners, and we have careers to maintain. We realized we couldn't let the publishing overwhelm the writing.

So we started Fiction River. We crowd-funded this project on Kickstarter in August of 2012. We figured if we couldn't meet our Kickstarter goal, then there wasn't enough interest in Fiction River to proceed.

We met our goal within the first week. We more than doubled our fundraising goal. The response exceeded our expectations. We're doing this project because of 314 people who chose to take a risk with us, and even more who couldn't afford to pledge but spread the word. Thank you, everyone!

We're hands-on editing some of the volumes, but others we're giving to our most trusted editorial friends. We act as the series editors, reading everything that comes in, but the other voices add a perspective that we would never get on our own.

This makes Fiction River diverse. The only thing we can promise is high-quality fiction. The genres will change. The focus of the anthologies will change. But the stories will always be the best we can find.

Because *Unnatural Worlds* is the debut volume, Kris and I had to edit it. We couldn't wait for a later volume. We edited it together, which led to some interesting moments, as Kris will explain in her editorial.

We hope you enjoy the debut volume of Fiction River. We had a lot of fun putting it together. And we plan to give you a lot of great reading in the future.

—*Dean Wesley Smith*
Lincoln City, Oregon
March 10, 2013

So I Lied

Kristine Kathryn Rusch

Writers lie for a living. Lawrence Block acknowledged that when he called one of his how-to-write books *Telling Lies For Fun and Profit*. Only when I lied, I wasn't lying to you folks.

I was lying to me.

Here's the lie. For fifteen years now, I have said I would never edit again. I said this for two very good reasons: 1) I never ever ever ever wanted to work for anyone else again, especially as an editor; and 2) I wasn't going to start another publishing company. I was done with all that owning-a-business nonsense.

I could not foresee the rise of electronic books, print-on-demand publishing, and crowdfunding. I had no idea that the publishing world would change so drastically that I could jump back into editing as my own boss without a huge capital outlay.

I am still surprised by this. Stunned, actually.

I did know one thing: I was never going to read slush again, and I will keep that promise to myself. I spent ten years in the slush-reading trenches. My time there is done.

So when Dean Wesley Smith and I set up Fiction River, we decided that we would ask our favorite writers to write stories for us. We have a lot of favorite writers, many of whom you haven't heard of. That's because we have taught business courses for writers since the late 1990s. We've seen a lot of fantastic writers come into our workshops, and write a lot of fantastic stories.

Some of those fantastic writers got picked up by traditional publishers. Other fantastic writers didn't get their work picked up because it slipped between the cracks or because it was a bit too daring.

What most people don't remember is that the first magazine/anthology series we ever did, *Pulphouse: The Hardback Magazine*, had a subtitle. It was *A Dangerous Magazine*. We published fiction that slipped through the cracks, fiction that many other publishers wouldn't touch.

In 1991, I left the magazine side of Pulphouse to edit *The Magazine of Fantasy & Science Fiction*. *F&SF* had (and has) a different mission: it needed to reach a broader base of subscribers. Sometimes I could slip in a dangerous story, but mostly I published stories by spectacular writers who wrote down the center of the sf/f field.

I hadn't realized how much I missed dangerous until we started editing Fiction River. This volume covers a broad range of the fantasy genre. Future volumes include hard science fiction, time travel, urban fantasy, mystery, and romance. We're not sticking to one genre nor are we sticking to one voice.

With that in mind, Dean and I decided to co-edit *Unnatural Worlds*. We wanted a diverse volume and what better way to do that than to have two editors. We agree on most things, but we disagree sometimes on what makes a story work.

Some of my favorites in the volume aren't Dean's favorites, and some of his aren't mine. Yet the volume all works together as a cohesive whole.

We also edited each other. I argued with him for weeks about my story, "Shadow Side." I kept asking if he wanted something else. He threatened to go into my computer files and drag out "Shadow Side" himself.

I asked him for a Poker Boy story. Dean couldn't understand my interest. Poker Boy is one of my favorite all-time characters.

If I could publish a Poker Boy story in every anthology I edit, I would. I know Dean would dig in his heels at that. So I am pleased that I managed to get one Poker Boy story out of him for the first volume of Fiction River.

The other stories in the volume run a range of emotions and subgenres.

We start with Devon Monk's "Life Between Dreams." Devon, best known for her Allie Beckstrom urban fantasy series, knows how to straddle worlds. Since we're straddling worlds with *Unnatural Worlds*, we figured Devon's marvelous short story was the perfect place to start.

Devon's story blurs the boundaries between fiction and reality. Ray Vukcevich explodes those boundaries. He always has. The great thing about Ray's writing is that he creates a world that no one else could ever invent. Dean calls Ray's world "Planet Ray" and I can't think of a better description. Ray is, in my opinion, one of the best and most underrated writers in the United States. "Finally Family" should show you why Dean and I both love his work so much.

I have yet to read an Esther M. Friesner story that I didn't like. She has written everything from heartbreaking science fiction to historical young adult fiction, and she makes it all look easy. When we asked Esther for a story, we had no idea what we'd get. She provides us with yet another new world, one that is uniquely Esther (but does continue, for a short time anyway, our bug-oriented theme).

"True Calling" marks Irette Y. Patterson's first fantasy publication, but I can guarantee it won't be her last. Set in our world only with magic (and cake!), Irette reminds us that the romance genre has taken on the word "paranormal" for a reason—and that reason isn't just vampires. It's also the gentle, heartwarming side of the genre that most of the traditional magazines dismiss, and which readers love so well.

Kellen Knolan's "A Taste of *Joie de Vivre*" is also a first short story sale, although Kellen has published two novels under a different name. Like Ray, Kellen is an original, and his perspective is truly his own. Someday we hope to say that Fiction River provided the first glimmer of Planet Kellen.

Annie Reed has been one of my favorite writers since I first encountered her work at one of our workshops. She has sold a lot of short fiction to anthologies and magazines, but I have a special place in my heart for her Diz and Dee detective stories. When she submitted "Here, Kitty Kitty," I didn't tell Dean how much I love the Diz and Dee stories. I knew he hadn't read one before, so I let him be the final arbiter. He loved this as much as I do. Diz and Dee give us a much-needed dose of urban fantasy and also one really hot elf.

We follow the hot elf with Poker Boy. (You'll see why when you read those two stories.) Then we give you my much more serious "Shadow Side." All three stories—from "Here, Kitty Kitty" to "Shadow Side"—follow three very different investigators, investigating three very different things.

Leah Cutter's story has no investigator, just one marvelously courageous young girl, who takes an important personal stand. I first read this story in June, and like all great fiction, it has become a cherished memory. After you read "Sisters," you'll never look at ceremonies the same again.

When we asked Richard Bowes for a story, I expected something like the New York tales he used to write for me at *F&SF*. Instead, he sent what seems like a traditional fantasy tale, with a witch and enchanted characters. But in typical Rick Bowes' fashion, he takes an expected world and makes it unexpected, keeping all of that emotion that makes Rick Bowes's fiction so very powerful.

Jane Yolen's "Dog Boy Remembers" took my breath away when I read it. The story seems so simple and yet it's not simple at all. Jane has long carved out a unique place in the fantasy genre, and no fantasy volume would be complete without her work. You'll remember Dog Boy long after you close this book.

David Farland wrote a Runelords story just for us. Runelords is parallel worlds fiction masquerading as epic fantasy. Epic fantasy is hard to write in the short form, but Dave, whose original incarnation was award-winning short fiction writer Dave Wolverton, is more than up to the task. "Barbarians" is a powerful tale that will inspire some of you to read the Runelords saga and remind the rest of you why you read it in the first place.

The breadth of the stories here astonish me. What astonishes me even more is that all of these authors were willing to work with us on our return to editing, despite other deadlines and commitments. We're lucky to have such a fantastic group of writers and the fruits of their incredible imaginations.

The worlds here might be unnatural, but they're also quite impressive. And I think Devon's title says it best. I feel as if this volume shows us the life between dreams.

—*Kristine Kathryn Rusch*
Lincoln City, Oregon
March 11, 2013

Readers love Devon Monk's Allie Beckstrom urban fantasy series and her Age of Steam steampunk series, but our favorite remains her short stories. You can find some of her best in the 2010 collection from Fairwood Press, A Cup of Normal. *She has a new fantasy series premiering soon called Broken Magic. "A Life Between Dreams" isn't part of any of those series, however.*

Devon says this was "one of those rare stories that sort of fell off my finger-tips. I had recently ended a nine-book series and found myself thinking about life's many endings and beginnings and all the small and large sacrifices and choices we make between them."

Endings and beginnings. How appropriate for the first volume of the Fiction River series.

Life Between Dreams
Devon Monk

Mary Still dropped the screwdriver back into the empty coffee can next to the jar of Moebius clock oil, and held her breath. From just beyond the open door of the garage she heard the distinct glassy *tink* of this reality colliding with another. Someone, or something, was crossing the boundary.

The sound could be nothing, just the random scrape and rattle of the joined universes steering a little too wide around the corners.

It could be the bosses, who said they'd be here in exactly one hour to see that the outpost was secure and to reassign her a new partner if Tom didn't return.

Or it could be Tom.

She hoped it was Tom. But she hadn't seen her partner for six months now, not since the job they'd almost failed in East London with the dreamer kid. She'd walked away from that with a much finer appreciation for the rules of dispelling ter-rors and imaginings.

Tom had just walked away.

She picked up a tire iron and a wooden cross, and moved back from the nineteenth century Regina music box she'd been restoring, even though she had yet to find a comb to make it sing. No need to lose paying customers just because she had to fight nightmare creatures from another dimension, or worse, her bosses.

She strolled up to the door and opened it. Being quiet and sneaky around terrors and imaginings never worked. Walls didn't stop them, doors didn't hold them back, and stealth was a waste of time.

Still, she hesitated there in the cool shadow of the garage and stared out at the Nevada sunlight pouring over the rocks and orange dirt in front of her shop. Highway 90 lay like a black snake warming itself over the arid land, curving down out of Goldfield up north and missing her place by an eighth of a mile or so.

Wind hissed through the sage brush and set the insects buzzing.

A man stepped up to the front porch of her shop.

He was medium build, brushing six feet tall and wore a black wool coat that reached almost to his knees, his jeans tucked into the top of hunting boots. His dark hair was brushed up and away from his face, even though it was several inches too long to hold the style, and he was in need of a shave.

Hands shoved in his coat pockets, he paused to read the sign above her entryway: *Still Curious Antique Restoration.*

"You put my name on the sign?" he asked.

"Yes," she said, not lowering cross or bar yet. "Good to see you, Tom. You owe me half a year's overhead on the place."

He turned his head, tipped down his sunglasses. "Good to see you too, Mary."

She swallowed against a mix of anger and relief that rushed through her. He still had a soul behind those eyes. He was still human. That was good. Very good.

"Are you going to put your sticks down yet?" He gave a slight nod toward the cross and crowbar.

"No. But you might as well go inside. The coffee should be done brewing."

He hesitated. Maybe he didn't want her at his back. She was angry, and he was pretty good at reading her emotions even though no one else ever was.

"Are you worried I'm going to knock you out when you're not looking?" she asked as she strode across the dirt, her boots kicking up clouds of cinnamon dust.

"It crossed my mind."

"You'd deserve it."

"Yes," he said, "I would."

And that was that. They were partners again. Everyone got their one time out, their one time to break away from the job and never come back. No one would chase them down if they decided to just quit.

Coming back meant the next unapproved time off would be in a coffin.

"That was your one chance, you know," she said as they stepped into the darker, but not much cooler, shop.

The place was filled with rare items she'd restored through normal, and inter-dimensional means. Shelves and corners were stacked with antiques and other valuables. Need a bellows for your harmonium or a Tiffany lamp base plate? She'd find it in this world, or cross a few boundaries and find one that was still intact in an alternate dimension.

The bosses didn't love the idea of trans-dimensional Dumpster diving, but a girl had to make ends meet between gigs of saving the world.

"To get away?" He paused to pick up a crystal goblet and ran his thumb over the water-smooth glass. He put it down, then briefly

11

brushed his fingers over the velvet of the case it was settled in. "I know."

She followed him, watching how he walked: subtle limp on the right, boots landing just a little too heavily on the floorboards, left arm pressed against his side. He'd been hurt, maybe still was, and he was exhausted. Would the bosses notice? Of course they would, they noticed everything.

"Where've you been, Curious?" she asked after they'd left the antique shop behind and pushed open the door that only unlocked for them.

"Over the edges," he said.

They were through the living room that she rarely used, and finally in the very modern, very well-stocked kitchen.

The warm, home-and-comfort smell of brewed coffee softened the stark white and chrome of the place. If she'd had a choice, the kitchen wouldn't look like a laboratory outfitted by Ikea. But this wasn't so much her home, as an outpost.

"Not where I'd go to get my head together," she said.

He nodded and dragged fingertips across the counter top as he walked to the coffee pot.

She didn't blame him for wanting to touch everything. Running off into dimensions that are almost exact duplicates of your world, but never quite right, meant that once you got home, you wanted to hug it, roll in it, and press reality tight against you.

Hold the people there tightly too.

"That's not why I left." He poured coffee in one white china cup. "Not to get my head together." He filled a matching cup, retrieved the cream and watched the pure white muddle the darkness as he poured.

"All right. Why?"

He turned with the coffees in his hands. "You'll want to be sitting for this, Still."

She rolled her eyes and plunked down in a chrome and white chair next to the chrome and white table.

He placed her cup on the table in front of her as if afraid to actually touch her yet, then held his cup under his nose and inhaled. His eyes closed and the tension he'd been trying to hide drifted away, leaving his face in the meditative expression of peace.

If touch in the home dimension was good, food was even better. And sex...well, it was worth coming home for.

He finally took a drink and made a pleased sound in the back of his throat. When he opened his eyes again, he gave her that smile she'd fallen for too many times, then leaned back against the counter.

She noted he kept most his weight off his right foot.

"You remember our last job?" he asked.

"Hard to forget almost dying."

"And the kid there in East London?"

"Harder to forget the boy with terrors so strong he could have ended this dimension."

She said it easy, flat, but it had been the most frightening job of her life. They'd nearly not made it back from fighting the monsters that kid had dreamed up. His terrors had crossed into twelve dimensions before they could stop them, and had done permanent damage to this reality too.

That earthquake and tsunami? Yeah, that was the East London kid dreamer.

"I went back to see him."

She raised an eyebrow. "That's a little outside protocol." It was a lot outside of protocol.

"He started dreaming again."

It happened sometimes. They could do certain things to make sure terrors and imaginings didn't plague people, but occasionally it wasn't enough. And when that happened, protocol said they had to remove the person from their home reality, drag them out to a dimension so distant, their terrors were weakened and unable to affect any reality.

They became a name on a missing person report, or sometimes were replaced with a near-dimension version of themselves.

"Why didn't you call me? I could have helped."

"I didn't relocate him out across edges."

"So you killed him."

"No."

Her stomach clenched. "What did you do? It's relocate or kill, Tom. There isn't any other option."

The look on his face said that there was.

"What did you do to him, Curious?"

"I made a deal."

"With him?"

"With his terrors."

A second or two ticked by while she tried to process that. "What?"

"I put the kid down into a deep sleep and called them out. Then I told them I wouldn't destroy them, wouldn't hunt them if we could come to an understanding."

"So you destroyed them."

"No. We came to an understanding."

Crazy. No one negotiated with imaginaries. No one made deals with monsters.

Except, apparently, her partner.

"What deal?"

"They'd leave the kid. Empty out completely. And take me instead."

"And you believed them? Believed the promise of monsters? Why?" She had a hard time keeping her voice down. "Why would you do such a stupid, dangerous thing?"

"He's my son."

14

Mary Still closed her mouth and shook her head, trying to make sense of what he was saying. They were partners, yes. They'd had sex. But they'd never admitted they were in love.

"When?" she said quietly. "He must be six or seven?"

"He's six. I met his mother in France, spring that year," he added.

Seven years ago. They'd just been assigned this warden outpost that summer, met for the first time at the briefing before taking up their new assignment as partners.

"How long have you known?"

He took another drink of coffee, the tension folding the corners of his eyes and drawing lines between his eyebrows. "Figured it out six months ago. When he almost killed us."

"Do you want to be in his life?" she asked.

"His mother married a couple months after we met. He already has a father who thinks he's his own. I was just her last chance fling."

"You know this is bad," she said.

"I know."

"You know we can't have children. That if we do—"

"—they'll become conduits for terrors and imaginings across multi-realities."

No wonder the kid was so strong. He had warden blood in him. "He's a trans-dimensional beacon," she said. "Every terror in the known realities can find him."

"Me," Curious replied. "Every terror in the known realities can find me now."

"Then why haven't they?"

"They have." He finished his coffee. "I have the bruises and broken bones to prove it."

"Why haven't they found you now, here?"

He twisted, winced when he couldn't quite reach the counter to rest his cup there. "Well, I haven't slept in three days, and I haven't stayed in one reality for more than an hour or two."

"So you're running."

"I'm finding an answer to my problem."

"What answer?"

"You."

"No," she said.

"No? I haven't even asked you anything yet."

"No, I will not kill your son, and no, I will not kill you."

He held her gaze. He was good at reading her emotions. It should be loud and clear just how serious she was.

"Killing me," he said slowly, "would make this an easy clean-up, an easy ending."

"No," Still said again. "So what's plan B?"

"Who says I have a plan B?"

"Because, Curious, you always have a plan B."

"All right. I turn myself in to the bosses, tell them everything."

"Who will kill you *and* the kid just to be safe," she said. "No. Next. Plan C."

He lifted his hands and pressed his thumb knuckles into the inside corner of his eyes. His hands shook. "Plan C," he said. "I'm open for suggestions."

"To begin with, you get some sleep."

"No," he said.

"And I'll call Horse."

Curious pulled his hands away from his face. "God, no. Horse? What are you thinking?"

"I'm thinking you need sleep and Horse and I can handle whatever comes crawling out of or across reality while you do it. We'll take care of it before the bosses show up."

"That's not a solution."

"Yes, it is. It's a short-term solution. Once you get some sleep, we'll work on a long-term solution."

"Horse owes me money," he grumbled.

"I'll be sure to tell him that while he's saving the world from you. Go."

He started off to the bedrooms, and she pulled her phone from her pocket and dialed the nearest warden in this reality, Robert Horse.

"Mary Still, it's been some time," Horse said in a voice as broad as his shoulders. "You ready to switch out partners and leave Curious behind?"

"Hi, Horse," she said. "I need some help. Can you get over to the shop in the next ten minutes or so?"

Horse was stationed in Idaho, somewhere up near the border with Canada. Distance wasn't that much of a problem for wardens. After all, they had to locate and get to outbreaks of terrors and crossovers from other dimensions as quickly as possible.

Luckily, once you knew the differences and variances of other dimensions, it wasn't difficult to map a route that could get you from any place on earth to another in about fifteen minutes.

"Should I bring my cross and guns?"

"Would you leave them behind if I told you to?"

"No. I'll be there in ten. You seen Curious lately?"

"Yeah, that's my problem."

Horse was quiet a second. "He still got a soul?"

"Yes."

She could hear his exhalation of relief.

"Well, then how bad can it be?"

"Just come soon, okay?" She thumbed off the phone.

The sound of the shower turning on told her Curious was going to scrub the grit of other realities off before crawling into bed. Good. That would give her five minutes.

And five minutes was all she needed.

Mary picked up the cross she'd left on the table and stuck it in the back pocket of her jeans. Her gun was strapped against her ribs where she always carried it.

It was early March, and a Wednesday—not exactly high tourist season—but just in case, she walked back to the shop, turned the sign to "Closed," locked the door, and dimmed the lights.

She had a little boy to see.

Mary Still set her feet and took a deep breath. Walking into other dimensions took some getting used to. Without a lodestone, a person was doomed to be lost, to never quite know if they were headed toward or away from their home reality. She placed the palm of her right hand over the lodestone she wore on a leather thong around her neck, and with her left hand tapped her fingers in the sequence that would trigger the shift in dimension.

Then she started walking. Right through the wall of her shop that was a wall of an antique store, a gas station, a grocery store, a hospital, then wasn't even a wall any more, each step taking her miles or hundreds of miles, across hills in some dimensions, rivers in others, and strange bottomless canyons filled with swirling stars.

She knew the shortcut to London, and took it until she was walking down a street, rain and sudden, biting cold making her wish she'd thought to wear a coat or even long sleeves.

Brown brick buildings stacked up on either side of her, wooden fences in various states of paint and disrepair soldiering along the alleyway as she headed to the apartment where the East London kid dreamer was not dreaming.

A tap of her fingers and she sidestepped this reality until she found one where the door was open, then entered the third apartment from the left, top floor, into a cluttered but tidy home.

She didn't want to be seen, so she stayed just on the edge of where her home reality and the next met. Dogs and cats and other animals would sense her here, but most humans wouldn't.

The East London kid dreamer was in his bedroom, sitting on the floor, surrounded by action figures and cars. He had Curious's mop of dark hair, but his eyes were brown in a cherubic, freckled face.

Mary paced a circle around him, looking for the glow that signified someone plagued by the terrors and imaginings. This kid had been practically on fire when she and Curious had found him six months ago caught in the paralysis of nightmares and terrors. But now—nothing.

He had that slightly elevated aura that all kids under the age of thirteen carried. No one, not even the bosses, would suspect that he was anything more than a normal kid.

How the hell had Curious pulled that off? You couldn't undream a person.

She knelt in front of the boy so she could see his face more clearly.

He looked up as if he'd heard a sound. And that's when she saw it. Curious had somehow erased the kid's ability to even have a nightmare. Oh, he might have a bad dream, but the deep horrors that called terrors and imaginings into the world would simply not be possible.

She didn't know where her partner had learned that, but it sure wasn't in the rule book. Great. If the bosses found out about this—any of it—Curious would be dead. The only good thing to come out of it was that the terrors would never find the kid again.

"Good luck kiddo," she whispered.

His gaze almost settled on her. He smiled and she felt something inside her break. He looked so much like Tom.

Mary made it back to the shop and into her home dimension before Horse arrived. Curious was out of the shower, so she went down to his bedroom and knocked softly on the door.

"You awake?"

"Are there monsters trying to eat your face?" His reply was muffled.

"No," she said.

"There ya go."

She stepped into the room. He was lying in bed, under just the top cover, his arm draped over his eyes.

"I looked in on the kid."

He didn't move his arm. Didn't say anything for a moment or two. She sat in the chair next to the bed, suddenly tired and wishing she could crawl under the covers with him to hold him against her, solid and real.

"Why?" he asked.

"I wanted to see how you did it. And I wanted...wanted to see the only kid—in any reality— we can call our own."

He swallowed hard, then stretched his other arm out across the bed toward her, his hand open.

She pressed her palm into his, lacing his fingers. His entire body tightened a little and he exhaled a held breath. She must be the first real person he'd touched in awhile. Maybe in six months.

"We can't ever see him again," she said softly.

"I know."

"He'll never know you."

"I know. I'm sorry, Mary. To put you in this mess. To bring it here for you to clean up."

"I can handle it."

He finally dragged his arm away from his eyes and turned his head to look at her. She'd never seen him so deeply tired. "You shouldn't have to."

"We're partners, Curious," she said. "All the way to the end."

"If I die..." he started.

"No," she said. Then, to the stubborn set of his jaw that told her he wasn't going to let it go that easily: "You owe me, okay? Secluded tropical beach—real world— private chef, and no work for a week."

That got a smile out of him. "Seriously? A week? Do you think I can pull off the impossible?"

"Yes."

The distinctly glass *tink* of realities being crossed rang out from just beyond the door, interrupting whatever it was Curious had been about to say.

"Heard you two were having some trouble," Horse said. "Didn't expect it to be in the bedroom. Although it's not that big of a surprise."

Curious scowled. Mary gave his hand a squeeze before letting go and standing to face the warden.

Horse was a tall, rangy man with overly prominent cheekbones and hard edges everywhere else. He wore his long white hair tied back in a single braid beneath a gray cowboy hat that didn't exactly match his dockers and Mr. Roger's green zip up sweater. He was anywhere between ninety and a hundred-and-three, which was saying something since the life expectancy of most wardens hovered closer to the fifty marker.

"Thanks for coming, Horse," Mary said. "We owe you."

That was enough to stop Horse mid-step. "Before I've done anything? It must be bad."

"It is," she said. "Curious took on a dreamer's terrors."

Horse laughed. It was loud enough to cover most of the swearing Curious set off into. Mary waited for the old guy to get his breath back.

"My boy, you are a cracker. Let me get a look at you." He crossed over to the foot of the bed and stared down at Curious, who had propped up to a sitting position and was glaring at him.

All the laughter drained from Horse's face. "Dreamer light. I should turn you in for this, Tom. You too, Mary, for not reporting him."

"Help us or leave," Mary said evenly.

Horse made his decision with a nod. "You, personally, are indebted to me, Tom Curious."

"If you do what Mary says, yes," Tom said.

"And I don't owe you money from that damn poker game any more."

Curious gritted his teeth. "Fine."

"Good," Mary said before the agreement went sour. "Time for you to sleep, Curious. Do you need any help?"

He shifted down to lie flat on his back. "I could sleep through the end of the world."

"Let's hope you don't have to," Mary said.

Curious closed his eyes. It didn't take more than three breaths before he was out.

"You know who this dreamer is?" Horse asked.

"No."

"If you're lying to me, Still..."

"I'm not."

That was the one advantage to people not reading her well. She could get away with a lot of falsehood if necessary.

"I always thought that boy was a little too unstable for the job," Horse said.

"He's my partner, Horse. I'll stand by him until the end."

"Of course you will, Mary. Of course you will."

The terrors arrived, slipping through the walls, oozing through the floor, dropping from the ceiling. They crawled out of Curious while he screamed.

Mary pulled her gun.

"Remember to cross the t's and dot the i's," Horse said, drawing his own weapons.

"I always do."

They waded into the terrors, brandishing crosses. It took faith or will power to banish the terrors, and while any religious or focusing symbol would do, Mary preferred the cross. The only thing that stopped the imaginings were silver-coated bullets, but the smallest bullet would do, therefore the term: dot the i's.

Solid creatures with strange assortments of limbs and skins and mouths, with too many eyes, or none at all, launched at them, hungry to destroy. They sizzled to dust and smoke at the slightest brush of a cross, and faded to screams when the silver bullets struck true.

Mary wasn't sure if Horse would be able to keep up, but the old guy worked tirelessly, shifting over edges and back to keep the outbreak contained in this one room and then holding here while Mary did the same.

Dozens and dozens of beasts shuddered into existence. So many, she almost lost one on a simple shift. There were too many for her and Horse to handle. And the bosses would be here in minutes.

She didn't know when Curious had stopped screaming, but when he stood at her side, wearing pajama pants and a T-shirt, gun in his hand, she realized he'd been awake and on his feet for awhile. He shouldn't be able to do that. No dreamer woke up until the terrors and imaginings were gone. But he wasn't just a dreamer. He was a warden.

It felt like it took them three sweaty hours to dispatch the remaining monsters, but only fifteen minutes passed. Then it was suddenly very, very quiet in the room.

"That everything you got, boy?" Horse panted and wiped sweat off his face with his forearm. "Cause I could do this all day."

Nothing but the dark ichor and dust of the beasts remained. There was no time to clean it up now.

Curious holstered his gun. "How long before the bosses arrive?"

"About five minutes," Mary said.

"Bosses?" Horse said. "What are you two doing standing around? Curious, get dressed—a suit and tie. You too, Still. And a little lipstick wouldn't hurt."

She'd punch him for that comment later.

Mary ran to her room, scrubbed her hands, face, and arms, brushed the dust out of her hair, then slipped into a tailored dark green suit and fashionable boots. She pulled her hair up with pins. And yes, quickly applied lipstick and some mascara.

It took her all of three minutes. By the time she was striding into the kitchen, Curious and Horse were there waiting.

Horse had cleaned up and looked completely unfazed by today's events as he made himself a sandwich.

Curious wore a charcoal gray suit, and had shaved. His blue eyes no longer looked so tired, nor haunted, though there was still a slight glow of something like dreaming around him. It was faint enough, the bosses might overlook it. Especially since there just was no reason to suspect a warden of dreaming.

"Do you think we can do this?" she asked.

"We'll be fine," he said. "But you'd better do the talking."

Mary nodded. She made a cup of tea to keep busy.

The leaves had steeped for less than a minute when the *tink* of scraping realities snapped in the kitchen.

Mary would have known the bosses had arrived even without the sound. She always sensed them the way one does a predator hidden in the shadows. A cold chill slipped down her spine and her heartbeat picked up.

She carefully hid her fear behind an unbreakable wall of calm, and turned.

"Good day, sirs," she said. "Welcome to post four thirteen, we are prepared for inspection."

Three bosses stood in the room—all men in their mid-sixties, and all in black suits and long black jackets. The man in the front was darker skinned than the rest and taller, while the man to his left was heavy, and finally, the man to his right was albino-pale. They wore sunglasses, which they removed in unison.

She wondered if they practiced that move, or if they were just naturally creepy.

Mary was careful not to allow any change in her expression. Everything was riding on this. Riding on her ability to lie straight to the boss's faces—which she had never done before.

Their eyes were hard, clever, and completely soulless. Somewhere in the fifty plus years of serving as wardens, these men had lost that irreparable thing that made them human.

Mary was staring into her future, the future of every warden.

Even Horse put his sandwich down and stood, straight and attentive. Curious at her left clasped his hands behind his back, breathing easily like he wasn't still sporting injuries and hadn't just had an army of terrors and imaginings use his head for a subway tunnel.

"There were terrors and imaginings here," the tall man in the front said.

"Yes," Mary said. Short answers meant less of an opportunity for them to sense the lie.

"Explain."

"They followed Curious when he came back today." Mostly true.

"Where was warden Curious?" The heavier boss to the left asked in the same dead monotone as the first.

"He was across edges."

"Why?"

"He—"

"No," the first boss said. "Tell us, Warden Curious. Why were you gone six months across edges?"

Oh God. This was it. Curious might be many things—amazing and frustrating things—but he was not a good liar.

"I was looking for something," he said. "Looking for a solution to a problem."

"What problem?"

Mary stayed outwardly calm, but her mind was racing. Should they run? Wardens with souls are fast but the bosses without souls could cross edges even faster and had eyes everywhere.

Fight? They couldn't kill the bosses—well, technically, they could, but it would be immediately sensed by the other bosses down the link they shared, and then she, Curious, and Horse would all be dead.

"I was looking for this." Curious put his hand in his suit pocket and pulled out a beautiful steel music box comb.

Mary gasped. "That's the comb I need for the Regina I'm fixing."

"I know." Curious chanced a glance away from the bosses to throw her a smile.

"You didn't tell me."

"Well, it was a surprise."

"Enough," the heavier boss said. "We do not condone such actions, but as it has caused no hardship across realities and provides a cover for operating the outpost, we will not discipline you for such."

"Thank you, sirs," Curious said.

"You have also returned in time to continue as warden of outpost four thirteen," the first boss said. "Do you accept your duty from this day onward?"

Mary held her breath, waiting for his reply.

"Yes, sir, I do," Curious said.

"Then it shall be so." The boss turned his drill-point gaze to Mary. "Are your records in order?"

She nodded, trying not to show her relief. They weren't out of the fire yet. "Yes, sir. Except for the recent job, which I will input after this inspection."

"Very well. Why are you here, Warden Horse?"

"Ms. Still asked me over," Horse said smoothly. "I stayed to settle a monetary debt between Mr. Curious and myself. And when the t's and i's showed up, I lent a hand, as is protocol."

None of that was a lie. None of it was the full truth either. But Horse delivered it with such easy authority that Mary made a note to pay more attention to what the old man said in the future.

"We will inspect the outpost for stability," the second boss said.

The bosses spent the next half hour looking through the living areas, then the antique shop, and finally strode out to the garage where Mary had been working on the old music box just an hour ago.

Curious handed her the steel comb and she set it carefully on a piece of soft cloth next to the box. The bosses' sharp eyes missed no detail. They could see the comb was indeed the item she was missing.

"Our inspection is complete," the first boss said.

Mary tried to dampen the hope that they might have made it through this safe, together, and still partners. Hope was dangerous and made a person sloppy.

They followed the bosses out of the garage. Once they reached sunlight, the bosses paused.

"Is there anything else?" Mary asked.

"Everything is as it should be," the first boss said.

"I agree," the second boss said.

Mary waited for the third boss to speak. He hadn't said anything this entire time. Now he studied them, and smiled enough to show teeth.

It was a cold expression—a wolf baring fangs for the kill.

"Why do you glow, warden Curious?" He said it softly, but it stopped them all as surely as an explosion.

"What do you mean, sir?" Curious said.

Mary lifted her hand toward her lodestone. She might be able to grab Curious and get them both off-reality faster than the bosses would follow. Might.

"You glow as if you dream," the third boss said again. "But a warden never dreams."

Curious shut his mouth and glared at the bosses.

This wasn't good. Wasn't good at all. There was no half-truth to hide this, no way to deny what he had done.

"It's my fault," Mary said.

Three soulless gazes shifted to her.

"Nonsense," Horse said.

"Horse," Mary warned.

The old guy was still behind them, and planted his hand on both of their shoulders. Mary was going to regret breaking his arms across edges when she slid out of here, but he should know better than to try and keep them pinned for the bosses to kill.

"It's not *just* your fault," Horse said cheerfully.

"Bad decision," Curious said.

"It is both of their fault," Horse said a little louder, "because they refuse to admit it to each other."

Mary frowned. Curious didn't take his eyes off the bosses, but she could tell he didn't know where Horse was going with this either.

"Explain," the third boss said.

"They're in love," Horse said. "Been dancing around it for months now. It's what sent Tom out across edges for that music box bit, and what made Mary hold on until the last minute for him to come home."

"Love?" the third boss sneered.

"You know how it messes with the sight, Glass," Horse said. "Throws off light that looks like dreamer light. And, beg your pardon, but you bosses are color-blind when it comes to the subtleties between love and dream."

Had he seriously just insulted the bosses and called one of them by name?

Mary held her breath, fingers poised to tap a sequence to get them out fast.

"I see." The third boss, Glass, seemed disappointed. "Is this true? You are in love?"

"I—," Curious started.

"Yes," Mary interrupted. She didn't know if it were true or not, but it didn't sound like a lie. Didn't feel like one either.

The bosses held her gaze for a long, painful moment. Then they put sunglasses over their eyes again, turned, and walked toward the highway.

"We do not condone love," the first boss said.

"But as long as it does not interfere with your jobs, warden Curious, warden Still, we will not forbid it," the second boss said.

"Yet." That was from Glass.

The bosses tapped fingers, cracked reality, and were gone.

Mary spun to face Horse. "How did you know they'd fall for that?"

His eyebrows hitched up. "I am an old man, Mary. There's very little in this world I don't know. You ought to keep that in mind. Now, if you'll excuse me, I'm going to go finish my sandwich."

He strolled off to the house, whistling a show tune.

Mary stared after Horse and waited for her heart to stop racing. They had survived.

"So we don't have another inspection for six months," she said. "By then we should be able to figure out a long-term solution for this dream thing you have going."

"Mary?"

She turned at Curious's quiet tone.

He was waiting, every line in his body tense with doubt. Maybe with hope too; dangerous, dangerous hope. "Were you telling the truth? About us being in love?"

She could lie to him. It would make everything easier. But they were partners. They were in this together.

"I think I was, yes."

He nodded and looked down at his boots. When he looked back up, he gave her that smile that turned her inside out. "So where do we go from here?"

"Anywhere we want to," she said. "Together."

"To the end." He held his hand out to her.

"To the end," she agreed.

She took his hand and held tightly to him as they walked beneath the antique shop sign above trans-dimensional outpost four thirteen, to start their life together again.

Ray Vukcevich won't say exactly what inspired "Finally Family," but evidence points to the local crows. "I bet this story came from me looking out the big windows at the lawn below," he writes, "and my crows scratching around for breakfast. When I walk out there on the way to the post office, they all look around like oh, it's just him again. While I'm gone, they flutter up into the trees above my parking space and decorate my car. I know they do that on purpose just to demonstrate who is really in charge."

Whoever might be in charge, let's hope they provide more inspiration for Ray, whose latest collection, Boarding Instructions, *recently appeared from Fairwood Press. His other books include* Meet Me in the Moon Room *and* The Man of Maybe Half-a-Dozen Faces.

Finally Family

Ray Vukcevich

1

Bug Boy

Bug Boy couldn't tell them that he was really a Bulgarian and had been blown into Japan by the crows during the earthquake in Pernik last year. He didn't speak a word of Japanese, and no one he met recognized the language he did speak, so he quit talking.

Everyone did the best they could when it came to Bug Boy— a place to sleep, stuff to eat, even English lessons from that young woman, Kameko who was actually an orphan from America and had no more Japanese than Bug Boy had himself. Whenever she spotted him, she always turned a big smile on him like she was searching his face with a flashlight. That made him blink his big black eyes.

The day the next big quake shook Japan, Bug Boy was riding a bicycle very early in the morning. Was he delivering newspapers? No, he was not. In fact, if the Newspaper Boy saw him, he would be in some trouble. There is no way Bug Boy could be mistaken for anyone else, and the Sisters would be very interested to hear that he had been out on Bicycle Number Two when the sun wasn't even quite up yet. The Newspaper Boy rode Bicycle Number One, of course.

Bug Boy was naturally nocturnal, and it was unusual for him to be out in the sharp, new air when there were so many black birds gathering and looking for something to eat.

Not that the birds could make a meal of Bug Boy who was the size, if not exactly the shape and smell of a regular boy like oh, say, the Newspaper Boy who was not quite five feet tall but solidly built with serious eyes and a scar on his left cheek shaped like the letter I if the letter I were bowing at his nose. Bug Boy's eyes were black, not exactly faceted, but you might say "reflective" in certain lights. Some Sister might flip on the cellar light and yikes there would be that gleam in the black eyes of Bug Boy who would be down there looking for tasty bits stunned stupid and slow from the stuff the Sisters sprayed around the baseboards which had almost no effect on someone as big as Bug Boy.

Or another of those Sisters might be doing a bed check with a flashlight which was a different flashlight from the smile of the English teacher. Yes, that bed was occupied, check and check again for this one and for that one, and here we are coming up to Bug Boy's nest pushed away from the others, and yes, he's really in it tonight, but then the beam would cross his face and those black eyes would sparkle when they should have been closed and him sailing some dreamy sea in a little boat not much bigger than a rowboat but with a little sail like a pale blue triangle. Go to sleep, Bug Boy!

Bug Boy hoped he would be back by the time the Sisters called them down to breakfast. He hoped he would have parked Bike Number Two and sneaked back up the side of the building and through the little window and into his place at the end of the line as the boys filed down (minus the Newspaper Boy who would eat later) for breakfast.

You might think Bug Boy was wearing a leather jacket as he leaned over the handlebars and stood up on the pedals and pumped hard down the nearly dark street.

Look at him go.

What's your hurry Bug Boy?

Oh, never mind. We don't want to know.

You'd be mistaken about that leather jacket.

When Bug Boy got around all the corners and into the little park, he stopped and looked left and right, back and forth, up and down, and then he let the crack in his back widen, and he spread his wings, and a foul odor lumbered out so heavy you might imagine you could actually see it. Bug Boy knew better than to open his wings anywhere near other people. This reluctance to open them was the cause of his odor problem. Because he could not open them often enough, stuff just built up in there next to his skin which looked and felt like uncooked chicken, and it was like you yourself would be if you never got to take your socks off, say. That would be no bed of roses we'd be smelling when you finally did get to take them off and wiggle your toes in the cool air.

Bug Boy let the bike fall over on its side. Then he ran around in circles, jumping and flapping his arms, and slowly opening and closing his wings to fan out the awful odors. The morning air felt so cool and moist on his back that he couldn't help bursting out with a little happy chirruping.

2
Kameko

Her students all sat there looking up at her and waiting for her to say something interesting. Or anything at all, really. All she had to do was talk to them in English. The job was not terribly difficult.

She loved her students. She loved this amazing city. But life was so hard here, and she was so lonely. Everything was very expensive. It might have been better if she spoke the language. It might even have been better if she looked like she shouldn't really be able to speak the language. Everyone was so nice to regular foreigners, she thought, but she looked just like everyone else until she opened her mouth. Then people seemed shocked, although they were masterful in hiding it, as if she had just lifted her skirt to show them the ugly scar on her upper left thigh from falling out of a tree when she was twelve. Gramps had been so angry at the backyard for letting her fall, and the backyard had been so contrite and crushed with guilt that they had had super strawberries, some as big as baseballs, long after the season was over.

Japanese might be the language of her dead mother, but she didn't think she would ever learn it. She tried to memorize a new word every day, but then when she tried to use such a word, she found that it changed when you put it in a sentence in ways she just couldn't seem to get. Oh, and the "wa" and the "ga" were driving her nuts.

Her grandfather had been right, even if he hadn't insisted on it—coming to Japan when all she knew about the country and the language was what she had learned from anime might be a big mistake. There weren't many ninjas about, for example. And no one seemed to really care about your blood type. Japanese men were either a million polite miles away, or they were pinching and groping her on the trains.

She might have listened to her grandfather's gentle suggestions, but she had gone out to the backyard while he cooked dinner, and his crows had come to her and told her yes, she should go to Japan, told her they could take her right now if she wanted. All she had to do was become in tune with the crow culture of the place she wanted to go, and presto change-o whoosh! Away she'd go. But what did she know about Japanese crows? Nothing really. Didn't they all have three legs? The Yatagarasu? Did they play soccer? Ha ha! You silly girl! The crows made such a racket of cawing and flapping and laughing at her that Gramps ran out still holding his tongs to see what the matter was.

In the end she flew to Tokyo by jet instead of crows and made her way to the Ueno neighborhood where she would be teaching English at an orphanage run by Catholic nuns. Actually, someone else, a trained teacher would be providing the instruction. All Kameko had to do was talk to the students in English. The simplicity of her duties made her feel even more isolated and set apart from the other teachers, the real teachers. She had a very small apartment with tatami mats and cushions and a low table and a futon. It was perfect. She would never have been able to afford such a place in Tokyo without help from her grandfather. The neighborhood had plenty of crows, and they were very different from the crows at home. These were big and aggressive. Don't even think about messing with us or we'll rough you up! They were all the time dive-bombing people they didn't like. The city put blue netting over the garbage cans on collection days to keep them out of it. That didn't really work. The crows were smart and worked together to get under the netting.

"Okay," Kameko said. "Today we will be talking about pizza."

Peas Sue!

Peas Saw!

Just as she turned to write the topic on the board, the floor moved. Kameko knew it was an earthquake immediately. She had mistaken the only other earthquake she had ever experienced in Oregon as a big truck passing by on the street outside. This one was unmistakable. This one was the real thing.

Time slowed.

A voice came on the intercom, and the students all got up, so slowly, and crouched down under their desks. Kameko was not sure what she should do. The room was shaking. The windows were rattling. Stuff was dancing off the big teacher's desk and falling onto the floor. There was a roar in the air but she couldn't be sure it wasn't just in her head. It would be stupid to just stand there and be the only casualty, but then she noticed the strange student whose name translated to "Bug Boy" had not gotten under his desk. Instead he was moving quickly toward her, very quickly—scuttling forward on too many legs, she thought. He was at her side almost at once.

He took her hand and said something in a language that was not Japanese. She shrugged and tried to smile at him but felt her smile flash on and off as the room continued to shake. He pulled at her hand, and she let him lead her to the classroom door. The earthquake seemed to be over by the time they got into the hall-way, but he was still pulling her forward urgently.

The aftershock hit just as Kameko and Bug Boy got outside.

So many things happened at once. The dark sky was alive with the flapping and screaming of the big gangster crows. The earth was shaking, and the tall buildings were swaying from side to side. She pulled away from Bug Boy and put out her arms for balance, but that did no good. She fell to the pavement. She saw Bug Boy looking up at the sky and waving his arms. He's got his jacket on backwards she thought as it seemed to open out at either side of his body just as the crows descended and covered him completely. Kameko yelled for help, but no one came. She grabbed her phone and called her grandfather, thinking it was a crazy thing to do even as she was doing it.

"Earthquake!" she shouted when she saw his face on the little screen. "The crows!"

3
The Backyard

When Cassie was alive she liked to tell the story about how my back-yard was in love with me and had tried to sabotage our romance. She would tell about the night she came home with me and first met the backyard.

Yes, I had owned this house all those years ago, and after I'd married Cassie, she and the backyard came to a kind of détente. It remained my territory. It liked our boy Johnny, but he never really felt comfortable back there. He knew the backyard would be whispering in my ear about anything he got up to.

But that first night Cassie and the backyard did not like one another. Okay, okay, I was flattered in a perverted way over two women fighting over me, even if one of them wasn't strictly speaking a woman. In fact, I never ever referred to the backyard as "her" while Cassie was alive. In those days, I had a patio table out there on the deck with a couple of wonderful huge white wicker chairs with comfortable cushions I was always careful to bring in when I wasn't using them so the Oregon rain would not ruin them.

I'd left Cassie sitting in one of those chairs while I went inside for wine.

I heard her squeak like she'd seen a bat or something, and I'd yelled, "What?"

"Nothing," she'd called. I decided we could use some snacks, too, so I put some cheese and crackers on a platter.

From Cassie's viewpoint, things had not been so serene. She used to describe the sudden drop in temperature as I left her in the wicker chair. Branches snapped. Bushes shook as creatures crept through them. Something scampered over her foot. The patio light above the sliding glass doors dimmed. A sharp wind shook everything and then just stopped suddenly leaving a wet, dead smell floating in the air. A hummingbird flew down in front of Cassie. She carefully raised a hand toward it. It dropped onto the tabletop, obviously dead.

"What?" I'd shouted.

"Nothing!" she'd said.

She didn't know quite why she did it, but she opened her bag and nudged the body of the dead hummingbird into it. She snapped the bag closed and put it in her lap. I came out all goofy smiles with the wine and the cheese and crackers. The air was cool and sweet with the smell of spring flowers.

Johnny married a wonderful woman named Natsuki from Japan and they gave us a granddaughter, a beautiful baby, my Kameko. But then a drunk driver killed both Johnny and Natsuki. Natsuki had been an orphan and had no family at all, so there were not so many hurdles for Cassie and I to jump when adopting Kameko.

Those were wonderful years really, and I treasure them. Cassie's heart failed suddenly, when Kameko was ten, and I finished the job of raising her alone. Well, me and the backyard.

The hummingbird wasn't really dead, Cassie would say, zeroing in on the climax of her story.

The backyard loved Kameko almost as much as I did, maybe even more than it loved me. Cassie and Johnny would have been amazed to see it. I never worried about Kameko when she played back there. Picture this. She's three-and-a-half and wearing the white, red, green, and orange tie-dyed dress we'd bought her at the Saturday market, and she's barefoot, and she's in the backyard talking up to a tree. Her jet-black hair is long down her back. She raises one small fist and shakes it in the air. Or maybe she's talking to a squirrel up in the tree. Whatever it is, it's getting a piece of her mind.

So there he was, Cassie would say, with his crackers and cheese and wine, grinning like a bear. The backyard had gone completely silent. It was a deep listening quiet that you couldn't help but notice. Any little sound you made yourself bounced around like a scream. And in that deep quiet came a muffled desperate cry from Cassie's lap. She pulled her purse onto the table and opened it, and the hummingbird shot out like a bunch of angry bees! The backyard blew out a huge sigh of relief that brought all the rustling and whispering night sounds back all at once.

She'd say I said, "Was that a bird?" And I suppose I might have said that. I don't remember the details she remembered. I remember that I was already in love with her and that I ached for her and that I was wondering if she would spend the night with me. So she had a bird in her purse? I could live with that.

Cassie would say the backyard was trying to make me think she was a thief. The backyard was trying to say look look she snatches helpless hummingbirds out of the air and puts them in her purse. Tell her to go away! Tell her to go away!

Well, that didn't happen, I would always say—my only contribution to the telling of Cassie's story.

My phone made the special sound that meant it was Kameko calling. An odd time for her to call. Shouldn't she be in school? It would be tomorrow morning in Japan. Maybe she was on a break. We were totally video these days so I put on a smile and took the call ready to see her face swim up on my small screen.

I could see something was terribly wrong.

"Earthquake!" she shouted. "The crows!"

I thought she meant my crows here who were suddenly everywhere. How could she see that? My crows. The ones that always came back to the backyard. The ones who were cautious but not afraid of me. The crows who had told Kameko they could take her to Japan. Did they promise she would find her mother? They poured into the backyard in a huge heap. I had never seen them do such a thing. It was as if they had all pounced on something.

"He's gone!" Kameko said on the phone.

"What?" My eyes were jumping back and forth from the phone to my crows in the backyard. What had they caught?

Then the crows all suddenly leaped away from what they had been covering and took to the air. A boy, I thought.

The figure unfolded itself and beat at the air with its own dark wings. I made some kind of startled sound, and it turned black eyes on me, and then it jumped up and scurried toward the rhododendrons. The backyard closed around it like a hug. Not a boy, I thought.

"Gramps?" I looked down at the phone again. Kameko swept the camera in a wide panorama, but I couldn't make much of the blurry images and couldn't tell if things were still shaking.

"Is the quake over?" I asked.

"I think so," she said.

4
The Bulgarian

Kameko wondered if the backyard would like this new man in her life. She wondered if the creature her grandfather had always called "The Bulgarian" would make an awkward appearance. Maybe Grandfather's crows would swoop down and take them all off on an adventure. Maybe Gramps himself would choose this night to show up as a ghost for the first time. That would have been just like him. She smiled to herself. It had been ten years since he died. She had been living in another city, but when she inherited the house and the backyard and the Bulgarian, she moved back to Eugene, Oregon. After all, a translator could work anywhere, and with the money Gramps had left her, she could afford to take only the jobs that interested her. She had a knack for capturing the flow and feeling of Japanese literature and making it accessible to English readers. She could do that in the other direction, from English to Japanese, too. She had a pretty good reputation. Things were going well.

She would serve poached salmon with local kale and little red potatoes tonight.

"Mike?" she called.

"Yeah?"

"You doing okay out there?"

"Fine, fine." Did he sound a little tense? The backyard was probably grilling him in subtle ways he would not actually recognize but would feel at some level. The Bulgarian might scuttle naked from shadow to shadow just to mess with his mind.

Well, wasn't meeting the family always a little tense?

She supposed she was using this evening as a test to see if Mike might be Mr. Right or just another tumble in the hay. He was pretty delicious. Everything was cooking nicely. It wasn't time for the fish yet. She poured out a couple of glasses of wine.

Should she maybe put out some cheese and crackers?

Nebula-award winner Esther M. Friesner has published 39 novels and nearly 200 short stories. She is also an editor and a playwright. Lately, she's ventured into the realm of historical young adult fiction with the popular Princess of Myth *series.*

About this story, she writes, "I've always enjoyed mucking about with mythology, especially Greek myths. They've always been a glorious garden of 'Yes, but what if…?' for me. One such garden party inspired me to write 'Thunderbolt,' a reimagining of Helen of Troy's childhood abduction, which, in turn led to my writing Nobody's Princess *and* Nobody's Prize*. I'm also quite the fan of Victorian/Edwardian literature, especially the language. Oh, the wonderful language! 'The Grasshopper and My Aunts' lets me combine the two—happily, I hope."*

The Grasshopper and My Aunts

Esther M. Friesner

It wanted but an hour of noon and my governess was already locked in the library with my aunts, weeping. I could not forbear to smile. Before this, my best efforts at freeing myself from those young women entrusted with my so-called education usually did not show any results until well after luncheon.

If I put my ear to the door—and I did—I could hear my aunts Domitilla and Euphrosyne taking it in turns to try persuading the poor, distracted girl to stay on in their employ. It was not working. Apparently Miss Cubbins had a mortal terror of any creature with more than four legs and fewer than two, the sole exception being rodents. The grasshopper I had introduced to her embroidery basket that morning fitted the former category most admirably. Had I been previously aware of the pathological nature of her fear, I might have found some other manner of expressing my impulses towards girlish mischief.

43

Upon reflection, no. She *had* insisted I learn fractions. Some offenses call for blood; blood and grasshoppers.

The library door was made of good, thick oak, harvested from the ancient forests of Dyrnewaed, our ancestral estate. Family tradition had it that the sage, Merlin, had been pent entranced in one of the trees that once clustered the grounds of the manor. If so, his chances for undisturbed eternal slumber ran aground during the reign of Elizabeth, on the day that Hermes, Lord Wielward, decided to sacrifice his oaks in order to fully refurbish and titivate his home, in hopes of attracting the Virgin Queen's attention and favor on one of her many royal progresses. The trees fell, the manor house was transformed, tongues wagged, and the queen took notice. Her next royal progress descended upon Dyrnewaed like a swarm of insufficiently perfumed locusts, but once she took a closer look at my ancestors' domestic arrangements, her favor failed to follow. Thus did Lord Wielward's foolish aspirations nigh bankrupt our family for generations to come, though at least he contrived to retain his life and (greatly reduced) freeholding.

It was said that if you put your ear to one of the doors that came from Merlin's oak, you could hear the old wizard bitterly declaiming "Serves you right!" with much relish. If so, his Celtic *Schadenfreude* was now being overshouted by my aunts' remonstrations with Miss Cubbins. I knew I was going to be punished, but wanted some advance warning of the severity. *Better the devil you know,* as the saying partially goes, although at Dyrnewaed the conclusion of that adage is: . . .*even if the demon in question does take it upon himself to arrive at formal dinner parties with his latest crowd of brimstone-reeking casual acquaintances and throw off poor Euphrosyne's seating arrangements entirely, the swine!*

As I fretted over my impending chastisement, the balance of the kerfuffle within the library shifted abruptly when Miss Cubbins declared: "I beg of you, my ladies, do not entreat me to stay.

The magnitude of my terror on discovering the horrid insect which *your* niece deliberately secreted amid my embroidery was such that I flung the entire basket so far that it cleared the hawthorn hedges. I heard a distinct splash, which leads me to believe it landed in—"

"—the spring?" There was a marked transition in the tone of Aunt Domitilla's voice. When she inquired, "Are you telling us, Miss Cubbins, that you pitched your miserable sewing basket into *our spring*?" it was like listening to an articulate scalpel.

"Yes, and I fear my needlework must have been ruined beyond all—"

In a breath, the library door swept open, knocking me sideways. I had barely time to scramble to my feet before I saw my governess fly across the hall, to crash into the wainscoting between a tapestry of Phaeton's plunge into the sea and a portrait of Her Majesty, Queen Victoria. She slid down the wall in a heap, whimpering. Meanwhile, Aunt Domitilla presented herself in the doorway, her ice-white hair come all undone from its combs, her cheeks a scorching red, and a series of bulging veins turning her temples into an approximation of my hand-drawn map of the rivers of Belgium. Her blazing gray eyes seemed to shoot sparks capable of fricasseeing a full-grown vole.

"You—you *struck* me!" Miss Cubbins cried.

If there was one thing Aunt Domitilla hated, it was someone who insisted on wasting her time by stating the obvious. She strode from the library doorway to tower over my unfortunate governess.

"And *you* tossed a basket into our spring," she shot back. "Wretched creature, are you so base, so beyond all hope of human decency that you have forgotten the single dictum that my sister and I laid down for you at the onset of your employment here? *Nothing* is to come into contact with the waters of that source. Not one thing, not ever, and no exceptions!"

Aunt Euphrosyne emerged from the library and laid a delicate hand on her elder sister's arm. "Now, 'Tilla, it was an accident," she murmured. Her powdery pink-and-white face was composed into the picture of maidenly reserve she had so often urged upon me, to no avail. Her ersatz golden curls trembled ever so slightly as she bowed her head, interceding for Miss Cubbins. "You know as well as I that our darling Melantha's governess would never have done such a thing deliberately."

"I know nothing of the sort!" Aunt Domitilla countered. "One person's convenient 'accident' is another's Trojan War. Or do you believe that Eris exclaimed 'Oopsie-daisy! Silly butterfingers me,' when she flung that golden apple among Thetis and Peleas' wedding guests?"

Miss Cubbins picked herself up and gathered the remnants of her dignity. "My ladies, I apologize for what truly was a mishap. I shall fetch the offending basket from the spring at once, following which I shall take prompt leave of your service. I hope you will find it in your hearts to give me a good character, and I wish you every bit of luck you may require in finding some unhappy—*deserving* young woman to replace me." With this, she turned on her heel and headed for the front door, chin held high.

She did so without awaiting Aunt Domitilla's reply. She ought to have known better. My elder aunt was used to issuing directives and had an inborn aversion to receiving them. She pounced upon the governess, age-gnarled hands seizing Miss Cubbins' shoulders and forcing the young woman to spin around and face her, nose-to-nose.

"You will go nowhere without my leave," she growled. "Nor shall you have any letters of recommendation, in aid of securing future employment, until first we view the effects of your trespass." With that, she dug her fingers into the governess' arm and hauled her away, leaving Aunt Euphosyne and me to follow as best we might.

Aunt Domitilla had a ground-devouring stride that soon carried her and her hapless prey out of our musty manor house and down the patchily graveled drive. She ignored Miss Cubbins' endless litany of complaint and protest. In vain too did Aunt Euphosyne beg her sister to slow the pace a trifle as she struggled to keep up. My youth afforded me no such difficulties, and I ran merrily alongside my elder aunt and her captive.

"*What* are you smiling about, Melantha?" Aunt Domitilla demanded as we all swerved sharply to the right at the end of the hawthorn hedge and doubled back around it. "I am not ignoring your role in this disaster. Ungrateful child! Is this the thanks poor Euphrosyne and I merit for lavishing the benefits of a Classical education upon you?"

I tried to re-form my expression to one of sincere contrition but failed gloriously. "I am sorry for any inconvenience I may have caused you, dear aunt."

"Inconvenience?" Aunt Domitilla snorted and raised one grizzled eyebrow in a look of unbridled irony. "The Black Death was an 'inconvenience'. *This*, my lass, has all the earmarks of being a fully realized catastrophe. I hope that you are proud of yourself."

"She tried to teach me *fractions!*"

"Then it is a great pity she did not succeed, Melantha, for I have every expectation that you shall need the very skill you scorn when all Hades breaks loose and our mortal bodies are chopped into sixteenths at best."

"Oh, piffle." I thrust out my underlip, a childish affectation part and parcel of my thirteen years. "If we meet some dreadful fate, what good will it do to be able to identify the fractions into which we've been divided?"

My elder aunt stopped her tracks and dropped her grip on Miss Cubbins. "It will give us a sense of *intellectual satisfaction*," she replied loftily. "A virtue about which you neither seem to know or care, might I add. Ah, I weep for your generation. No: I weep for mine and the foolish notion that one must take responsibility for the orphaned children of one's kin."

"For the orphaned *heiress* of Dyrnewaed, you mean," I said *sotto voce*.

Aunt Domitilla's thin lips grew thinner to the point of vanishing altogether. "What was that, Melantha?"

"Only that it was poor Pappa's kindness, as master of this estate, that allowed you and Aunt Euphrosyne to live with *us* and not the other way around," I replied much too sweetly. "You have no claim to this property."

Such deliberate goading was likely to earn me a slap, but I deemed the game worth the candle. I conjectured that once my elder aunt struck me, she would regret it and thus commute the punishment for my original offense. Better a slap for sauciness than whatever penalty awaited me for assaulting a governess with insects.

My plans came a cropper. Aunt Domitilla remained uninfuriated, her hands unraised against me. "So this is the thanks we get," she said in a flat voice. "You fling in our faces the fact that Euphrosyne and I are beholden to your late father—and now to you—for our daily crust. Our constant service to this family since the day of our arrival is not worth a mention, nor a whisper of gratitude. So be it. Let this day mark the end of our dependence."

Aunt Euphrosyne gasped and laid one hand to her shallow chest. "'Tilla, what are you saying?"

"I am saying that Miss Cubbins will not depart Dyrnewaed unaccompanied. We shall go with her. No doubt our niece is perfectly capable of managing things here without further help from us."

"But she's a *child*, 'Tilla!" Euphrosyne exclaimed. "The staff can help her handle the ordinary aspects of the estate, but what about the rest of it? We still have no idea which side of her mixed blood she favors, nor if she possesses a whit of her mother's innate ability or her father's talent. Worse, she has no idea of the family trust and duty! If we leave matters in her hands, horrors will ensue."

I did not care for my younger aunt's hysterical reaction concerning my capabilities. "'Horrors'?" I echoed with disdain. "If you're talking about what's in the wine cellar, we are old friends. Or are you speaking of the entity sharing coffin-space with great-great-granduncle Leander? It behaves nicely when it's not hungry and I have been punctilious about feeding it with all due caution. If you've heard any complaints from the village, do not rush to judgment. Sheep and children go missing for all sorts of reasons. I *know* you are not referring to dear Scylla, down at the gatekeeper's cottage. Poor thing, her mind wanders so badly these days that on my daily visits it is all I can do to remind her I am her former nursling and not her noontide refreshment."

I turned to Miss Cubbins, who had gone a peculiar tint of ashy grey. "Wha—wha—what are you saying, Miss Melantha?" she stammered, trembling.

"Never mind her," Aunt Domitilla said crisply. "*She* is thirteen and omniscient. But I repeat myself. Let us rather repair to the site of your transgression, Miss Cubbins, that you may behold the results of an ill-considered excess of emotion when confronted by a simple grasshopper. We shall then observe how well our niece deals with the results. I trust it will be most enlightening, at the proper distance."

With that she renewed her hold upon my erstwhile governess' arm and plowed onward.

There was not much farther to plow before our small group reached the grassy banks of that spring whose continued purity was of such moment to my aunts. I knew the place very well. My earliest memories were of summer afternoons spent lolling on the greensward while Pappa stood with arms outstretched over the waters, chanting words I neither knew nor had any interest in knowing. The glimmering mist that arose from the center of the pool on those occasions was a lovely shade of bronze, interspersed with flickers of crimson. After Pappa concluded the formalities, we would share a feast of treacle tart and tea, taking every precaution that not one crumb touched the water, though again I was ignorant of the reason and disinterested in learning it. Sometimes he would cut a few of the reeds that bordered the eternally flowing source in order to amuse me by creating a shepherd's pipe upon which he played many a jocund tune. (Dear heavens, what awful, *awful* music!)

I remembered the spring and the pool. I remembered the verdant banks and the nodding reeds.

I did not remember the willow trees that grew so tall they veiled the sun from sight, nor the fluffy-bolled cotton plants choking the edges of the water, nor—most clearly of all—the naked man. I am quite certain of that. My aunts might call me a scatterbrained hoyden when so disposed, but even so, the presence of a completely bare-bodied stranger has a tendency to stick in one's memory.

"Hello?" he ventured. Miss Cubbins took one look, shrieked, and keeled over insensible. "What's wrong with her?" the nude gentleman asked. He stood knee-deep in the water, strands of long, black hair clinging to his finely shaped head and lean, muscular chest and shoulders. His eyes were a delectable shade of green, reminiscent of the verdant carapace of—of—

My inability to pinpoint the answer tormented me until Aunt Domitilla inquired primly, "Sir, are you now or have you ever been a grasshopper?" and I was much relieved in my mind.

The handsome youth frowned. "Who *are* you, woman?" He turned his head left and right. "Where am I, anyway? This doesn't look like the mansions of Olympos or the plain of Ilion."

"I should hope not," I interjected. "It is England's green and, so we are frequently assured, pleasant land." This answer only succeeded in deepening the wrinkles of perplexity marring the smooth perfection of his brow. I endeavored to amend his puzzlement by adding: "You are in Albion, not Ilion, dear sir, an isle in the northwestern ocean well beyond the Pillars of Hercules. It would be my pleasure to provide details, but first, would you care for tea or some trousers?"

He scratched his head. "Never heard of either, but I'm willing to eat anything once."

Aunt Domitilla glared. "Wicked child, is this how you confront incipient disaster? By offering it tea?"

"Tea and trousers," I pointed out. "He clearly stands in need of both. But pray, what disaster is this? You cannot mean it is beyond your capability to thwart! Dear aunt, I have seen you hold off entire gaggles of gargoyles with a single knitting needle. Imps and cacodemons doff their caps in your presence. One word from you caused the succubus troubling our butler's son to leave off her vile nocturnal activities and obtain employment at the local workhouse. By the way, you have yet to explain the details of those rather boisterous night-time tomfooleries of hers to me, and you *promised*."

"Do not confuse matters of family *religion* with matters of family *trust*, Melantha," Aunt Domitilla said stiffly. "I assure you that the person presently dripping before us embodies a great threat to the latter."

"But *how*?" I insisted. "It is plain that the poor fellow can not possibly be carrying any concealed weaponry."

My elder aunt rolled her eyes. Turning to our newly arrived guest, she asked, "Young man, as you were recently a grasshopper, have I now the pleasure of addressing one Prince Tithonus, son of King Laomedon of Troy?"

"That's me, all right."

"Further, were you previously the paramour of Eos, goddess of the dawn?"

A lascivious grin spread slowly across Tithonus' finely chiseled features. "*I'll* say. And if she'd been as on top of things in the brain department as she was in the bedroom, I'd still be the first thing up in the morning."

"*Mister* Tithonus! Language!" Aunt Euphrosyne left off chafing Miss Cubbins' wrists in a vain attempt at returning the governess to consciousness and jerked her head up, scandalized. "I will thank you to note that there is a *child* present."

"Who, her?" He winked at me. "Pretty little poppet. Give us a kiss."

Aunt Domitilla pursed her lips. "I believe I liked you better as a grasshopper."

"You never met me as a grasshopper."

"Nonetheless."

It was at this juncture that Aunt Euprhosyne's attentions succeeded in reviving Miss Cubbins. My former governess sat up and looked around groggily. "The naked gentleman is still among us," she observed. "I believe I shall swoon again, on that account."

"You will swoon when and if I require it of you" Aunt Domitilla snapped. "In any case, you will not do so until you have acknowledged the effects of your hysterical reaction to what was a formerly harmless insect." She indicated Tithonus.

Miss Cubbins blinked. "You call that an insect?"

"Hello, darling," Tithonus said cheerfully. "Don't tell me *you're* a child, too?"

Before Miss Cubbins could give a suitably indignant answer, Aunt Euphrosyne spoke up: "You mustn't mind Prince Tithonus, Miss Cubbins. We had no idea he was upon the manor grounds or we would have forewarned Melantha against using any vermin matching his description as part of her pranks."

"Who are you calling vermin?" Tithonus cried. "I didn't *ask* to become a grasshopper. I *wanted* immortality. Is it my fault that silly bitch—?"

"Mister Tithonus! *Must* you?"

"—that silly *biddy* Eos forgot to beg me the gift of eternal youth as well as eternal life? Do you know how awful it is to live on and on and on, trapped in a body that can't die but keeps on aging?"

"I can almost imagine it," Aunt Domitilla said dryly.

"Well, it *stinks*!" Tithonus stamped his foot, sending a splash of water flying out of the spring. My aunts gave a small backward jump, no doubt to preserve their raiment from haphazard dampening. "You wrinkle and you weaken and you tell the same boring stories over and over and you start to smell funny and then you get so dried up and shrunken and tiny that *someone* gets the bright idea to turn you into a grasshopper because you're nine-sevenths of the way there already!"

"I beg your pardon, but nine-sevenths is an improper fraction," Miss Cubbins pointed out in her punctilious fashion.

"There are *improper* fractions?" My ears perked up. Perhaps I had been too hasty in objecting to the subject.

"Melantha, there is a time for mathematics and a time for moral improvement," Aunt Domitilla decreed. "Learn to distinguish between them."

"And after all that—" Tithonus went on. "—after so much suffering and humiliation, what do you think Eos does? She drops me! Acts like I never existed! Tosses me out of her celestial mansion and onto this godsforsaken dab of dirt. You'd think the trollop would at least shelve me somewhere with a decent climate, but *this* place—?" He made a rude noise.

"Perhaps you will find England's weather less objectionable once you have spent time here in your restored form," Aunt Euphrosyne offered. Ever the conciliator, she added: "We will happily offer you the hospitality of Dyrnewaed until you have become acclimatized to your renewed humanity."

"Are you not forgetting something, Euphrosyne?" Aunt Domitilla asked with a lift of one eyebrow. "The doors of Dyrnewaed are not ours to open, as Melantha has so *kindly* pointed out."

"Dearest auntie, please don't be such a sourpuss." I slipped my arm through hers and gazed into her face in a most beguiling manner. "I didn't mean any of those naughty words. You *must* stay on. I would be lost without your guidance."

"We shall all be lost, soon enough," Aunt Domitilla replied in dark, foreboding tones. "Look around, girl! Use what portion of your brain was our late sister's bequest to you! Do you notice *nothing* besides the unclothed prince before us?"

"Of course I notice more than that!" I replied crisply. "I see those trees and those cotton plants. I would have to be blind to ignore them."

"And is that your limit? Have you only thought, 'Ah, trees and plants have sprung up unbidden and at full maturity. What a merry lark!' and never once asked yourself '*How* did that happen?'"

"My basket. . ." Miss Cubbins stared at the willows. "My basket was woven of osier wands, and my embroidery—it was pure cotton in both cloth and floss. When it landed in this pool, do you mean to say that it and all contained therein became—?"

"As once they were, yes," Aunt Euphrosyne said gently. "This spring encompasses the power of restoration for those living things which were transformed against their desires. A touch of its waters returns them to what they were and what they long to be again."

"Embroidery floss has *longings*?" Miss Cubbins looked ready to dash off at any moment and beg admittance to Bedlam.

"If it did not, the waters would have no effect upon it," my younger aunt said in her soft, unprepossessing voice. "*Quod erat demonstrandum*." She indicated the gently nodding cotton bolls.

"Good thing you weren't carrying lunch in that basket, eh, girl?" Tithonus chuckled.

The governess clasped the cameo brooch at her stiffly starched collar. At first I thought she was distressed at the thought of a ham sandwich suddenly regenerating itself into a wheat field and a living pig or portions thereof, but her thoughts tended elsewhere: "Merciful heavens, the tales of this accursed house and misbegotten family are true: You are witches!"

"How *dare* you, you ignorant minx!" Aunt Domitilla exclaimed. "Witches, are we? By the eternally nibbled liver of Prometheus, it is a blessing that circumstance has removed you from your post before you had the opportunity to infect our precious niece with such thick-witted drivel."

"If only we *were* witches," Aunt Euphrosyne said with a heartfelt sigh. "Things would be so much easier. At best we might expect a steady income from the sale of love philters and potions for gentlemanly enhancement, and at worst a burning at the stake."

"We are *custodians*," Aunt Domitilla said. "The spring and many other features of Dyrnewaed's grounds have powers that attract the attention of otherworldly beings—we can attest to that. We have accepted the responsibility for keeping watch and ward here, with great help from the centuries'-long enchantments shielding this place from the *direct* view of supernatural creatures. Without such spells we would have been overrun ages ago."

"But where's the harm, auntie?" I asked in all innocence. "If a creature wishes to use our spring to revert to its original form, why don't we permit it? One splash and done!"

"Dear Melantha, you are too young to realize that it would not end with that initial splash," Aunt Euphrosyne chided me gently. "Most metamorphoses should on no account be reversed, for they encompass generations. What dreadful impact it would have upon the population of this island if Arachne managed to dip one pedipalp into this pool! She would not be the only one affected. Every spider of her bloodline would become a young woman with overweening pride in her talent as a weaver. Most of them might find employment in the mills of Manchester, but the rest would be a burden on society."

While this exchange continued, Tithonus sloshed to the edge of the spring and stepped out onto dry land. "My toes look like oil-cured olives," he muttered. "And I'm still hungry. Hey! One of you women stop yapping and bring me bread, wine, oil, and a nice collop of roast lamb!"

"I am sorry, Your Highness." (Aunt Domitilla did not sound sorry at all.) "Your refreshment will have to wait."

"For what?" the Trojan prince snarled testily.

"For the inevitable. When Miss Cubbins' basket hit the water, ripples ensued."

"Well, of course ripples—"

"I do not speak of *physical* ripples alone."

Tithonus looked bewildered and was not alone in this befuddlement. Miss Cubbins and I were equally confused, but my elder aunt saw no need to elaborate. Fortunately, Aunt Euphrosyne took pity on us and explained:

"My dears, imagine a blazing fireplace entirely hidden from view by a pair of heavy draperies. Now picture what might happen if someone dropped a smidgen of gunpowder into the flames. Even the smallest explosion would be heard on the far side of those draperies, and the cloth itself well might ruffle or bell out, and so—"

"—people would suspect that *something* was behind those draperies, even if they could not see it, and they might draw nigh, in order to investigate it more closely," I concluded.

"Oh, my sweet Melantha, if it were only *people* with whom we shall have to deal now!" Aunt Euphrosyne looked mournful.

"Wait, wait." Tithonus pinched the bridge of his shapely nose, eyes shut tight in furious cogitation. "You're saying that when the basket hit the water, I *exploded*?"

My aunts exchanged a *look* and sighed in tandem.

"*Men*," said Aunt Domitilla.

"*Myths*," Aunt Euphrosyne amended. "Though I shouldn't be one to talk."

Before she might say more, a faint rumble arose from beyond the stand of poplars marking the western edge of the manor grounds. The necessary presence of these trees as a windbreak was all that had saved them from the Elizabethan "improvements" committed by Lord Wielward, but now their luck seemed to be at an end. The proud trees swayed as though caught up in a tempest. Towering trunks groaned under the strain before they snapped and fell. Some simply shuddered where they stood before bursting into showers of splinters, as though obliterated by an artillery barrage. Miss Cubbins squealed.

She might have saved her breath for more inspired screaming. It wanted but an instant more of arboreal destruction before the *real* horrors came.

They poured out from between the ruined trees in a mob of fur and feathers, scales and squamous skin. Seven swans came swooping in above a lumbering she-bear, a sharp-toothed weasel, an assortment of cruelly-horned cattle, and a slither of nasty-looking snakes. The beasts carried such an air of unnatural bloodthirst as to turn a reasoning person's spine to jelly. I vow there was a mouse amid the throng that looked capable of tearing my throat out and using my esophagus for a skip-rope!

"This is only the beginning," Aunt Euphrosyne murmured. "These are but the metamorphosed beings who happened to be in the neighborhood. Once word spreads, we shall be inundated!"

As the creatures neared, I noted fresh cause for alarm. "They're *huge!*" So they were, each at least thrice the size of ordinary beasts of their breed. If the mouse had startled me before, now it absolutely terrified me. I flung myself into the sanctuary of Aunt Domitilla's arms.

She thrust me away unceremoniously. "For shame, Melantha!" she said with cold severity. "Is this how the mistress of Dyrnewaed behaves in a crisis? Where is your inbred gumption? Were you not born daughter to the hereditary primate of the *Ecclesiam Omnium Daemonum* , whilom prelate of Our Lady if Dis, Somerset, as well as to our sister Celaeno, whose dark wings obliterated the sun and whose foul droppings were the nonpareil of loathsome filth? Shall you not fulfill the promise of your parentage?"

My jaw went slack with shock. My mother was famous for her foul *what*? My father once headed the Church of All *Whom*? (Well, I suppose that sort of religious affiliation would explain the things in the wine cellar, and the crypt, and dear old Scylla's peculiar taste in beverages, but I always thought we were just schismatic Muggletonians.) Head reeling, all I could manage to do was wail: "But—but *Mamma's given name was Cecily!*"

"Is *that* what you have gleaned from my words?" Aunt Domitilla was fit to be tied.

"Now, 'Tilla, it's our own fault for having sheltered the child from her heritage." Aunt Euphrosyne was ever the voice of reason. "It is rather a lot of family secrets to absorb so abruptly. You should have done it more gradually."

"As I intended, dear sister, once the girl showed us she'd mastered her *mundane* studies." Here she glowered at Miss Cubbins and me in equal measure. "Which might have been accomplished ere now if Melantha had been a more attentive pupil supplied with a *far* more doughty teacher."

Miss Cubbins crumpled. "My lady, I swear by all I love to be the doughtiest of governesses to Miss Melantha in future, if only you will save us from our present peril!"

"Oh, fine," said Aunt Domitilla, and threw me into the spring.

The spot into which she cast me must have been the deepest part of the pool, for I submerged fully. I had only an instant to realize my situation before the waters closed over me. As I fought my way back to the world of air and light, I thought I heard the muffled sound of two additional splashes. My head broke the surface in time to see that I had heard correctly: my aunts were just emerging from the wavelets beside me.

My aunts. . .my goodness, they *were* a sight! Domitilla and Euphrosyne spread dripping black wings and tossed back their ebon tresses as fierce shrieks broke from their feathered throats. As they took flight, I saw that their still-human faces were now youthful and lovely, their feet transformed to talons, their breasts indecorously bare. Her Majesty would *never* have approved.

As for me, the spring had wrought similar though not identical changes. My shoulders felt oddly heavy, possessed of strange new musculature. I flexed things I did not know could be flexed and was rewarded by the leathery crack of my own unfurled wingspan. I know not by what instinct I soared from the pool into the sky, only that I did so. Vanity and curiosity in equal measure made me look down as I ascended, so that I might see my reflection in the water.

Gracious, wasn't I the most extraordinary creature! I had my aunts' dark wings, but these sprang from a lithe, reptilian body, and my familiar human face showed a mouth filled with fangs. Flames flickered in my nostrils, and for some reason my clawed hind paws were sheathed in black gaiters that went quite nicely with the scarlet cassock veiling my immature bosom from view. Part harpy, part dragon, part demonic clergy, all added up to make me one very odd duck indeed.

Odd, not effective. As my aunts attacked the approaching wave of creatures with talons and certain unsavory bombardments, I struggled to find a way in which to help them. The very notion of a harpy's traditional strategy—to rain mythic guano upon one's opponent—revolted me to the point where my innards simply would *not* cooperate. I lacked Pappa's clerical training, which meant I could not summon any of his former infernal parishioners. I might have used my draconic strength directly, but single combat would not be efficient. While I battled one beast, a horde of others could reach the spring.

The spring! Inspiration struck me instantly. I turned in midair and dove back toward the source, scooping up a large mouthful of the transformative water, splashing poor Miss Cubbins willy-nilly in the process. Beating my wings frantically, I flew back around the manor house and in one wild, mad, make-or-break feat of valor. . .I spit on the front door of Dyrnewaed.

"What sorcery is't that wakes me from my unsought slumber?" With lightning-tipped staff in hand, the graybeard wizard Merlin stood amid the wreckage of the heavy oak panel that had contained his spirit since before Great Eliza's reign. "Reveal your name unto me, O mage and savior supreme!"

"Introductions later, magic now," I shouted, snatching him up in my claws and whisking him back to the embattled ground between the woods and the spring.

To his credit, Merlin did not waste time giving arguments or demanding explanations. His cool blue eyes took in the situation in a trice, his supernatural sense allowed him to perceive where to place his loyalties, and his magic enabled him to raise a spell on the spot. It leaped from his staff and rocked the ground it struck, causing a wall of warding to erupt around the troublesome water. Undetectable to mortal senses, the barricade thrummed with sorcerous power that blasted all of the attacking creatures off their feet, out of their flight paths, and halfway to perdition.

My aunts alone were spared from the general eviction. They hovered in mid-air, astonished by the sudden depopulation of their theatre of war, until their eyes lit upon the wizard. They drifted to earth with the grace of autumn leaves and bowed before him.

"You have our thanks, O Merlin," Aunt Euphrosyne intoned. Her harpy voice was considerably more impressive than her tremulous human one. "What dread agency set you free from your ages-long durance to aid us in this, our most desperate hour?"

"The dragon-thing spit on my door," the wizard replied simply.

"Melantha!" Aunt Domitilla ruffled her feathers. "Spitting in the house? And you, a lady born and bred. What next? *Public nose-blowing?*"

"Excuse me, dear Aello," Aunt Euphrosyne murmured, calling her sister by what I presumed to be her true name. "If we are being accurate, our sweet Melantha did not spit *in* the house so much as *on* it."

"Do not chop prepositions with me, Ocypete," Aunt Domitilla replied in the same wise. "The fact remains that the child's intemperate actions have caused a dreadful upset in our domestic arrangements. We now have a legendary wizard for whom to provide, as well as the dawn-goddess' castoff lover. However shall we manage to introduce *them* to the vicar and the local Hunt? O, we are socially ruined! I shall never be able to contribute my tatting to the parish jumble sale again, and you *know* how it piles up!" She flapped her wings in despair.

"Does this mean you will be staying at Dyrnewaed?" I asked innocently.

"Of course we will!" Aunt Domitilla (née Aello) snapped as we all wended our way back to the spring. As my aunts had chosen to walk rather than fly, out of deference to Merlin, we made a rather comical procession. Harpies are cruel grace itself when airborne, but on the ground they tend to waddle. "It would not do to leave you unchaperoned with both a legendary wizard and a prince whose manners thus far have been less than—"

She stopped in her tracks and stared. Miss Cubbins stared back, her face pale, her expression sheepish, her hair serpentine.

Tithonus was pale as well, though this was due to his having become as fine a piece of marble statuary as the British Museum might covet.

"Oh my," said Miss Cubbins, while her hair hissed and writhed. "I am most terribly sorry. I did not mean to turn the gentleman to stone, but when Miss Melantha splashed me, it simply could not be helped."

"A gorgon!" Aunt Euphrosyne exclaimed. "Did we know she was a gorgon when we hired her, Aello? I'm sure *I* was unaware of the fact."

"Apparently, so was she," my elder aunt remarked with a wry smile. Turning to Merlin, she added: "I am gratified to perceive that your magic has protected you from the effects of our governess' coiffure."

"Shieldings and wardings, Madam," Merlin said smugly. "Never cut corners on your shieldings and wardings, I always say."

"Indeed."

At Aunt Domitilla's behest, the wizard turned his powers to restoring us to our human guises. Despite the social niceties, the governess went first. As her fellow Mythics, we were immune to her petrifying gaze, but my aunts declined to become the empirical proof of whether our mortal bodies would be equally unaffected.

Later, over tea, it was arranged that Merlin should stay on at Dyrnewaed as a long-lost uncle, newly back from the Afghan border. Miss Cubbins also agreed to remain, with the proviso that half a glass of spring water accompany her to all of our lessons, a visual memorandum for me to remain on good behavior or—as she so crudely put it—else. I thought it beastly of my aunts to approve this, but had no choice in the matter.

As for Prince Tithonus, Merlin's magic had no effect on him, alas, nor did repeated aspersions with the spring's restorative waters. My aunts had him removed to the conservatory, for shelter from the elements, and Miss Cubbins frequently brought me there for lessons, though certain aspects of his undraped physique proved distracting for us both.

"Perhaps he has no desire to return to the flesh," I remarked. "At least in this state he will retain his youthful vigor."

"You need not speak of *flesh* quite so knowingly, Miss Melantha, nor to *stare* at the poor gentleman so attentively," my governess chided, but she was goggling at the prince's vigor as much as I. "Now open your Latin book to Ovid's *Ars Amatoria* and let us begin."

Ah, the delights of a Classical education!

Irette Y. Patterson writes science fiction, fantasy, and romance. She lives in Atlanta, Georgia. "True Calling" is her first professional fantasy sale.

Irette says the inspiration for "True Calling" comes from her mother. "My mom does not bake," Irette writes. "She doesn't even keep butter in her refrigerator. Once a year, though, she breaks out her hand mixer and makes my dad a birthday cake with homemade lemon filling and fluffy frosting. I can't help but think that the effort she puts into making that once-a-year cake involves a lot of magic."

True Calling

Irette Y. Patterson

Cat waited for a moment as she stepped into the bakery, the bell dangling from the door announcing her arrival. Trays of baked goods surrounded her. Silver trays with goodies packed to the edge—baklava, chocolate sponge cake layers held by ganache and lemon cupcakes with cream cheese frosting, the lemon filling betrayed by the dollop of neon-yellow filling on the center right on top. In front of her were the clear glass display cases of more yums available for sale. Sample cakes were displayed at a slant on the wall behind the cashier.

No. This was no place where you sauntered in. You gave it its proper reverence. The bakery sat there on that strip of a road having been there before the area devolved into strip clubs and all-night pancake places. It had history. And family. And presence.

The fact that she could get a baklava with its honey oozing against her finger and sticking to the sides of her mouth would have been reason enough to choose this bakery for the event.

The real reason, though, was that it felt *right*. She wasn't from the Path side of the family so she couldn't read another person's

65

thoughts. She wasn't an engineering whiz like the Freeman girls. And life would have been so much easier as an aura-seeing Bow. As a Hart she specialized in the heart of the home and family. And this place was filled with love and family.

"Move it, Chick," a voice came behind her pushing her aside.

Cat sighed and moved so that her friend could step in. "Really?" she said.

"Look. We got to get back to work. The board is meeting today and you don't know when they're gonna need us to run some numbers or something." Her friend Kesha brushed past her to the cashier, "So. Let's see this cake that you're getting for a man who doesn't know you exist."

"We are not getting into this right now."

"Uh-huh. I don't know why you just don't make the doggone cake anyway. You make everything else."

Kesha was, well, Kesha; she never met a wig she didn't like and it sometimes overpowered her tiny frame. Sometimes Cat thought that they looked like frick and frack. Kesha had the figure of a model. Cat had the figure of someone who was, well what she was, short plump and with, she thought, curves in all the right places. She liked her shape and knew that if she got too thin, Auntie would probably reign down terror on her for not being the "appropriate" shape. She truly believed that your shape and size could impact the amount of power like a singer who needed to be a big girl in order to blow those notes.

Cat loved her aunt, but the woman did go overboard regarding things. Everything she said wasn't true. Like the whole baking thing. You could bake but you didn't bake for just anybody, and you certainly didn't bake for a guy friend. You just never knew what would happen.

Uh-huh. Yeah. Auntie could be a bit on the paranoid side.

"Are you listening?" Kesha snapped her fingers in front of her. "He's going to break your heart, boo."

"We're just friends," Cat said.

"'Uh-huh," she said.

Cat smiled as the lady came from out back. She wore a white blouse and black slacks with her long, black curly hair pulled away from her face.

Maybe she should have gone to Publix. But no, this was special. Everything else was ready for the party. The cake was the last thing, and she even had little helpers to help her set everything up. This was it.

Cat walked up to the counter. "I'm here to pick up the Falcons cake."

But the response was what concerned her; there was none of that immediate reaction or recognition.

Cat kept smiling. "The cake that has the Falcons jersey on it. I'm supposed to pick it up today."

"I'm sorry, ma'am, did you have an order for this?"

"Yes," Cat said, she dug in her purse for the order form and for the receipt of the deposit. "Here it is. I even sketched out what I would like."

The lady looked at it and rubbed her chin, all the while the bell rang announcing the entrance of another customer. "This doesn't look familiar at all. We don't have a cake that looks like that back there."

"Are you sure? The lady who I spoke to—"

The lady peered closely at the receipt so that the paper almost met her nose and then put it back, "Ah, that's the problem. Dolores took your order. She's gone now. Well, we had to fire her." She shook her head, "Precisely for reasons like this."

"You wouldn't happen to be able to whip up a cake out back, would you?"

"No," she looked past Cat to the couple of women—a mother and daughter—that were behind her. Cat looked at the daughter's hand. There was the engagement ring, but no wedding band. Then she looked at the shop. She had thought it would be a good idea to get the cake here because they made groom's cakes and wedding cakes, and groom's cakes in the South could be just about anything because it was supposed to represent the groom. Usually it was chocolate, which worked with Brad just fine because that was his favorite.

"Excuse me," the lady said, "I have an appointment." She gave the paper back to Cat. "I'm sorry about that. Maybe next time you'll keep us in mind." She opened up the cash register. "Here's your refund." She squeezed Cat's shoulder. "I'm really sorry about this."

"Sorry." Cat looked at the cash wadded in her hand. It looked alien there along with the laughter of the two women with the baker.

Kesha entered her view. Eyebrow raised.

Cat held up her hand. "Don't. All right? I can just pick up a cake after work."

"You? You're just going to pick up any ole cake? From any ole bakery? You won't eat mall chocolate chip cookies."

"I can make them better at home. It's a waste." The pat answer slipped out before she could take the words back. She shook her head. "Look. Don't worry about it. Just show up tonight. Everything will be fine."

"Uh-huh."

Thankfully there were no emergencies at work. She was out the door on time at 4 p.m. and made it to her car and out to the interstate headed home in record time. Just like the Waffle House, Atlanta had grocery stores with bakeries on just about every corner. *If* she could just go to any old bakery. Which she couldn't. Because Kesha was right.

Dang it.

Hmmm. Berry's Food City on Mt. Zion had good cakes. She'd attended a wedding where they made the wedding cake. Serviceable and on the way home. Just what she needed so that she would still have time to go home and start the cuteification process. Because she was going to prove to Brad that she was wife material and then everything would be all right.

The bakery was located to the right of the store entrance, past the display of cards and the ready-to-eat section. It was empty with one lone man in glasses and a plastic hair net staring from behind the counter. The instrumental version of Culture Club's *Do You Really Want to Hurt Me?* taunted her from overhead.

"Excuse me," she said. "You wouldn't happen to have a cake, would you? I'm looking for a quarter sheet cake that is, uh, manly?"

"Do you have a particular design that you're interested in?" he asked.

"Not really. This is just a last ditch effort because of something that was a mistake. I kinda need it for tonight."

"Well, that would mean that you would need to look at what we already have here.

They looked at the ready-made cakes. All of the themes were way too feminine for a rugby player. Barbie. Pink and purple "Happy Birthday" on a quarter sheet cake. And then there was the round cake with yellow roses. Brad liked lemon, but—she shook her head. No, no this wasn't going to work and every second that she spent here she was wasting time.

She smiled. "Thank you," she said and left. She glanced at her watch; it was the digital one that she used to work out. She only had about two hours of leeway. He didn't necessarily need a cake. There was going to be plenty of food there. His roommate had already started setting up the decorations. He'd been very helpful planning the surprise party along with Brad's friend Joe.

She had this idea of how it would all play out in her mind. She would have some cheesy '80s music playing because that's what he loved, and when he was used to everyone saying surprise she would come out of the kitchen with her hair pulled back from her face, in a cute top that hugged her curves, fitted jeans and high heels. You definitely had to have the hooker heels and the hooker red lipstick. Because she was going after him. It wasn't going to be just a cake, it was going to be a declaration.

But all that took preparation. And time. Which she did not have. She could spend the next hour or so calling, hoping and praying and then winding up with who knows what. Or she could do what she knew she needed to do.

In ten minutes, she was home and had turned on the oven. She made sure that her oven thermometer sat on the middle rack. Baking was a science. That was something that she and her cousins definitely knew and one thing that you learned quickly. It was basic and it was simple.

Most people had a sweet tooth and would eat something sweet put in front of them. An easy way to spread goodwill whether you happened to be a hearth witch or not (Auntie would say that they were not witches being Christian and all. But you could say all kinds of things when you owned the church the family attended and paid the preacher's salary.)

She pulled the half-apron made from cupcake fabric from where it hung on the door of the pantry and tied it around her waist. She turned the radio to the R&B station. Luther Vandross was crooning a song that was one big pickup line. Perfect. It was the same steps she always took when baking. The ritual was comforting and anything done time after time could build the magic, which is what she was looking for.

Then came the eggs and butter to be brought to room temperature.

She looked at her pantry. She had originally wanted a chocolate cake but she didn't think that was going to work. You had to use what you had. That's something that she believed in. Any self-respecting hearth witch would have lemon in her refrigerator. It was absolutely amazing what lemon could do. You could use it to season, to clean. And now that she thought about it, she knew what cake she was going to make. It was simple—just one step up from a box cake, which she had to admit were pretty doggone good. The problem was that a box cake was a box cake.

She stopped as she felt the eggs. They had lost the chill of the refrigerator, but still not there yet.

This was not supposed to be a special cake. She didn't know if she could stop herself from infusing anything into it. She'd used that mixer plenty of times to bring cookies to co-workers and for special occasions when she had intentionally wanted to do something—when she was trying to throw in a heap of happiness, as Auntie would say.

But she didn't know about this one. It was a birthday cake. It wouldn't matter this one time. There weren't really dictates, they were just suggestions, right? She thought that as she took out the flour. Besides, no matter what Auntie said, something that she could not tolerate was a box cake no matter how delicious.

You need to make things with love, she would say. Baking is very serious business and so was her heritage, her birthright.

She looked on and worked. Once she knew what she was going to make, it was simple. She'd done it many times before. She carefully measured the flour. Whipped the butter and decided to add just a bit of lemon juice in the batter while she was making the lemon filling. Brad liked lemon so he would like that. Since she was making it from scratch, she decided to pull out an old favorite—coconut cake with lemon filling and fluffy frosting.

It was intensive, but worth it and way better than something she could buy.

Yes, in more ways than one, a voice popped into her head. She squashed it as she squeezed the lemon for the filling.

This would be fine. It was just a plain birthday cake and who knows what would happen? It would probably be a blessing for the whole company. And if he did like it, what was the harm in that? Everyone knew that you had to prove yourself to men these days, and the most valuable wife was someone who was skilled at the arts of the hearth, who knew how to make a house a home.

She looked down at her apron dusted with flour. This was love. Her cousins may have loved their sewing machines. Others, the garden, but she loved to be in the kitchen, with flour flying everywhere.

Three layers should do it. Women would be invited and they would probably want to share a piece because it was so thick. Maybe a separate cake? No, she had doubled the recipe so she would have enough for cupcakes. Like the ones at the bakery.

She stopped. Why hadn't she thought of that before? They would be easy to transport and—no that would be an experiment for another time. She knew what she needed to do and how much time she had. The cake would be cutting it close as it was. She would have enough time to get the thing cooled down and frosted.

She placed the batter-filled pans in the oven and when that was done, set out to make the filling and the fluffy frosting. She was humming along as the kitchen grew cozy as she liked to think of it when something was baking.

And soon it was time and ready. She poked holes in the cake to let the filling seep through. She took a tester cupcake to experiment on; she would after all make notes for the next time. And she needed to know about the lemon. Hmmm, a bit lemony but he liked it that way. It would be a nice fluffy dessert with the frosting. She bet she could get some of his friends from the gym to try it.

She pulled everything together and looked at the time. Just enough to stick it in the cake transport holder and make it over to his house.

She texted Brad's friend Joe—*Need 10 more minutes.*

Return text—*OK.*

She splashed her face, took off her apron and hung it up and looked at herself in the mirror. She was flushed and happy. It would have to be enough because she didn't have time to get production ready. He would be so surprised. She giggled to herself and headed over there.

She stepped into the apartment and there were already about ten people there, including Kesha. Joe had assured her that these were good ones, that he would be happy to see all of them. She didn't know these people from his other life outside the office, but that was what it was about, after all. It was his party so he should have the people who he wanted.

The only people he hung out with outside of work were her and Kesha anyway.

And it looked great. Stealth, well, that was possible and Joe would tell Brad that he needed to borrow something at Brad's apartment.

She made the rounds saying hello to everyone and then ran into Kesha who ooed and ahhed at the cake.

"You baked," she said and her eyes narrowed. "And this is your special cake."

"Oh, it's nothing," Cat said eyeing the hummus and wanting to introduce herself to everyone.

"Baby—"

The ding on her phone sounded then. She looked down. They were coming.

"Y'all everyone. They're coming!" she said.

Then turned the lights off and said, "We'll all yell surprise, OK?"

The guests nodded and got into position. She was so excited. She lived for times like this. So awesome.

The door opened, the voices, "Brad, man, I'm sorry but I needed you to help with these."

"No problem, we'll get them right now."

And then everyone burst forward. "Surprise!" they said in unison.

And he did look surprised. He turned back to Joe who moved quickly out of the way and then to the rest of the folks assembled. When everyone else rushed forward, she held back. I mean, you could take a girl from home but you couldn't disrupt home training. And what she really noticed now that she was looking for it were magical touches all over the apartment. From when she bought the decorations and how carefully Joe had hung them up and now seeing the cake on the table—she'd stuck candles in them but hadn't bothered to go do a big reveal with someone bringing it forth—she saw that a haze of goodwill hung all over it.

Even Kesha must have sensed it and she wasn't even family in any way, shape or form.

Brad broke out of the group and came toward her still smiling and gave her a big hug. She hugged him back.

Joe broke in, "She's the one who was the ringleader for all this. She's the blame."

"Hey, thanks, Girlie," he said.

She smiled back. "Now let's cut this cake," she said, a bit overwhelmed by it. She'd brought the serving utensils, but they made do with paper plates. She knew that no one was going to clean up after all this and she wanted to make it as nice as possible.

Between that and the alcohol, she was sure that someone was going to break out the karaoke. Food, friends and song. That is what made an event.

Cat kept trying to catch his eye, but his eyes kept going to a cute strawberry blonde in the corner with the perfect makeup and standard cute top and jean uniform of the going-out crowd.

Whenever he looked up from talking with someone, his eyes went to her. Cat served the cake, brought out sodas and kept everything going. By the time she came back to the main room they were singing a duet, the cake eaten on the side.

In her mind came the voice again, that damned voice of reason. "They look like they would make a good couple."

And they did. Auntie had said that she had the touch, that she could see the invisible bond forming between people. But she always also said that Cat wouldn't be able to tell who would bond her heart.

And the cake that she had wished happiness and love into, it had given him the courage to go after the one he had really wanted.

And it wasn't her. At all.

Joe stepped to her as he followed her eyes, "They look good together, don't they?"

She smiled because what could you do? You never let them see that your heart is breaking, and he was a guy, so hopefully he wouldn't see it anyway, "Yes," she said, "they do." She shook her head. "I think the kids are gonna be all right."

"How about you?"

She pulled back at the question. She didn't know what he meant by that. "I'm good," she said, not meeting his eyes which were a little too dark and saw her a little too clearly. "I think that we're out of napkins."

"I'll get them," he said. "You've done enough here."

But she didn't want to stay there and watch everything that was going on. She wanted to hide, to feel useful as it became more and more apparent that these people were his true friends. Yeah they'd gone out a couple of times as friends, but if he were putting this party together the other ones belonged here, not her.

At the end of the night Brad snapped up Strawberry Shortcake to take her home.

She looked at the cake. Only a quarter of it was left. The damned thing had done its job. She shook her head. Auntie told her that her calling would sneak up on her like that, just like her future husband. It will knock out the blue, she said. And she'd been right. A matchmaker. Of all the nonsensical things.

Joe was there, he'd helped her take down the streamers and everything else.

"Great party," he said.

"Yep. All the work paid off."

When she took the cake to put it in the carrying cake holder he covered her hand with his. "Hey," he said laughing, "Uh, where are you goin' with that cake?"

"Home. I thought everyone took what they wanted."

"Not me." He looked at her closely. "Did you do something to your hair?"

"Maybe flour," she laughed. "I had to whip that thing up in no time flat. I'm not sure that I look equally presentable."

"You just look different."

"No, no. Same me." She couldn't take his gaze so concentrated on the cake again. "You really want it? You seem pretty in shape to want this."

"You made it from scratch, right?"

"Yes, even the filling and the frosting. No box cake this one."

"Then, yes, I want it. My grandmother always said that a homemade cake is like a love offering."

"Your grandmother said that?"

"Yes, she did."

"Well, you can have it then. I think I'd like your grand-mother."

He smiled, "I'll clean the plate and bring it over to you."

"Just tell Brad and he can drop it off at work."

"But I have to repay you for doing all this for my buddy. Maybe lunch sometime?"

She blinked. Lunch? He seemed like a nice guy. No. He probably was a nice guy. Took direction well and was helpful. This was the guy who was the real possibility, the one who was right in front of her instead of the one who would never be.

The "no" was right on her lips. Her tongue right at the bottom of her front teeth.

She looked down at her empty cake carrier. She had gone in full and now left empty. But she didn't have to.

And there were more ways to take chances than going to Vegas.

"Joe," she said, "lunch sounds really good."

The smile that he gave her was worth the answer. She turned and there was Kesha sucking her teeth and arching her eyebrow. Cat gave her a wink as she held the cake carrier in her hand to carry out to her car. It suddenly occurred to her that Kesha had been single for way too long. And she liked red velvet cake.

Maybe this matchmaking thing was gonna turn out to be all right.

Kellen Knolan's job as a teacher introduced him to Young Adult fiction. "The one thing I noticed," he writes, "was how constantly dour many of the characters seemed to be. Why weren't there more stories about the kids I knew? Alternately fun, serious, worried, goofy—and yes, dour. I moved [the kids] to Nexus, Louisiana, where everything is fantastic fiction, save for the internal lives of the kids themselves."

"A Taste of Joie de Vivre" marks Kellen's first appearance in print, but certainly not his last.

—————

A Taste of *Joie De Vivre*
Kellen Knolan

A sweat ball crawled slowly down Ashley Foret's back.

Starting as a tiny droplet at the base of her neck, it had built mass but not momentum and was now firmly planted at the base of her spine. Lacking the inertia to move over the bulge of her butt, its tortured tickle grew as other sweat balls gravitated towards it. Considering reason No. 36 it sucked to be overweight, Ashley still found a small smile forming on her face: three dozen reasons was nothing compared to how many reasons it sucked to be the Nexus High School mascot.

Clad neck to toe in a furry tiger suit, Ashley was every component of miserable. The summer heat of Louisiana's Cajun Country in full force, it was 89 degrees with humidity to match. While it was vacation for most everyone else, all the fall sports were back at practice. Even the cheerleading squad was there, despite their coach being on leave.

Walking to school along the edge of the city of Nexus's commercial district, Ashley once again laughingly lamented out loud the lack of streetlamps in this part of town: "Where's a good backscratcher when you need one?"

79

That Ashley could have a sense of humor about anything was testament to both her demeanor and the culture in which she was raised: Pure blood Cajun with roots going back to the Acadians settlement in the swamps two-and-half centuries ago. *Joie De Vivre*, her grandmother always said, "The Joy of Life," as a cure for everything.

When Ashley lamented being overweight, it was her Maw Maw who'd say "Who dat want be skinny mullet anyway?" in her heavily accented Cajun. Annoying at times, incomprehensible at others—fat or skinny, hair or fish, Ashley still had no idea what the expression had to do with wanting to be thinner—Ashley nonetheless listened. It was Maw Maw who'd gotten the family through when Ashley's mother, Maw Maw's only child, died in a car accident driving back to Nexus from New Orleans on I-10.

Not that Ashley always listened right away. At fourteen years old and about to be a freshman in high school, it was her job to be a pain in the butt—and Maw Maw's job to set her straight, as when Ashley said she was going to decline the offer to be the school mascot after failing at tryouts: "I wanted to be a cheerleader!"

"Don't you make a *bahbin*!" Maw Maw shot back.

As often the case, Ashley was momentarily lost with her grandmother's words. It wasn't the accent; she'd lived in Cajun Country long enough to understand all but the thickest accents. It was what a *bahbin* was, and stopping for a moment to once again consider the mishmash of French, English, Native American and African tongues, it took her a second to remember just what the expression meant: "I am not pouting! I just wanted to be a cheerleader, not the mascot!"

"*Co faire*?" Maw Maw asked. "Everyone see you the same."

"Why?! That is why! Who wants to be seen as the fat girl in the fur!" Ashley cried. "Who wants...? Oh, God, I am so sorry Maw Maw..."

Like many of the older people in Nexus, Louisiana, Maw Maw was hairy, strangely so. Just one of the litany of birth defects that had afflicted the residents of the town for generations, all the older people in town seemed to be afflicted with something: Webbed feet and hands, translucent skin that seemed to almost glow from underneath, hairy faces and hands—even on the women. In many places it would have been a curse—but not in Nexus, or, as it was called many years ago: Recontere.

Because in Recontere, Louisiana they simply went with it, celebrating their differences instead of being afraid of them. *Laissez les bons temps rouler*, they called it: "Let the good times roll," and through decades of poverty, storms and deprivation, the people of Acadiana Cajun Country had, and no more so than the afflicted generations of Recontere.

For years Recontere had been a refuge for all kinds of people who might be shunned anywhere else. Whether born there, a refugee from the many traveling circuses that traveled the backroads in the mid-20th century, or just someone who grew tired of being a spectacle somewhere else, Recontere was where they gathered to live their lives and if a few nickels could pass their way, tell their stories. As it happened there were many nickels in those days, and after a time these men and women came to be known throughout Acadiana as "The Storied."

By the dawn of the 21st century, however, those days were long over. Inside town whatever had produced the birth defects had stopped. Outside, circuses had stopped traveling, and in their rush to get everywhere on the interstate, people had long ago stopped descending into a small town along the swamp just to listen to a story. Town leaders had even abandoned the name Recontere, a semi-combination of the French words for Encounter and Story, and changed the name of the town to Nexus.

Why they'd done that was a mystery to Ashley who'd heard the basics of the story many, many times; Acadians were fiercely proud of their history. But it was a story without an ending. Each time Ashley thought she might get a chance to ask her unanswered questions, Maw Maw would start into a slow tirade using words that Ashley knew her grandmother would not want her to know. Sometimes Ashley even saw tears, as Maw Maw lamented the distant strip of interstate highway that had stolen both her daughter and her way of life. The only time Ashley ever saw the *Joie De Vivre* leave her grandmother, Ashley always longed to know more, and was always afraid to bring it up.

Until the day after cheerleading try-outs when Ashley apologized to Maw Maw for blurting who wanted to be the fat girl in the fur.

Laughter filled Maw Maw's voice. "In the fur I am fat! And you! *A bon couer* and practice! And not shave so much, *es bon!*"

And she was right—not about the need to stop shaving; Ashley thought she had enough social problems without being all hairy, too. But about doing something whole-heartedly, which is why Ashley took the mascot job and walked to school every day in sweltering heat to make sure she was at practice on time. Maw Maw having given up her driver's license long ago—you could walk most everywhere in Nexus, anyway—it was Ashley's only way to school with her father working the offshore oil rigs for the next week.

Almost within sight of Nexus High School, Ashley lamented having to walk for reasons beside the heat. Mainly that moving at such a slow speed allowed her to observe what a crap-fest this part of Nexus actually was. Boarded up buildings, vacant houses, overgrown lawns: Each a reminder of the glory days of Recontere, all they served to do now was punctuate that more than just the interstate had left the town behind, whatever its name might have been.

Wishing one last time for a lamppost to scratch her back on, Ashley couldn't help but notice at her feet a rusted-out hole where one used to stand. Mindlessly kicking it, Ashley went to Plan B for scratching her itch: flogging her back with the tiger head in a random attempt to hit the sweat ball. It worked—sort of.

"Hey, ya fat fur ball!" screamed a voice from a passing car. "That's costume abuse! You owe me laps!"

Snapped from her contemplation of sweat balls, swinging animal heads and the dismal state of Nexus, Ashley looked up just in time to see Niki Bordelon's brunette head duck back inside Portia Comeau's BMW Mini as the two headed for cheerleading practice. The captain and assistant captain of the squad, respectively, they had the power to make good on their threats. Heck, Niki and Portia were the reason Ashley was already in costume in the first place: Everyone was expected to arrive at practice ready to go.

Normally, this rule didn't apply to the mascot; it was one thing to expect girls to arrive in tiny skirts and T-shirts, it was another to expect someone to do so in a full-body fursuit. But then there was nothing normal about the Nexus High School Cheerleading Squad these days; that much had been clear since the coach's car blew up in the parking lot the last day of school—while she was in it.

* * *

Miss Lynette Dugas, cheerleading coach, demonically frightening math teacher, and anal-retentive car owner, was known throughout Nexus High School for all of these things. A first-year teacher, she was insanely bitter that she'd had to "come crawling back to Nexus," as she put it, to find a teaching job. Her career plans putting her in New Orleans but her grades and teaching acumen making her employable nowhere but her backwater hometown, she was unfortunate proof of just how few people wanted to call the place home these days. Taking her frustrations out on her students almost daily, she was reviled by nearly everyone, who took to calling her "The Dragon Lady," a term she actually seemed to embrace.

So when the students of Nexus High School felt the thump of a distant explosion inside even in the far corners of the school building, a few dared actually hope it might be her in the flames. Her car nearly vaporizing as she closed the door, the fireball had literally melted some of the letters off the signs in front of NHS hundreds of feet away. (The school was now officially a "RUG REE ZO") The car, a brand new black Camaro, was left a metal hulk of melted tires, leather, and engine parts. The car's personalized license plate, Louisiana tag "DRGNLDY" was found on the roof of the gazebo in Brasseaux Park, more than a block away—with the bumper still attached.

It was a miracle that no one in the school was hurt or even injured, largely because the parking lot was still empty of people during sixth period when Miss Dugas went home early because of illness. More importantly, however, was that she always parked on the far edge of the parking lot with instructions (and well-known threats) that no one was to get anywhere near her car. A parking lot designed for a much larger staff and school population, Miss Dugas's Camaro was nearly a hundred feet from any other car when it exploded.

And that wasn't the strange part.

The strange part was that she walked away from it. Literally standing up amidst the flaming wreckage of her car approximately five minutes after the explosion, she simply walked out of the flames and over to the paramedics. Ashley, hundreds of her fellow Nexus Tigers, and the fire department now gathered in gaped-mouth silence, it was fellow incoming freshman Drew Broussard who spoke first: "Damn, she's hot."

"That is so wrong," Ashley said.

"Why?" Drew asked. "Because I'm gay? I can appreciate the feminine form."

"No, you jackass," Ashley said, "because what's left of her clothes are still on fire."

"If you call a sports bra and panties clothes," Drew said, now cocking his head slightly sideways. "At least I think it's a sports bra. With the flames it's kind of hard to tell—"

"Drew!" Ashley said, as members of the fire department began to run towards Miss Dugas. "The woman is on fire!"

"No, just what's left of her clothes. She's just fine, and I do mean fiiiiinnnnnne, although how the hell that's possible, I have no idea," Drew said. "I knew she wasn't human."

"DREW!"

"Hey, you're the one who called her a dragon lady," Drew said, sounding not the least bit unhappy. "It's not my fault you were right."

"She's still a human being," Ashley said. "I'm sure there are better things that could be said."

"Yeah: She's hotter than I thought," Drew said, now starting to laugh. "That firefighter just knocked off her bra…"

* * *

Recalling the incident, Ashley was somewhat ashamed to find herself laughing. Partially because she had to admit Drew was right; Ashley herself had gotten a "C" from the mercurial math teacher for nothing more than using a wooden pencil instead of a mechanical one.

More, though, it was because Miss Dugas had been completely uninjured by the accident. No burns, no scars, nothing. Well, not the physical kind of scars, anyway. Rumor was that even though she was officially returning to teach and coach come fall, she desperately wanted to leave since virtually the entire town had seen her naked. But so what? She'd wanted to leave town since the minute she got here; the town and school would be better off without her, Ashley decided. And besides, if looking for a new town where no one would have seen her naked was the goal, she was screwed. It had gone viral on YouTube about three weeks ago.

Be that as it may, even absent for the summer Miss Dugas's presence was still felt throughout the cheerleading squad. Her captains, Niki and Portia, ran it just as cruelly as she would have. Certainly, cheerleading squads had always been a cauldron of rank, title, and mean-girl behavior. But where most cheer coaches tried to minimize these behaviors, Miss Dugas at best looked the other way, and at worst encouraged them. Now, with her gone, Niki and Portia had free reign to treat everyone like crap.

In the beginning, Ashley hoped the school administration would put a stop to it. But given the chaos following the explosion and the administration's desire not to bother the only math teacher it could find, it pretty much refused to do anything. Coupled with the fact that Niki and Portia weren't doing anything illegal, just mean, the principal figured it was "girls being girls," and let it go at that.

It was more than that, of course; making people run laps in sweaty suits in Louisiana's summer heat was likely dangerous. But Ashley refused to give Niki the satisfaction of hearing her complain or seeing her quit—another thing she'd learned from her Maw Maw. That's why, even though Ashley once again found herself on the cheerleading craplist, she trundled on to practice, knowing exactly what awaited her. Not because it was bad, but because it was normal.

Finally reaching the edge of the school parking lot, Ashley walked through the middle of the dirt that used to be Miss Dugas's parking space. The corner of the lot yet to be repaved, Ashley figured it wouldn't be. In all her years in Nexus she'd noticed that things that fell apart tended to stay that way, whether through a lack of money or enthusiasm she didn't know, that was just how it was.

Stopping for just a moment to make sure Niki and Portia were out of their car and onto the football field, Ashley was relieved to see her friends, Kayla and Autumn, were still in the parking lot. As always, Kayla had her jittery hands wrapped around an iced mocha. While Autumn's hands were rock-steady, perfect for applying yet another layer of mascara.

Having all tried out together, Ashley was relieved her friends had made the squad, even if during practice they weren't actually allowed to talk to each other. Calling to them, she was surprised to see them completely ignore her as they continued huddled in conversation. Hoping she hadn't become a social pariah to even two of her best friends, she approached quietly trying to hear what they were talking about.

"…I've heard she can only go out at night…" Kayla said.

"And that she has to wear one of those Arab sheets during the day…" Autumn said, completely unaware that Ashley was opening her mouth right behind her: "It's called a burqa, guys," Ashley said knowingly. "And who in the world in Nexus is wearing a—"

"SSSHHHHH!!!" Both girls said to Ashley. "There's a reason we're trying not to get noticed!"

"You're trying not to get noticed," Ashley said to them both. "It's the only way not to do laps around here."

"This is different," Kayla said. "Madison is a vampire and no one is supposed to know."

"Madison Gaudet is a vampire?" Ashley asked, her eyebrows now fully raised. "That's horrible!"

"I know," Kayla said. "No one's supposed to talk about it."

"Well, I can see why," Ashley said, the sarcasm beginning to drip. "She's the best garlic-oyster cook Schucker's restaurant has. If she's a vampire she'll have to stop doing that, although I do suppose this means they always have someone for bussing tables on the night shift, doesn't it?"

"I'm serious," Kayla said. "I heard my grandmother talking about it on the phone this morning."

"Your mom watches reality TV and thinks they're documentaries," Ashley said. "That doesn't say a whole lot."

"Not all of them!" Kayla said, defensively. "She knows *Swamp People* is stupid."

"That's because she knows half the people in it," Ashley said, acknowledging that on at least that Kayla was right-on. Everyone in Acadiana hated that show. "But seriously, a vampire? Did she switch demographics and start reading *Twilight*?"

Here, Autumn decided to chime in: "You know, Madison's not the only one I've been hearing strange things about. Marc and Destiny, too: I've heard rumors about those two, weird rumors…"

"Let me guess," Ashley said. "Werewolves."

"Yes!"

"Well, werewolves had to be in there somewhere," Ashley said dismissively. "Anything else? Witches? I mean, what's a good story without a little Harry Potter these days?"

"No," Autumn said, "no witches. But I did hear Destiny Doucet's a mermaid…"

"You have lost your damn mind," Ashley said, not willing to engage their silliness any longer. "Or your grandmother has. Autumn, I know your and Kayla's grandmothers talk all the time. Every senior citizen in this town does."

"You got that right," Autumn said as she and Kayla turned to walk away. "But before you get all high and mighty, you should know it was your 'Maw Maw' our grandmothers were talking to."

* * *

Running the last of her four quarter-mile laps around the Nexus High School track, Ashley still couldn't believe what her friends had been talking about. Not because she thought they were crazy, but because there was some little part of her that knew they weren't. For one thing, she had heard her grandmother talking on the phone this morning in hushed and whispered tones—and now she apparently knew who with.

Certainly there had been no talk of werewolves, vampires and mermaids; Ashley would have remembered that. But she did hear her mention the Roux-Ga-Roux, a mythical werewolf-like being that supposedly lived in the swamps. Dismissing it at the time—and largely still doing the same now—she was more intrigued by what else her Maw Maw had talked about: The Raconteur. French for storyteller, Ashley had heard the word on and off for years in town. In a town known historically for storytelling, that made sense.

But this morning was different, odd. And now that she thought about it, it was a term she'd heard more often of late, each time in circumstances she thought strange at the time. Forming a pattern, they distracted her, which was good. It kept her from noticing the sweat balls forming once again on her spine.

The first time she'd heard the word had been just before Mardi Gras, when the entire town along with the nation had been engrossed in the disaster in San Francisco. The aircraft carrier *Jefferson* had struck the south pillar of the Golden Gate Bridge, setting off a cascade of explosions and destruction that eventually caused the collapse of the bridge's roadway into the ocean. The carrier itself, disabled by the destruction of its command bridge, had then slammed into Alcatraz Island. Hundreds were dead or missing, and even months later, the *Jefferson* remained beached on its side in the bay.

Locally, however, the talk had been about someone seen on TV in the moments after the disaster: George Robichaud, the patriarch of one of the founding families of Rencontere more than two hundred years earlier. Missing for more than 40 years, helicopter cameras had filmed him lying in a young girl's arms, both of them marooned on the island of asphalt still clinging to the north tower of The Golden Gate Bridge, his hands cradling her face. National speculation focused on who these two survivors of the disaster might be. Speaking something to her before he passed out, his words were uncertain to a nation looking for something hopeful out of national tragedy.

In Nexus, however, there was no debate about what he'd said: "Tell them: The Raconteur has returned"—and within weeks he had. Still in a coma from his injuries, he was now a patient at Recontere Hospital, where from the moment of his arrival, a vigil had been going on outside his window. At first hundreds of people with candles and now just a few, every night there was someone outside his window. Led always by the town elders, the last of The Storied.

Ashley had been there several times, always with her Maw Maw. Each time Ashley wanted to ask, "Why are we here?" And each time she would stop, once again seeing that look of longing and pain that came whenever her grandmother talked about her history or that of Recontere and Nexus. It was the look Ashley had seen this morning, too, though this latest time it seemed tinged with something different. Ashley wanted to call it hope, but knowing the misery the topic caused her Maw Maw, she had a hard time believing tha—

"Ashley!" Niki and Portia bellowed together from their seats in the stands. Their make-up shaded from a melt-off, their sneers were symmetric, as well. The rest of the squad now forced to wait for Ashley in the heat, it was almost as if the captains were dragging it out on purpose. "Get your furry ass over here!"

Enviously, Ashley eyed Niki opening a chilled bottle of water, already knowing it wasn't for her. It was for Princess, Niki's perpetual accessory and pet Chihuahua. Four pounds of constant motion and urine, the last thing the dog needed was more fluids.

Snapped out of her reverie, any thoughts of hope—for anything—were snuffed out by Niki's next words. "OK, nap-time/lap-time is over: Get your head on."

"I'm really not supposed to wear it when it's this hot," Ashley said. "It's 40 degrees warmer in there and—"

"Are you saying you don't want to be the mascot?" Niki asked, sounding clearly hopeful. "Because I'm sure there are a lot of other fat girls that would love to hang out with the cheerleaders if you can't hack it."

"No, I can hack it," Ashley said, refusing to give in. "If I could just get some water."

"Fine, but take Princess with you," Niki said, pointing down at the small Chihuahua at her feet. "And don't you dare drink before she does. Now get your head on!"

Putting on her head and taking Princess by the leash, Ashley thought it ironic that Niki was giving her control of the dog. Vision in the suit was terrible; in an effort to make it look like a real tiger they'd made the vision and comfort of the person inside secondary. Ashley was as likely to step on the dog as she was get it water, and while that would be a bad thing for her cheerleading career, it made her smile nonetheless. As many times as the dog had peed on squad members' personal things, it would be divine justice. Not that she really wanted to kill the dog, but she had to admit Princess was far more suited to satisfying gator snack than ideal pet.

After getting water for them both, Ashley returned Niki's pet/accessory to Niki's shaded spot in the stands and once again took her place at the end of the cheerleading line. Not considered part of their official routines, Ashley was still expected to stand there, in formation. It was another way of torturing Ashley. She knew that Niki and Portia would never let her perform at an actual game. No, Ashley would be relegated to the stands to be punched, prodded and kicked by fans of the opposite team and by children from her own town.

Once again lulled into boredom by the need to just stand there in the heat, Ashley couldn't help but think about Madison, Marc and Destiny and the rumors that clearly were making their way through town. All around fourteen years old, each was about to enter their freshman year at NHS. That was really all they had in common—that and Farallon Robbins.

Farallon was the daughter of George Robichaud, and why she had an Americanized version of her Cajun surname no one really knew. But when it was clear George wasn't going to recover quickly, George's sister, Jenna, had flown out to California to get Farallon and her half-brother Jayson, to bring them back to Nexus. Both of them odd ducks out of water in the bayous of western Louisiana, they were nevertheless making friends quickly.

Among Farallon's most immediate friends, Ashley knew, were Madison, Destiny and Marc Broussard. Not only spending a lot of time with her, they had been spending a lot of time with The Raconteur himself. Not because of him, per se; he was still in a coma. But Farallon had allowed them into her father's hospital room, something no other non-family members were allowed to do. Maybe they'd caught some weird disease from him, and the old people in town were letting their imaginations get the best of them.

Ashley dismissed that thought quickly, however: Her good friend Drew, along with Sabrina Thibodeaux, and even Jayson and Farallon Robbins themselves, weren't the subject of any rumors whatsoever. Wouldn't they have been affected as well?

"Fuzz-buns!" Portia screamed at her, interrupting her thoughts. "Why aren't you stepping left with us?!"

Immediately, of course, Ashley had no good answer, though fairly quickly one presented itself. In the heat her plastic feet had stuck fast into the track. And nothing she could do could move them. "My feet won't move. I seemed to have melted into the track."

"And this is my problem, how?"

"Well, you could help me," Ashley said, and before even thinking went on, "isn't that what a captain does?"

"Listen, fatty-fur," Niki said, now clearly asserting her authority. "When you can jump higher, move faster and cheer better than anyone out here, you can be the captain and decide what one does. But until you feel like officially challenging me for the job, don't tell me what my job is. Got it?"

"Yes..." Ashley said, still very mindful of her predicament. "But could I please get someone's help getting unstuck?"

"Well, since you asked so nicely," Portia said, clearly having no intention of returning the favor. "Princess, go help her."

Watching the dog, Ashley was at once impressed and horrified: Almost on cue the dog lifted her leg and peed on Ashley's leg. Still stuck to the track and basically blind, Ashley could do nothing but listen to Princess's collar bell jingle as she felt a warm, wet feeling crawl down her left ankle. Getting more embarrassed by the minute, suddenly being Madison and forced to wear a burqa around didn't seem quite so bad; at least as a vampire she'd have a reason for things to suck.

Finding herself laughing inside the costume at her own terrible pun, Ashley once again was glad she had Maw Maw in her life. Deciding to make the best of it and not give Niki any satisfaction, Ashley refused to move even the slightest. Instead, she took the offensive—of sorts: "I'm impressed, Niki. How'd you train your dog to do that?"

"I didn't train him at all," Niki said to Ashley, as if that meant more for her brains than the dog's. "It's just a matter of taste I guess, and I must say I'm surprised."

"Why is that?"

"Because I would have thought you didn't have any," Niki said, once again staring at the dog. "But clearly Princess likes something about you…"

Having no idea what Niki meant, Ashley still couldn't see what was going on through the tiny eyes of the costume. Soon, however, she got her answer as she heard a jingling collar and felt a warm trickle down her other ankle.

* * *

Dawn arrived early the next morning, Ashley thought to no one in particular as she awoke the next day. This was good, as it was a pretty stupid thought. Cracking her eyes open, however, she had some idea of where the thought had come from: She could see the sun rising outside her window.

A true believer in the value of summer vacation, Ashley was lucky if she rose before lunch, much less breakfast. And yet there it was: Dawn breaking over the trees—and the ruins of the rice co-op. It had burned down less than a year ago, and true to Nexus form it was still a debris-filled heap, with the emergency fencing even having fallen down in places. She heard it made a nice homeless shelter.

This morning, however, it made a nice silhouette for the oranges and pinks of dawn, and as the ambient light crept through the oak tree outside her window she could even see a couple of robins high in their nest. She had to admit, there might be something to this morning thing.

Stretching her arms out, Ashley was surprised they didn't ache. (By the time Autumn and Kayla had finished yanking her out of the asphalt yesterday, Ashley was surprised her fingers were still connected to her wrists.) More, Ashley was taken aback at the sight of her arms: They were furry.

That was a first: She was so tired last night she'd fallen asleep in the costume. Except that made no sense. Her Maw Maw had peeled her out of the costume.

Confused, Ashley tried to clear her head by rubbing her eyes. Again, shock: Not only had Maw Maw never gotten her out of the costume, Ashley had actually fallen asleep with the head on.

What the hell?

Sitting up now in bed so she could get the head off, she gently tugged on the ears and muzzle to make sure she wouldn't damage it any more than she must already have. (She could not imagine how many laps she might get if Niki and Portia could tell she'd slept in the costume.) Not even budging, however, Ashley found herself tugging harder and harder until she found she was actually hurting herself.

What the hell?

Deciding she'd better get to her mirror, Ashley swung her legs out of bed and jumped onto the floor—and nearly bounced out of the room. Crashing into her bedroom door, she heard a sickening crack as her shoulder crashed into the hardwood frame next to the doorknob. Pushing herself off the floor, she expected to find her collarbone broken. Instead, she found the doorjamb shattered and splintered, and as she rose to a standing position she found no aches whatsoever. Even the pains from yesterday's miserable practice were gone.

Making her way slowly to her full-length mirror, Ashley stopped to look at herself and saw what she expected—and what she could not have imagined. She was in the costume all right, head-to-toe. But it wasn't a costume anymore, it was her.

She had become the tiger.

Opening her mouth to scream, Ashley could hear her voice coming out; it sounded the same as it ever had. But where there used to be a mascot's black fabric void, there was now a tongue and a tiger's teeth to match. And now, once again looking at herself in the mirror, Ashley could see that where a mascot had cold, plastic eyes, she still had hers: green and deep.

She definitely owed Kayla and Autumn an apolog—

CRASH!

Before Ashley could even think about it, she had suddenly sprung sideways and out through her bedroom window. Shards of glass bouncing easily off her fur, she found herself flying into the branches of the oak tree outside. Feeling completely in control of her body while feeling no control of her urges, she found herself circling and climbing the trunk all at once, madly moving towards something. And then she saw it—and then she didn't.

Like popcorn from a bag, Ashley began mindlessly crunching before she even realized what she was doing. Finding herself actually licking her paws, she decided chewed robin was a lot like Maw Maw's coffee: Good to the last drop. It did not, Ashley noted bemusedly, taste like chicken.

Almost nauseated, and yet feeling very satisfied with herself, Ashley moved back down the tree and pounced back into her bedroom. Sitting now on her haunches, she gazed at herself again in the mirror, this time a robin's carcass hanging out of her mouth. A third errant foot sticking out of her teeth, she knew she'd eaten more than one. Transfixed, she didn't even notice her Maw Maw's reflection materialize in the mirror until Maw Maw was completely in sight. Spinning around, Ashley couldn't even begin to think of what to say—and she didn't have to.

"*Oh, Cherie!*" Maw Maw said, tears in her eyes, a broad smile on her face. "*Vomment ça vas?*"

"How am I feeling?" Ashley asked. "That's all you have to say?! I'm a tiger! I just leapt out the window, ate a bird family, and then jumped back in! Doesn't that bother you?"

"I never liked robins, anyway," Maw Maw said, her quiet voice beginning to calm Ashley in spite of herself. "*Vomment ça vas?*"

"What is it with feelings? I'm feeling…! I'm feeling… I'm feeling great, actually," she said, as she considered her furry paws and felt her tail starting its slow swing back and forth. "Maw Maw, what the hell is going on?"

"The Raconteur has indeed returned."

* * *

For generations in Recontere, Louisiana, the Raconteur had not so much told stories as created the people to live them. Some became Roux-Ga-Roux, werewolf shape-shifters. Others became nearly translucent, their glowing skin becoming "The Dancing Lights," or *Feu Follets*. These "myths" of the swamp and more were The Storied of Nexus, living a life unlike any other. Truly, *Joie De Vivre* in its purest form.

And then it stopped. The latest Raconteur, George Robichaud, had disappeared in the early 1970s. With him went the stories and the characters his family had always created to live them. The last generation, that of George's father, were the last Storied. Years passed, generations grew older, and soon tales were created to explain why women like Maw Maw were so different than their children and grandchildren. Burdened with a secret they could share only amongst themselves, they grew quieter every year as their grandchildren moved away and their generation died—and Recontere died with them.

Children like Ashley grew up knowing the words *Joie De Vivre*, but never really living them—until this morning, when Maw Maw explained it all.

Now, there was one thing Ashley wanted to do.

* * *

Running around the track before cheerleading practice—Niki said her costume looked like she'd slept in it—Ashley walked to the end of the cheerleading line when she was done, just as she had dozens of times before.

"Fur bag!" Niki bellowed. "Go get my dog some water!"

Happy to oblige, Ashley took the leash of the suddenly quivering and back-pedaling dog. Straining on her leash, it seemed Princess had decided that strangling herself was preferable to being anywhere close to the terrifying scent coming from Ashley.

"What the hell is wrong with you, dog?" Niki asked without an ounce of compassion, as the dog began to whine even louder. "And what do you want, fuzz-wuz?" Niki sneered, clearly impressed at her ability to call Ashley a different name every time.

"I was wondering if you could tell me after practice what the rules are for officially challenging for your job?"

"Sure: lose about 40 pounds," Niki said, laughing for a few moments before stopping. "Wait, you're serious, aren't you? You realize for every minute of mine you waste after practice I'm going to make you run a lap?"

"OK," Ashley said. "That sounds fair."

"Sounds ridiculous," Niki said. "Go run a lap now for wasting my minute. And another 12 after that for wasting a minute of every girl on this team."

Willingly beginning her run, Ashley was on her third lap before she heard Niki starting to yell: "Hey! Where's my dog? I paid good money for that thing!"

"Maybe it's with someone else...?" Portia said.

"Someone else? Who else has my good taste? They wouldn't even sell you a dog on the internet..."

Smiling, and then outright laughing, Ashley continued her run, joyful that Niki's disappointments were only beginning. The soon-to-be former captain was right about one thing, however, Ashley thought as she picked a jingle bell out of her teeth: The dog really did have good taste.

Annie Reed is an award-winning mystery writer, but her most popular stories are about Diz and Dee, who run a detective agency in a Seattle-like place filled with magic. Last year, Annie went to an anime convention with her daughter.

"The cosplayers at the convention blew me away with the creativity and variety of their costumes," Annie writes. "When I got the invitation for Unnatural Worlds, *I thought it would be the perfect opportunity to introduce Diz & Dee to anime and cosplay. My daughter, of course, takes total credit for providing me with the inspiration for 'Here, Kitty Kitty.' She's not too far off."*

Here, Kitty Kitty

Annie Reed

I dove behind my desk as my miniature Zen garden went whizzing past me. The garden's stone base slammed into the wall right about where my head had been a split second ago, sand rained down into my hair, and I wondered what else I'd left lying around the front office that the little fairy might decide to throw at me.

My name's Dee, and I'm a private investigator. Clients usually don't show up at my office and launch deadly weapons at me. Along with my partner, Diz, I run D & D Investigations. People—and by that I'm loosely referring to elves, leprechauns, Greek gods, and my family—hire us to find loved ones who've gone missing. We rent office space in a shabby building on the inland side of Moretown Bay. The neighborhood's seen better times, but I like it. A masseuse with a unique flair for marketing and questionable taste in aromatics has a shop across the street, and there's an Asian store next to the office run by a very nice lady who two days ago introduced me to the little fairy currently hovering over my desk and yelling at me in Japanese.

I don't speak Japanese. I think my dog might since his usual Golden Retriever grin was dialed up to a near giggle.

"Want to let me in on the joke?" I asked him as I crouched behind my desk clutching my battered executive chair like it was a shield.

Dog didn't say anything. He only speaks to me in my visions. And yes, that's his name until he tells me otherwise.

We'd been having a nice afternoon at the office, Dog and I, up until the fairy barged through the door. Diz was off doing whatever tall, grumpy, gorgeous elves do—by themselves—after they crack a case with their partner. Dog had been curled up asleep in a small patch of actual sunshine coming through the front windows. I didn't blame him. Clouds, rain, and mist are the norm in Moretown Bay. Rare slices of sunshine should always be celebrated with a good nap. My cat was probably doing the same thing in my upstairs apartment unless she was still pouting. She hasn't quite forgiven me for allowing a dog to invade her life.

Faced with an office full of sleeping animals and no cases to work on, I'd been trying to distract myself from obsessing over my terminally single state, this time with Zen meditation. Diz told me recently that I should learn to live in the moment and enjoy the process instead of focusing so hard on the results. He thinks that might help me control my visions. I'm not an elf or a fairy or any other brand of magical folk. Vanilla human, that's me, only with a seriously unreliable touch of precognition. Since I suck at living in the moment, I thought learning Zen meditation might help; hence the little desk-top sand garden I'd purchased at the Asian market two days ago.

I'd been sitting at my desk raking lines in that stupid little plot of sand for what seemed like hours, trying to stop thinking about my partner's pointy ears and the one time I'd witnessed the tantalizing curve of his towel-covered derriere and just be in the moment, when our latest supposedly happy client flew in the door, picked up the Zen garden, and threw it at my head. I ducked just in time. She's got quite an arm for someone only ten inches tall.

"Okay, okay!" I said from behind the safety of my desk. Which, let's face it, isn't all that safe when the fairy hurling weapons at your head can fly just about anywhere she wants to. "I get that you're angry. Want to let me in on why?"

After all, Diz and I found the ceramic figurine the fairy had hired us to find. We don't normally track down missing objects, but Mrs. Takahashi, the nice lady who owns the Asian store, had asked...well, nicely. Two days after we were hired, we delivered the four-inch tall, white ceramic figurine of a cat to Mrs. Takahashi, who thanked us profusely and assured us she would give it to the fairy right away.

That had been two hours ago. It was pretty safe to say something had gone wrong, I just had no idea what.

The office door flew open again. I risked taking a peek around the corner of my desk to see what new trouble had descended on my quiet afternoon.

Mrs. Takahashi stood in the same spot of sunshine Dog had been sleeping in before he decided, like me, that hiding behind my desk was a pretty good idea.

Short and slender and about sixty years old, Mrs. Takahashi was the most well-liked person I knew. Even my cat liked her. I didn't know if there was a Mr. Takahashi. I don't think anyone did. From what everyone told me, Mrs. Takahashi and her store had been part of the neighborhood long before Diz and I opened our business. She was kind and patient and pretty much kept to herself. I'd never even heard her raise her voice.

Until now.

At least she wasn't yelling at me. The little fairy who'd tried to bean me with my desktop garden had turned her tirade on Mrs. Takahashi, who sounded like she was holding her own in the argument. I couldn't tell for sure since Mrs. Takahashi wasn't speaking English either.

"Think we should make a run for it?" I asked Dog.

He sneezed and shook his head.

Yeah, probably not a good idea. It's not wise to annoy fairies. It's even worse to run from them.

I raised my hand, wishing I had a white flag I could wave. "Truce?" I asked.

The rapid-fire argument ceased.

When I poked my head up from behind my desk, both the fairy and Mrs. Takahashi were staring at me. The fairy had her hands on her tiny hips. She was dressed in a white leather skirt and matching lace-up vest that bared her belly and managed to leave her wings unencumbered. Black hair frizzed around her head like dandelion fluff dipped in India ink. She wore white chunk-heel boots, and she was hovering about six inches away from Mrs. Takahashi's face, the beat of her wings making Mrs. Takahashi's grey hair flutter in the breeze.

The fairy was beautiful—most fairies are—but her outfit made her look like one of the ball-joint dolls Mrs. Takahashi kept in a locked case behind the checkout counter in her store. The dolls looked like a cross between someone's Asian schoolgirl fantasy, with their pleated skirts and white blouses and knee-high socks, and the delicate-faced characters I'd seen on the covers of the manga books Mrs. Takahashi sold. I'd asked her once why she kept the dolls locked away since they were the only things she kept under lock and key. She said they were very expensive, and then she quoted me a price for the smallest doll that was more than a month's rent for my office and apartment combined. I don't think she's ever sold a single doll. I can't say that I'm surprised.

Since the little fairy didn't look like she was about to throw anything else at me—at least for the moment—I quit using my chair as a shield and sat down in it instead. "So," I said. "Someone want to tell me what's going on? In English?"

Mrs. Takahashi inclined her head at me. "So sorry. It appears you and your partner were duped."

Duped?

She gave a quick sideways glance at the angry fairy. "The little statue you found was not the right one. She says you have tricked her. She is very angry."

"I got that part."

My scalp was starting to itch. I rubbed at it, and sand sifted down on top of my desk. It wasn't bad enough my hair frizzed when it was damp, which was pretty much all the time, now I had a headful of sandy dandruff. Too bad that wasn't the sum total of my problems.

Fairies are difficult beings to do business with. "Doing business" is perilously close to bargaining, and fairy bargains rarely turn out well for the non-fey involved. The only reason I'd agreed to find the little ceramic figurine for this particular fairy was because Mrs. Takahashi had asked. Nicely.

"Please tell her I'm very sorry for the mix up," I said to Mrs. Takahashi. "My partner and I, we weren't aware there would be more than one figurine that fit the description she gave us. We'll be happy to keep looking for the right one."

I waited while Mrs. Takahashi translated. When she finished, the little fairy still looked angry, but at least she no longer looked lethal.

"I do have one question," I said. "If there's more than one white ceramic cat figurine like that one out there, how can we tell when we've got the right one?"

While I waited for the translation, Dog came over and rested his head on my leg. I petted him and he wagged his tail. Sometimes I almost think he's just a dog.

The little fairy's response was short. Mrs. Takahashi kept looking at her like she expected the fairy to say something else, but the fairy just gestured in my direction.

Mrs. Takahashi shrugged. "She says you'll know."

"We'll know?"

"Yes. That is all she'll say."

We'll know.

Oh, great.

Diz was just going to love this.

* * *

"We'll know?"

Diz did not love this if his pacing back and forth in our front office was any indication. Well, that and the glower.

My partner's not the most Zen elf in existence, which, when I thought about it, made his advice to me to enjoy the process definitely a pot say hello to kettle kind of thing. Back when Diz and I were both detectives with the Moretown Bay Police Department, he was bad cop to my sympathetic cop. Since he's built like The Rock before The Rock became a movie star and has the intense stare to go with the muscles, Diz was a natural at bad cop.

I got stuck with Diz because no one else in the department could put up with his bad disposition. Although to be fair, he got the short end of that deal. No one wanted to partner with me either since my only qualification for the magical side of police work was a smidgen of precognition that kicked in whenever it felt like it. All this "be in the moment" stuff was supposed to help me control my precog visions. So far it had worked once, which was the vision where I met Dog. I'd thought he was just part of the vision—a part that talked back to me, no less—then Dog had shown up at my door and made himself at home.

As soon as Mrs. Takahashi and the fairy left, I'd called Diz to give him the bad news. While he was on his way back to the office,

I reviewed every step of our investigation, trying to spot where we'd messed up.

The little ceramic figurine was a family heirloom. The fairy said she had to leave it behind when she immigrated to the United States with her family. As soon as she'd scraped the money together, she arranged to have the heirloom shipped to her. It had been bundled with a shipment of goods from Japan headed for Mrs. Takahashi's store and other retail outlets not only in Moretown Bay but throughout the Pacific Northwest. The shipment had arrived on a cargo boat as scheduled, but when Mrs. Takahashi's portion of the shipment arrived at her store, the box containing the ceramic figurine was missing.

The fairy was convinced pirates had stolen it. In my experience, the days when pirates stole trinkets just because they were pretty were long past. Modern pirates only stole merchandise they could sell without a hitch. Protection spells cost a bundle, and unless a pirate expected a big payday at the end, stealing small stuff from a fairy just wasn't cost-effective.

I was pretty sure the shipment had been misplaced. I've worked with shipping companies before, and if you don't pay extra for homing spells, there's no telling where a package could end up. Diz and I spent a day and a half running down every package that had arrived on that shipment until we finally found the little ceramic figurine, still in the box, in a comic book store in South Bay.

The fairy's figurine had arrived along with the rest of the store's order of manga and anime products. The guys at the comic book store had been too busy getting ready for a big trade show at the convention center to even unpack the shipment, so they didn't know they had one more box than they should have. The owner of the store had been more than happy to hand the figurine over without a fuss when he learned it belonged to a fairy.

I'd checked the shipping information on the box against the printouts Mrs. Takahashi had given us confirming that the box had been shipped from Japan. The numbers matched. The box had been opened, but Customs opened a lot of boxes coming from overseas. The figurine looked like the one in the photo we'd been given, and that should have been that.

In hindsight, it was pretty obvious what had happened. Somewhere along the way, someone had switched the figurine inside the box with an exact replica. But why? According to what Mrs. Takahashi told us, the figurine was only important to the fairy's family.

"How do we know the real thing's not still in Japan?" Diz said, not bothering to pause his pacing.

We didn't. But going to Japan wasn't in the budget—the fairy hadn't paid us a retainer, after all—so the logical place to start was Moretown Bay. We'd only tracked the package the first time around. We hadn't investigated anyone who worked on the cargo ship, in Customs, at the port, or with the delivery service, which was one honking long list of people.

Not to mention that if someone had swapped out the real figurine with a fake one, the real figurine could be hidden somewhere on the ship. Cargo ships probably had about a zillion places to hide a four-inch tall figurine.

Or whoever took the figurine could have pawned it in any one of dozens of pawn shops in the area.

Or sold it on the black market. I didn't know if white ceramic cat figurines were big on the black market, but no one knows why people take a shine to the things they do. Last year the hot new item had been zombified replicas of real-life political figures. As far as I was concerned, most politicians already looked like they'd been bitten by the undead, but stores couldn't keep those ugly little things on the shelves. The goblin gangs who ran the black market in Moretown Bay knew a hot property when they saw it, and pretty soon legitimate businesses had to hire armed guards to protect their shipments of undead politicians.

I thumped my sand-saturated head on my desk. Missing persons were easier to find than this. Our simple little case had just turned into a major investigation.

I didn't hear Diz pause in his pacing, but the next thing I knew, I felt the gentle touch of his hand on my shoulder. "I don't suppose you've had any luck..." he began.

He didn't have to finish the thought. I knew what he meant. He wanted to know if I'd had a vision.

"The sum total of my Zen is currently sifting through my hair onto my desk," I said. "And Dog isn't talking to me."

Diz wasn't one-hundred percent fond of Dog, mainly because he's pretty sure Dog wasn't one-hundred percent canine. Diz can sense when beings use magic. He described it to me once like feeling a tingle on his skin, anywhere from a slight sense of static electricity in the air to the sensation of being swarmed by a million ants all at once. It all depended on the intensity of the magic. He's learned to tune out low-level magic, otherwise he'd be twitchy all the time. Trust me. Twitchy and grumpy are not a good combination in an elf with his size and strength.

When Dog came into our lives, Diz told me he sensed some kind of magic in the Golden Retriever, but it was the low-level kind, not nearly the amount a shape shifter or changeling would generate. Most dogs don't put out any magical energy at all.

Just like Diz, I was pretty sure Dog wasn't a normal dog, but unlike my partner, I was okay with that. In the vision where I first met Dog, he'd been one of the animals in a live outdoor Christmas nativity scene. He'd looked me straight in the eye and told me—in perfect, non-accented English, no less—to get my butt out of the vision and get to work. It said a lot about Diz that he never questioned Dog's part in my vision, and that he accepted Dog in our lives on my say so.

"You need to relax," Diz said.

Dog came over and nudged my arm with his nose. I patted his broad back with one hand and sighed. Telling myself to relax was like telling myself not to think about the bean paste rolls I bought from Mrs. Takahashi. Which I now couldn't stop thinking about.

"It doesn't work that way," I said. "It's a human thing."

Diz snorted. He had so many "elf things," as he called them, like scaling the side of a building without the benefit of rope, I couldn't help but retaliate every now and then.

"Relax," he said.

"How am I supposed to relax? I have sand in my hair." No one could relax with sand in her hair.

I thumped my head against the top of my desk again, and that's when Diz started to massage my shoulders.

Diz had given me a shoulder massage once before, and it had been marvelous. His fingers are long and strong, and he seems to know exactly where to apply pressure. I wasn't sure how he'd learned to do that—he'd probably tell me it was another elf thing—but right about then I didn't care. Any day that included making one of the fey angry enough she hurled things at me was bound to make me tense, and Diz knew just how to work all the tight muscles in my shoulders and neck.

Dog nuzzled at my arm again, but right about then I didn't feel like I had enough energy to keep petting him. We had things to do, people to interview, a ceramic cat to find, and I should really get busy on that before the fairy decided she'd been patient enough, but I didn't feel like I had enough energy to do that either. All I cared about was the wonderful feeling of my tight muscles finally letting go. It was a marvelous feeling. It was an awesome feeling. I could live in this moment for the next hundred years and I wouldn't care one—

And just like that, I fell into a vision.

* * *

I've had precog visions since I hit puberty. My mother, after she got over the fact that her daughter wasn't exactly normal, treated my visions like the ultimate locator of lost objects. Heaven forbid if anyone misplaced a set of keys or couldn't remember where they left their wallet. According to my mother, I could just gaze into the crystal ball inside my head and find whatever had gone missing.

Well, my visions don't work that way. For one thing, I could never control when a vision decided to show up, no matter how much my Great Aunt Betsy needed her reading glasses. Besides, my visions showed me glimpses of the future. If Great Aunt Betsy had already lost her glasses, I couldn't help, no matter what my mother thought.

Most of my early visions were just hints of things, like a smell that didn't belong or a glimpse of something out of the corner of my eye. I still remember the first time I realized the smell that had been driving me nuts was really a vision. Two hours after I'd started to smell Chinese food, right down to the sweet and sour sauce and hot oil mixed with ginger, my father came home with takeout.

These days my visions ranged from an out-of-place smell to a full-blown 3D movie complete with digital surround sound. The vision where I'd met Dog had felt like I'd piggybacked someone's dream, which, as it turned out, I had.

Diz and I focused on finding missing persons instead of objects because my precog visions put me in the point of view of someone else. When I got lucky, that someone else was the person we were looking for.

This time when the vision hit, I found myself staring out at the world from the point of view of the ceramic cat figurine.

In the vision, I smelled absolutely nothing. Which made sense, considering that something made out of ceramic couldn't smell, but the total absence of smell felt so alien it almost kicked me back to reality, and I had to fight hard to stay right where I was.

I shouldn't have been able to see, either, but that sense worked just fine. I appeared to be in a huge room. Exposed pipes ran beneath a stadium-height ceiling, all painted white, and banks of fluorescent lights hung in neat rows extending as far as I could see. Books featuring Japanese-style cartoon characters on the covers packed the wire mesh shelves in front of me. I couldn't move my eyes or turn my head, but I thought I saw a wall of stuffed animals off to one side, only these animals were made of felt instead of the fake fur toys I remembered from my childhood. An annoying buzzing sound filled my head, like white noise only louder but muffled at the same time.

Something came into my field of vision—the top of someone's head with a pink headband on which odd-looking, droopy ears had been attached—and then a hand reached out to grab me.

As soon as I saw that hand, my heart kicked into high gear, my flight-or-fight instincts coming down firmly on the side of flight. I wanted to run right now, right now, *right now*, only I couldn't move, and Dog wasn't in this vision to help me. The world tilted to the side as the hand picked me up. I caught a glimpse of a teenage face surrounded by long, straight, strawberry blonde hair. Next to her I saw the dreadlocks of a pirate I knew all too well.

Oh, brother. I'd seen enough.

My heart still hammered double-time in my chest when I came out of the vision a moment later. "You can stop now," I told Diz. "The massage worked."

He stopped rubbing my shoulders. My muscles felt all tingly, and except for my heart, which had finally started slowing down,

I felt pretty darn relaxed. Too bad we had a figurine to find. At least I had a pretty good idea where to look.

"Remember the trade show the guy at the comic shop mentioned?" I asked.

"Vaguely," Diz said.

I wouldn't have remembered now except one word on the stack of flyers advertising the show had caught my attention, so I'd asked the guy behind the counter what "cosplay" meant. He'd told me way more than I needed to know. Or so I'd thought at the time.

"I think we need to head over to the convention center," I said.

My partner groaned. I guess he remembered after all.

* * *

"Aren't you a little big to dress up as a video game character?" the girl dressed as a bondage version of the Queen of Hearts asked Diz.

He glowered at her. She giggled and asked if she could take his picture. She hadn't been the first, and I doubted she'd be the last.

The thousands of fans who'd descended on Moretown Bay for the Northwest Regional Anime Convention had taken over the entire convention center and all the fast food restaurants and hotels within a three-block radius. From what I could tell, at least half of them were in costume, or what my friendly comic store guy told me was "cosplay." Diz and I had to register as attendees to get inside the retail sales area, which was where I was pretty sure my vision had taken place. With the cute little convention name tag adorning Diz's normal outfit of cargo pants, boots, and a style of shirt that's more tunic than polo—today's color dusty green—no wonder people like the Queen of Hearts thought Diz was in costume. All he needed were a bow and arrows and a jaunty hat.

The convention center stretched over two city blocks and had six different levels connected by escalators, elevators, and glassed-in skyways that crossed the streets below. We had to ride up three sets of escalators, cross two skyways, and make our way through a never-ending line of people waiting for a chance to meet their favorite voice actors before we finally found what the convention called a "dealer room," which turned out to be an auditorium the size of three football fields and packed wall to wall with shoppers.

"Which way?" Diz yelled down at me to make himself heard over the din of the crowd.

I had no idea. Most of the booths in the immediate vicinity had been constructed of the same kind of wire mesh shelving I'd seen in my vision. The booths were jam-packed with everything from artwork to tee-shirts to costumes to realistic-looking swords to boxes upon boxes of vinyl and resin figures. I didn't see anything made of white ceramic.

"We're looking for a manga dealer," I yelled back. "And Captain Jack Sparrow."

Even with Diz's height, which gives him an advantage in a crowd, it took us nearly two hours to find the right dealer. I recognized the shelves of manga and the wall of flat stuffed toys from my vision.

I also recognized the strawberry blonde with the droopy headband ears. She was dressed in a white pinafore that could have doubled for lingerie, and her hair hung straight past the bottom of her dress. She was with a guy doing a pretty good imitation of Johnny Depp's character in the *Pirates of the Caribbean* movies.

Diz and I got to the booth just as the girl grabbed the little white ceramic cat. I'd witnessed some frenzied shopping in the dealer room, and I wasn't about to come this far only to lose the figurine to the anime version of Little Bo Peep.

"Stop right there!" I yelled at her.

I must have startled her because she let go of the ceramic cat like it was a hot potato.

Elves move fast. I've always known that, but Diz surprised even me this time. One moment he was standing alongside me, and the next he was on his back on the floor at the girl's feet. He caught the figurine before it hit the concrete.

"Outstanding!" the Captain Jack cosplayer said. "I believe I have a spot for you on my crew. Do you like rum?"

A short, rotund man with a dealer badge clipped to his shirt bustled up to Diz. "See here, you. Give that back. It's not for sale." He glared at the girl with the headband ears. "It's not for sale. Didn't you see the sign?"

Sure enough. The figurine had a "Display Only" sign taped to the front.

By the time Diz got up off the floor, still holding the figurine, Little Bo Peep and Captain Jack were gone. At least we wouldn't have to fight them for the figurine.

The dealer was another story. He held out his hand to Diz. "I believe that's mine."

Diz ignored him. "This is the right one," Diz said to me.

"How can you tell?" Three more white ceramic cat figurines crowded the wire shelf where this one had been. Other than the "Display Only" sign, all the figurines looked identical.

Diz made a fist with his other hand. That was the signal he used when he sensed magical energy but didn't want to say so out loud. The first figurine we'd found had no magical energy at all.

I turned toward the rotund man. "Why isn't this one for sale?"

He glared at Diz, but the glare didn't last long. He clearly wanted the figurine back, but like a good many criminals before him, he decided he'd have better luck with me.

"It's our display piece," he said.

"It looks just like the rest of them."

"It's the first one. It's our good luck charm."

I gestured toward the shelf, about to point out that he had three other good luck charms.

Only now four white ceramic cat figurines crowded the shelf, all identical.

I raised an eyebrow at Diz, and he nodded. He'd seen the same thing. "It replicates itself when it feels threatened," he said.

The flight-or-fight sensation I'd felt when my vision put me inside the ceramic cat, that was right before the figurine used its magic. One way for something to hide in plain sight, especially when that something couldn't move on its own, was to surround itself with a whole bunch of somethings that looked the same. I guess I knew now where the first replica we'd found had come from. This poor little inanimate ceramic cat must have felt seriously threatened when Customs opened its box.

Or was it so inanimate? I'd never heard of an object that could use magic on its own.

I took a stab in the dark. "You know," I said to the dealer. "It's illegal to trap a magical being inside an inanimate object. The penalties for things like that are pretty severe. Am I right?" I said to Diz.

"Severe," he said, cranking up the wattage on his glower.

The color drained out of the dealer's face.

"I wouldn't want you—" I began, but I was interrupted by another guy with a dealer badge who'd just worked his way through the crowd.

"What's up, Harry?" he asked the guy I was grilling.

I turned to glare at the intruder and found myself face to face with the owner of the comic book store.

Hadn't even opened the package, my ass. More like found the goose that laid the golden egg.

"Hi, there," I said. "Remember me? I was just discussing with Harry here the penalties for trapping someone magical inside a figurine."

"They're severe," Diz said, right on cue.

The guy didn't even try to bluster his way out. "Take it," he said. "No charge." He snatched a stuffed toy off the display and thrust it at me. "In fact, take this, too. You see anything else you'd like? I got the latest compendium of *The Walking Dead*. You can have it, my compliments."

What was it with zombies? Maybe I should catch up with the rest of the world. After all, my nights weren't exactly booked solid.

"We'll let you off with a warning," Diz said. "This time." He arched an eyebrow, and damn if he didn't look like The Rock, only with much more hair. "Don't do it again."

He grabbed my elbow and steered me away from the booth before the owner could hand me anything else or wake up to the fact that we weren't undercover cops.

We made it out of the convention with only three more people asking Diz for his picture. When he got outside, the first thing he did was unclip the badge from his shirt and drop it in the trash.

So much for my partner's first foray into cosplay. Diz still held the little ceramic cat carefully against his chest, pretty much the same way I held the felt toy. I hoped my cat would like it. If I brought home one more strange thing she didn't like, I might find myself sleeping in my office along with Dog.

* * *

My cat loved the felt toy. In fact, I don't think she's stopped grooming it. I'm not sure all's forgiven, but it's a start.

The little fairy forgave us, too. I've never seen anyone so happy to get a little ceramic cat in my life. Joy radiated from every inch of her, her happiness so bright that it lit up the inside of Mrs. Takahashi's store and turned the fairy's hair golden blonde.

The fairy even cast a spell that removed every last granule of sand from my hair.

The rest of what happened with the fairy and the figurine I didn't witness, but I'm a decent detective and it was pretty easy to make an educated guess. The next morning when I stopped by Mrs. Takahashi's store for my sweet bean roll fix, I noticed that the case that held the ball-joint dolls was unlocked. Other than a little dust at the bottom, the case was empty.

"You sold them?" I asked Mrs. Takahashi as I handed her money for the roll. "*All* of them?"

She smiled at me in her normally reserved way. "They have found a home," she said.

"*All* of them? The same home?" I had a hard time imagining someone spending that kind of money on dolls.

Her dark eyes twinkled. "Every being has a home. Some, like your dog, find it on their own. Others need a little help." She placed the money I'd given her for the roll back in my hand and closed my fingers over it. "Thank you for yours."

It took me a moment, but I got it.

The dust at the bottom of the case was all that remained of the ceramic cat figurine—and the ball-joint dolls—that had housed the beings held inside each of them. The ceramic figurine hadn't been a prison. It had been a shipping container, just like the dolls— a way for the rest of the fairy's family and their pet to leave Japan. The pet inside the ceramic cat had been the last one to make the journey, and, more than likely, the fairy needed the pet's magic in order to work the spell to release the rest of her family from the dolls. Just like the being inside the ceramic cat had hidden in plain sight by replicating itself when it felt threatened, Mrs. Taka- hashi had hidden the dolls in plain sight in her store by putting them up for sale but pricing them so high that no one—especially no one in our neighborhood—could afford them.

I left her store smiling to myself. Sure, the fairies and Mrs. Taka-hashi had broken a bunch of immigration laws, but I wasn't with the cops anymore. Things weren't black and white in my world these days. I might be terminally single, but I'd helped reunite a family, and that was pretty darn cool. It didn't improve my love life, but I had a fresh bean roll, a kinda-magical dog, and my cat didn't hate me anymore. Right now, in this moment, life was good.

What do you know. Maybe I'd finally figured out Zen after all.

USA Today *bestselling writer Dean Wesley Smith pens several short story series. By far, the most popular series is Poker Boy. These standalone short stories rely on his offbeat writing skills (there is a Planet Dean as well as a Planet Ray) and his years as a professional card player. In the next six months, he will publish three Poker Boy collections. He's currently finishing the first Poker Boy novel,* The Slots of Saturn.

In addition to the Poker Boy stories, he has published more than a hundred novels under different names, and hundreds of short stories.

About Poker Boy, he writes, "One day, a decade or more ago, while I was sitting at a poker table, a guy who couldn't play a lick of poker and who was losing a lot of money to me and the others at the table, complained that the poker gods weren't watching out over him. I started wondering what the gambling gods would actually be like. So I tried to imagine if I woke up one day to discover I was a brand new superhero working for the God of Poker who worked directly for Lady Luck. Thirty or more Poker Boy stories later, I now have Poker Boy and his sidekick and girlfriend, Patty Ledgerwood, still saving the world, doing favors for Lady Luck, and generally having a great time."

———

That Lost Riddle
Dean Wesley Smith

Out of thin air I heard Stan, the God of Poker say, "Knock, knock."

It wasn't a bad joke. It was how he asked to come into my private doublewide trailer up in the woods in Oregon. It seems that when Stan teleported, he couldn't just drop in outside and then use the door to actually knock on. But he was a God, and my boss, so I supposed he could do just about anything he wanted, even make bad "knock-knock" sounds in thin air in my living room. I was only Poker Boy, a lowly superhero. Not much I could say about it.

I pushed aside the cold fried chicken I had been eating while sitting on my old green couch and watching the evening news out of Portland. "Come on down."

Stan appeared beside my couch and glanced around, shaking his head. He always did that when he came here. He just didn't understand why someone with as much money as I had (and as many superpowers) would keep an old, 1970s-furnished double-wide trailer in the Oregon Coastal Mountains, even if it was within a half mile of a casino.

It was the green couch and chair and shag carpet that did it for most people, not counting the fake wood paneling on the wall. I figured if I waited long enough the styles would come around.

The last time Stan had come here he suggested I put a felt painting of dogs playing poker on the wall. I was considering it.

My girlfriend and sidekick, Patty Ledgerwood, aka Front Desk Girl, couldn't figure out why I liked this place either, now that she knew how much money I really did have. I discovered I had a vast amount when Patty made me go through it and lay it all out for her. I hadn't bothered to total it in a decade. I just kept adding to it.

Even though I could afford a couple dozen mansions, I liked this old place, even though Patty said it smelled of faint mold and pine trees. It reminded me of my early days as a poker player and superhero. The old furniture and funky smell sort of kept me grounded. I said that to Patty once and she just shook her head and muttered something about how the place kept me actually in the dirt.

Needless to say, we spent most nights in her wonderful and very large apartment in Las Vegas, furnished with the best and most modern furniture, thick carpet, and views of Las Vegas that were tough to beat.

I usually only came up here while she was working and I was waiting for a tournament to start. Instantly jumping from Las Vegas to the mountains of Oregon was one of the many advantages of being able to teleport.

Stan didn't say anything after his disgusted look at my place. He was wearing his standard tan sweater, tan slacks, and loafers. He looked so nondescript, he could blend in anywhere and no one would notice him. I had a hunch if he stood in my trailer long enough, his sweater and slacks would turn 1970s green.

I took one more bite of the cold chicken leg, then stood and headed for the coat hanger beside the front door to get my black leather coat and black fedora-like hat. They were my superhero uniform that helped make me Poker Boy.

Stan only came here to get me when something was going wrong somewhere. Never a good sign. So the coat and hat were going to be needed for something very soon.

"So where to?" I asked as I slipped on my coat.

"You look like you need a drink," he said.

"What?" He knew I didn't drink. Never had and I sure couldn't see myself starting now.

I was about to say something about going back to my chicken and news when Stan jumped us to position beside a large white-marble pillar with people walking by. There were slot machines and a nearby restaurant. I could feel the power from the casino around us flowing into me.

The air smelled of prime rib and faint cigarette smoke. It took me only a second before I realized we were on the second floor, the mezzanine level, of the Eldorado Hotel and Casino in downtown Reno, Nevada.

To my left along the interior mall-like area was the Silver Legacy Hotel and Casino and beyond that the Circus Circus Hotel and Casino.

This interior mall area stretched for a very long three blocks and must have a couple dozen restaurants, shops and gift stores along its wide corridor. It was a nice place considering Reno's weather in the winter, allowing people to move between the three casinos without ever going outside.

I had always liked this interior mall and the feel of it. Some people said it reminded them of a huge cruise ship, only without ocean views and people getting seasick.

I glanced around. No one had noticed our arrival so I figured Stan had jumped us into a blind camera area.

"Back with your girlfriend in a moment," Stan said and vanished, leaving me alone.

I had no idea what the problem was, or why we were in Reno, but if he was going for Patty when she was still at work, I knew it couldn't be good.

I stepped away from the stone pillar and let my poker senses take in everything around me. A few people upset at losing, and one couple went past not happy, headed for the Silver Legacy. I caught part of a conversation about how the guy was angry with his wife flirting with another man. He was telling her so in no uncertain terms. It wasn't hard to miss, even without extra poker senses.

But I could sense nothing that would cause Stan to jump us to Reno and into the Eldorado.

Across from me was a brewpub full of younger patrons laughing and drinking. I'm not sure exactly when I started thinking of adults around age thirty as younger, but I did. Since I have been told that as a superhero, I have basically stopped aging at thirty even though I am over forty, I have no idea how jaded I was going to get by the time I reached one hundred.

Or two-hundred-plus like Patty. She still hadn't told me her real age. She just shook her head and said it didn't matter every time I asked. She didn't look a day over thirty either, but knowing there might be a few hundred years in age difference sometimes actually bothered me.

I felt a hand on my shoulder and the calming sense of Patty's touch. That was one of her super powers and I loved it.

And her. More than I wanted to admit to myself at times. We just fit together in seemingly every sense.

I turned around to look into her beautiful brown and very worried eyes. She was still dressed in the uniform of the MGM Grand Hotel front desk. A black skirt, white blouse and MGM dark vest with their hotel emblem on the right side.

Her long brown hair was pulled back tight as she kept it while working.

"Any idea what's going on?"

I shook my head, keeping my poker senses on full. I didn't quite have a "Spider-Sense" like Spider-Man did in the comics, but I had a pretty good ability to know when danger was approaching and right now I could feel nothing.

"Where is Stan?" I asked.

"He went to get Screamer," she said.

"This can't be good," I said.

She nodded.

A moment later Stan appeared next to the stone column in the dead camera area. Screamer was with him looking just as puzzled.

Screamer had the ability to touch someone and get into their mind and their thoughts. He didn't have a distinctive look, more like Stan with the ability to blend into just about anywhere. He usually wore old jeans and a sweatshirt with the UNLV logo on it and tonight was no exception.

Screamer had gotten his name from his ability to put images into other people's heads. He often worked for the police and could put images so bad and so real into a suspect's mind that he could make the most hardened criminal scream. What he did could never stand up in a court, but he had solved a lot of crimes over the years.

And he had helped this team save the world a few times as well.

"All right," Stan said. "Let's go."

He turned toward the short staircase leading down around an ornate fountain and into another section of the Eldorado Hotel and Casino mezzanine level.

"What are we doing here?" Screamer asked a moment before I could.

"Going for a drink," Stan said, his voice almost lost in the sounds of the multiple fountains.

Patty just shook her head and I followed them, keeping every sense I had on full alert. And that was a lot of senses, so many in fact I hadn't named them all. But the one right now I was trusting the most was my danger awareness sense.

And it was flat coming up blank.

We went past a gift shop, down another short flight of stairs, and toward what looked to be a combination bakery counter, restaurant on the right, and bar in the back on the left, tucked against the wall.

Suddenly Patty said, "Sherri."

Her uniform morphed into a black dress, her hair flowed into a perfect shape around her head, and black high heels replaced her tennis shoes she wore while working.

All in the space of one step.

I had no idea she could do that.

None at all.

And we'd been together now for a few years. If we survived whatever we were facing, we were going to need to have a talk about her powers.

"Oh, no," Screamer said as Stan headed toward the bar past the huge counter full of very tasty-looking pies and cakes and cinnamon rolls coated an inch deep in white frosting. The entire area smelled of fresh bread, making my stomach rumble and me wish I had taken a few more bites of that cold chicken.

"Come on, Stan, why?" Screamer asked.

Stan said nothing. Just kept walking.

Stan reached the bar and pulled up a barstool. Screamer sat on his left, Patty took the spot on his right, and I took the spot next to Patty.

I could still sense absolutely nothing wrong, but from Patty's sudden change and Screamer's comment, they were clearly sensing something I wasn't.

And that scared me more than I wanted to admit.

We sat there in silence with the sounds of the distant casino echoing faintly in the background. It must have only been a few seconds, but it felt like an eternity.

The bar was a normal wood bar, pretty wide, and even though it looked rustic, it was polished as smooth as glass. We were the only customers sitting at it. There were three empty stools to my right. It felt really, really strange to be sitting at a bar. I just never did this.

Bottles of varied booze lined the ornate back bar, blocking most of a mirror that made the area seem bigger. The top of the back bar was also a rustic ornate wood as were all the decorations on both sides of it.

This kind of bar could have been in any one of a thousand places. It actually seemed a little out of place with all the desserts in a huge counter ten paces behind us. It felt like it belonged more in an Old West saloon in a movie. A long ways from the smell of baking bread and ringing modern slot machines.

I was about to say something when a door into a back room swung open and a stunning woman emerged carrying a few bottles of vodka. She wore tan slacks, a white short-sleeve blouse, and an apron with the Eldorado Hotel logo on it. Her pitch-black hair was pulled back tight and I caught a glimpse of a dark tattoo on her shoulder and upper arm.

And she might have been one of the most beautiful women I had ever seen.

"Hey, Stan," she said, smiling in a way that could knock down just about anyone with its radiance.

Now my warning senses were going off and going off strong. If she was sitting across from me in a poker tournament, I would be very, very careful even being in a hand with her. She had power. More than likely she was a superhero or maybe a god.

But I caught no threat at all of danger from her. Just warnings about her power.

Stan nodded and didn't return the smile. "Sherri," was all he said.

She put down the bottles, wiped her hands on a white bar towel and slipped a bar napkin in front of Stan.

"Great seeing you," she said. "I suppose Mom sent you and your team here."

"She did," Stan said, again nodding.

"Well, I appreciate you coming," she said, smiling. "Thanks."

I wanted to shout out *"Mom?"* but then realized the only woman who could order Stan, the God of Poker around, was Laverne, Lady Luck herself. I now had a hunch suddenly who I was facing. I hadn't known going into a previous mission that Lady Luck had a daughter, so I suppose it shouldn't surprise me that she had two.

Or more for all I knew.

When this was over, I really needed to ask some very pointed questions about the family trees of some of my bosses.

Sherri put a bar napkin in front of Screamer, the smile turning a little sad on her face.

"I miss you," she said.

He only nodded just slightly, his gaze holding hers.

She missed him?

What in the world was going on? If this Sherri was Lady Luck's daughter, having both Stan and Screamer have strange reactions to her didn't seem like much of a good start to whatever we were facing here.

She shrugged and moved to a spot in front of Patty. She slid a napkin in front of her and smiled, the smile actually reaching her eyes. "Patty Ledgerwood I presume. I've heard so many good things about you and your work. You look stunning."

Patty smiled, blushed, and said nothing.

Sherri slid a napkin in front of me, her smile turning to something I couldn't read.

"So this is the famous Poker Boy I've been hearing so much about."

I kept my poker face and only nodded slightly.

She laughed. "You people sure aren't much for idle conversation, are you?"

"We're here," Stan said, his voice very controlled. "I don't understand why you are here, or what you need from us."

"I work here," she said, smiling. "I have now for about four years. Moved here from the Atlantis Casino. I worked there for ten years. Remember?"

She looked at Screamer and he just nodded.

She went on. "The management here keep offering to make me a bar manager, but I like keeping my hand in the drinks and talking with the customers."

Even though Stan had the best poker face that existed, I could tell he was surprised by that. If this was Lady Luck's daughter, I was surprised as well.

"And I didn't ask you to come here," Sherri said. "That was Mom's idea. She said you four might be able to help me with my lost riddle."

Stan said nothing, Screamer just shook his head, and Patty just smiled softly and stared at her.

Wow, was there a lot of history between these four. Clearly it had all happened long before I was born. And since Stan had been married to one of Lady Luck's daughters, more than likely he wasn't pleased to see this one either. So it looked like this was going to be up to me to figure out what she was talking about.

"So what's the riddle that your mom thought we could help you solve?" I asked. "And I assume I am talking with a daughter of Lady Luck. Correct?"

"Sherri," she said, giving me that beaming smile that I had no doubt melted some of the icing off a cinnamon role in the case behind me.

"The Queen of Clubs," Screamer said, his voice soft.

"Dear husband," Sherri said, a slight touch of hurt going to her eyes, even though she kept smiling. "You used to not like anyone calling me that name."

I was trying to deal with the fact that Screamer had been married to Lady Luck's second daughter at one point. Now all I had to do was figure out why Patty had a problem with her and I might have a clue what was happening.

"So the riddle?" I asked, pulling her attention back to me. "What's so important about it?"

"It's lost," Sherri said over her shoulder to me as she moved fluidly down the bar to pour some drinks for a waitress that had come up to the waitress station in front of a bar well.

Sherri seemed to move faster than anyone I had ever seen, yet the waitress never once looked up. After only a moment, which I guessed had something to do with her slipping slightly out of time to do the drinks, she came back toward us wiping her hands on a bar towel. "Can I get any of you a drink?"

My three teammates sat silently, so I said, "Sure. Bloody Mary mix with no vodka."

"Celery?" she asked as she moved to the well again.

"Nope," I said.

As she finished my virgin drink, I studied her. Not one sense of danger, nothing from her, and she wasn't blocking me in any way. In fact, I wasn't getting that much sense that she actually had many powers at all, even though I assumed she was a god. Could it be that Lady Luck's daughter was only a superhero like I was? That didn't seem possible.

As she put the drink on my bar napkin and again wiped off her hands, I asked her a simple question. "What's so important about finding or solving the riddle?"

"It will lead me to a second key holding the Four Faces of Janus."

"Oh," was all I said.

Stan just shook his head.

Screamer sort of snorted in disgust and Patty again didn't move.

We had already gone into Elysium, the capital of the ancient race of the Titans, to rescue Sherri's sister, Helen the Queen of Hearts, who had gone there to get one of the keys that held the Four Faces of Janus.

Supposedly, legend says that when the four keys are combined, they will open the time lock and allow the Titans to return to their rightful place in time and space. Or something like that. Mythology and facts were sometimes hard to tell apart for me these days. I really, really needed to ask more questions about all this.

One thing I did know, the Titans' major city existed in the same location as Las Vegas, only many, many eons in the future. So their coming back to this time would be a pretty large problem that I doubted anyone wanted to face.

"Are all your sisters looking for a key?" Stan asked.

"Sure," Sherri said. "It's sort of a hobby for all four of us. We're giving the keys to Mom for safekeeping when we find them. We have no intention of bringing them together, especially after seeing the wonderful city the Titans are living in."

"And you four have only found the one key, right?" I asked, trying not to be too stunned at Lady Luck having four daughters. I really, really, really needed to talk with someone about who had been married to whom and who was a child of whom.

"Just the key that you four helped my sister return with from Elysium," Sherri said, "although I feel that if I could find the lost riddle, I would be able to retrieve the second one."

Her bright smile had now vanished and she was clearly thinking about her problem. And I had zero idea what she was talking about when she said a "lost riddle" and my glowering team was sure no help at the moment.

"How can a riddle be lost?" I asked, slightly fearful I was walking into some trap.

Sherri just shrugged. "Lost in time, maybe. Never written down. Lots of ways a riddle can be lost."

"So it's just called "The Lost Riddle?" I asked.

She nodded.

Now all four of us were just looking at her as she headed back down the bar to the right to serve drinks to another waitress who had arrived at the station there.

"Someone want to tell me what's going on?" I asked.

"I think she's finally lost it," Screamer said, shaking his head sadly.

"She's fantastically beautiful," Patty said. "More than I even remember."

I stared at my girlfriend for a moment, realizing she hadn't been mad at Sherri, she had just been in some sort of fan-girl state with her.

"She's serious, all right," Stan said. "And she's as sharp as she ever was, trust me."

"So why do you hate her so much?" I asked Stan.

He laughed, softly, something I rarely heard him do. "I don't hate her. My wife, her sister, thought I fell in love with Sherri and caused all sorts of problems that led to me leaving Helen."

"You didn't?" I asked. "Fall in love with Sherri, that is?"

Again Stan just laughed. "I don't even really know her, to be honest. And Sherri's been married to Screamer here for a very long time."

"Over two hundred years," Screamer said.

"And she left you?" I asked.

"No, I left her," he said. "When I acquired this new power and could read all her thoughts every time I touched her. Staying together wasn't fair to either of us until we figured out how to deal with it all. We never got a divorce. It's been ten years now."

"So you are still married?" Patty asked, looking at Screamer, who nodded.

"Oh," was all I could say again. I had been working with this team now for some time and seen the inside of Screamer's mind more than I wanted to think about, and he had kept all this blocked from me. Clearly he had gotten pretty good at walling off parts of his own thoughts.

"She's so beautiful," Patty said, almost sighing. "We have to help her."

Now both Stan and I were shaking our heads at my girlfriend. Everything was screwy about this assignment and it was making me slightly annoyed. No one was in danger, I wasn't saving anyone, not even a dog, and I wasn't playing in a poker tournament. So far all I could see was a complete waste of a perfectly good evening.

Sherri again came back to a place in front of us. "Will you help me?"

"A couple more questions," I said. "So you need this riddle to find the Janus key?"

She shook her head. "I know where the key is at."

"So why do you need the lost riddle?" I asked, almost afraid of the answer.

"Stan," Sherri said, smiling at my boss, "If you wouldn't mind taking us all out of time for a moment, I'll answer Poker Boy's question."

He shrugged and an instant later the sounds of the casino stopped around us. And so did everyone and everything else.

I loved being able to step between an instant of time. One of my abilities was also to take myself and others out of the natural time flow. But Stan was a ton better at it and wouldn't have to strain to hold this for hours.

Sherri pointed to a place in the air behind her and an image like a three-dimensional movie appeared.

"That's new," Screamer said, looking puzzled.

"Learned it from you, actually," Sherri said, smiling at her husband. "It's a projection from my mind."

"I can't do that," Screamer said.

Sherri looked almost longingly at her husband. "We both have our new powers. I would love to talk later."

I was starting to get the clear understanding that she wasn't a god, but only a superhero like three of us at the bar. And she was learning new superpowers as she went along just as all superheroes did.

She turned back to the image she was projecting in the air as everyone in the casino remained frozen in their instant of time around us.

The image showed what looked like an old ghost town from a height of about a thousand feet in the air.

"Virginia City," Sherrie said. "South and slightly east of here."

The view came down and focused on some old buildings, then flew inside like a bird going through a wall. "Yellow Jacket Mine," she said. "Part of what most people think of as the Comstock Lode."

The traveling view of the image floating in the air went straight down, under some water and finally came into a flooded huge cave.

Sherri went on narrating the tour that was coming from her own mind. "The Yellow Jacket Mine broke into this huge cave and couldn't contain the flooding and had to retreat. No pump could ever clear it. It's over three thousand feet under Virginia City and the water temperature is over one hundred and fifty degrees."

At the bottom of the huge cave was a stone stand with a clear glass bubble covering it and protecting what looked like a very old key from the water.

"That's the second Janus key," Sherri said, her voice wispy.

"Why couldn't these stupid keys ever be hidden above ground?" I asked, shaking my head. My warning senses were going off big time just looking at that key so far down underground and underwater.

"So why the lost riddle?" Patty asked, the spell of Sherri's beauty clearly now broken by the little tour underground.

The image of the submerged cave vanished and Sherri just shrugged. "Not a clue what the riddle does," she said. "Or even what it is or why it's lost. I just know it's attached to this key in some fashion. And we don't dare touch the key until we understand what the riddle is all about."

I just shook my head. "This is a very strange hobby you and your sisters have."

Sherri laughed high and light. "Don't you think I know that? But after you guys helped my sister get the first one, Mom thinks it would be a good idea to get all four of them and get them really protected. So she's trying to help us."

I didn't want to say that having a key three thousand feet underground in one-hundred-and-sixty degree water wasn't already pretty protected, but what did I know? Lady Luck thought this was important for some reason. And she was Stan's boss and Stan was my boss, so by that reasoning I thought this important as well.

Stan let us slip back into the normal stream of time and the noise from the restaurant and distant casino slammed back into use like a tidal wave. And the wonderful smells from the restaurant came back as well, making my stomach rumble again.

"Okay," I said, trying to grab onto something that made sense in all this. "Tell me when I get this wrong."

Stan and Patty nodded and Sherri and Screamer just sort of looked at each other.

I ignored them and started trying to check off what I knew. "The four keys each have one side of the face of Janus on them. Right?"

Sherri and Stan both nodded.

"Apart they keep the doors locked, the Titans in the future, and the war between the Gods and the Titans stopped," Sherri said.

"Got that," I said. "And no one wants to start that war again."

"Exactly," Stan said.

"Does this Janus still exist?"

"No," Sherri and Stan said at the same time. They clearly did not like that question and I made a note to ask what happened to him at a later date.

"So why would anyone associate a riddle with a key?" I asked. "And then lose all record of the riddle? I've only been around this superhero and god world for a short ten or so years and I've come to realize that all you folks have very long memories."

"Good question," Stan said. "But the battle between the Gods and the Titans was long before any of our times. Long before Atlantis."

I nodded to that. I still have never asked exactly how many years all this stretched back. Another question for another time in my history lesson.

I leaned back and just stared up at the back bar. No one else said a word and Sherri moved back down the bar to serve another waitress with a tray full of dirty glasses and a long order of fresh drinks.

I tried to ignore my rumbling stomach and my desire for a cinnamon roll and just think.

On the back bar were a number of bottles of Jack Daniels, all with different colors and added names on the labels.

There were other bottles of the same brand, but different types back there as well. I stared at that for a moment and then it suddenly hit me what we were dealing with.

Being able to put things that made no sense together to make sense was one of my super powers, it seemed, and if I was right, I had just done it again.

"Stan, could you call Laverne to come and help us?"

He nodded and a moment later, without him moving, Lady Luck appeared, taking the empty stool to my right.

In my fondest dreams as a poker player, it never would have occurred to me that I would be sitting at a bar with Lady Luck herself.

Sherri finished the orders and came down the bar as her mother appeared.

"You want your usual, Mom?" she asked, smiling. Clearly the two of them had a good relationship.

"Later, honey," Lady Luck said. "First I want to hear what Poker Boy has to say about all this."

For the first time in a long time I wished I actually drank. I had a hunch I could use one right now. I took a deep breath and turned toward one of the most powerful gods that existed and asked the question I needed to ask.

"Do the keys have names besides one, two, three, and four?"

Lady Luck looked at me for a moment, then laughed and said, "I don't know, but I know who to ask."

She vanished.

I decided I could breathe again. It felt good.

I took a sip out of my Virgin Bloody Mary as Patty touched my leg and sent a calming sense through me.

"You think the key might have a name?" Sherri asked, clearly puzzled.

Stan just smiled and Screamer sort of smiled. They had seen me ask these kind of questions before that got right to the heart of a problem.

"Just an idea," I said.

It seemed like forever, but then suddenly Lady Luck was again sitting at the bar beside me.

And she was laughing.

"The one you all retrieved from the Titan's city under Vegas was called *Mystery*. The two that have not been found yet are called *Enigma* and *Dilemma*."

Then Lady Luck smiled at Sherri. "The one you found, dear daughter, is called *Riddle*."

Sherri clapped her hands together and did a little dance as she laughed and smiled. "It's not protected!"

"I'll get it," Lady Luck said, smiling at the joy her daughter felt.

She vanished and then a moment later reappeared holding the key that had been under three thousand feet of Earth and very hot water. She wasn't wet at all.

She started to hand the key to her daughter who held her hands up. "I don't want to touch it. Just get it safe and sound."

"I will," Lady Luck said.

Then she turned to me. "Once again, Poker Boy, thank you. And to your team as well for taking the time to help with this."

It never got old having Lady Luck thank me for helping her. Never.

Then Lady Luck looked down the bar at Screamer and smiled. "Talk to your wife. If you two got back together, she'd make a great addition to this team."

"Mom!" Sherri said, but Lady Luck was already gone.

For the first time Stan really laughed. And hard. And that also was a rare thing as well for the God of Poker.

"Great seeing you again, Sherri," Stan said. "And listen to your mother. We could use you." Then he vanished.

Sherri actually blushed.

Patty smiled at Sherri and then at Screamer and touched my leg. "Come on, I'm dressed up and I think I need to do some dancing."

"Dancing?" I asked, looking at her. In all our time together she had never told me she liked to dance. Ever.

She winked at me and squeezed my leg just a little higher and I got the message. "Oh! *Dancing.*"

A moment later we were in the living room of her apartment in Las Vegas, leaving Sherri and her husband alone in a crowded casino in Reno.

"Wasn't she beautiful?" Patty asked as she headed for her bedroom.

"Sherri?" I asked. "She was all right, but not as beautiful as you by a long ways."

"You sure know how to say the exact right things," Patty said.

She looked back over her shoulder at me and smiled a "dancing smile" as her dress vanished, leaving her totally naked and me totally speechless.

Hugo-winning editor and writer Kristine Kathryn Rusch also has a World Fantasy Award on her shelf and many readers' choice awards in both mystery and science fiction. She writes light paranormal romance novels under the name Kristine Grayson to escape the darkness of her nearly noir Smokey Dalton series, which she writes as Kris Nelscott.

Kris writes a lot of dark fantasy set in Oregon, usually on the Oregon Coast. But "Shadow Side" takes place in Southern Oregon. "When we attempt to take vacations," she writes, "Dean and I often go to historic hotels. One of the most frightening and spectacular trips we took was in the mountains near the Oregon Caves. Bats at twilight, a narrow windy road, and a locked hotel remain the most memorable part of that trip for me. So far, that terrifying experience has inspired three novels, and two short stories, including this one."

Shadow Side

Kristine Kathryn Rusch

Halfway up the mountain, Dan Retsler regretted returning to Oregon. He had a perfectly good job in Montana. The small town at the base of the Bitterroots had its own charm, and everyone now knew his name. He'd investigated his share of crime too—real crime, from shoplifting to domestic abuse allegations to more than the usual (to his mind anyway) number of shootings.

Yet, when he'd seen the advertisement for a police chief to handle a small town around the Oregon Caves, he'd jumped at the chance.

The Oregon Caves, he told himself, weren't the Oregon Coast. He wouldn't find selkies or ghosts or ugly mermaids or any other kind of fantastic creature that he failed to understand.

Instead, he'd be in the mountains, far from the ocean. Tourists would flock here, sure, but he had grown up in a tourist town. He understood how tourists fit into the local economy, and he knew how Oregon worked.

But as he turned west and south out of Grant's Pass, heading into the Coastal Mountain Range where the spectacular Oregon Caves threaded for miles, his stomach flipped, his shoulders tightened, and he nearly turned around.

He forced himself to continue by reminding himself that the committee expected him. He'd headed these hiring committees. He knew how much of a problem it caused when an applicant didn't show, particularly one good enough to warrant an interview.

He owed them that much. Besides, he was nearly there.

The committee set the morning meeting at the Marble Chalet, a place he'd never been to. He'd been to the Lodge at the Oregon Caves dozens of times. The Lodge was part of the National Park Service, and had actually been featured on PBS. His family loved to vacation there when he was a kid.

But everyone ignored the equally historic Marble Chalet. It had been in ruins for decades. In the flush 1990s, an enterprising private company restored it, and applied for a permit from the National Park Service to have a second public opening into the miles-long Oregon Caves complex, the opening easily accessible from the Chalet's parking area.

The Park Service decided a second opening was a bad idea. Retsler never found out why, but it made the Chalet a second-tier hotel by default.

If he took this job, he wouldn't work at the Chalet. He'd work in Marble Village, which the enterprising private company had originally built to house its workers, but which had grown like crazy. In the flush years before the century turned, a lot of Californians bought land and built homes here, so the village had more amenities than it deserved—from cell phone towers to high-speed internet. It had also lost a lot of amenities to the Great Recession, like the three-plex movie theater, although the faux vaudeville theater, which played old movies and second (or third)-run films did enough business to stay alive.

Retsler had found out some of this from a quick internet search. He remembered parts of it from his years living in Oregon, and the rest the town fathers had told him as they tried to entice him up here for the job.

They wanted an Oregonian; they made that clear. They were even happier that he was a native Oregonian, since such creatures were rare. They also wanted someone with experience in tourist areas.

He fit that bill.

He just wasn't sure about the rest of it.

The road forked outside of Marble Village, with the steeper, more difficult part heading toward the Marble Chalet. The initial signs heading to the Chalet were modern, with lettering that would reflect a car's headlights. But the closer he got, the signs changed, becoming rustic. Eventually, he realized these were the original signs, built in the 1930s, as the hotel itself got built as a WPA project.

For the first time, he actually felt a thread of excitement at seeing the Chalet.

He parked near the entrance to the lodge. A wide sidewalk led him around the rocks. He stopped, his breath gone.

Flower baskets hung from cut and polished Old Growth logs, harvested before anyone realized the old trees had to be protected. The logs formed the brace for a gigantic canopy that covered the walkway leading into the lodge itself. The rock way, made of cut marble, had to have come out of the Caves—again, before anyone knew this stuff had to be preserved.

The front of the lodge looked Swiss as interpreted by a group of provincial West Coasters who'd never really seen anything outside of the United States. The brown-and-white slats, along with the decorated shutters, seemed authentic enough, but the big logs that formed the foundation of the gigantic building ruined any tiny Swiss intimacy.

The word "Chalet" was wrong too. This wasn't a tiny house with a steep roof; this was a large resort with hundreds of rooms, surprising in its audacity. He wondered if there had ever been a time when all of these rooms had been occupied.

He doubted it.

The big wooden doors stood open, and he stepped into a large lobby. It took a moment for his eyes to adjust to the dimness. More flowers stood on tabletops and along both edges of the reception desk. A single dark-haired woman stood behind it. She smiled when she saw him.

He introduced himself so that he could check in. She handed him an old-fashioned metal key with a beautifully carved wooden fob attached. The fob declared his room number in large font.

He had no idea that ancient keys like this still existed in working hotels.

"They're waiting for you in the River Room," she said.

He pocketed the key when her sentence registered.

"River?" he repeated, not liking the word. He knew there had to be water up here, but he had come to associate water with trouble—at least in Oregon.

"Well," she said, her smile widening, "we couldn't very well call it the River Styx Room, now could we?"

His heart rate sped up. Why the hell would anyone name a room after the river that in Greek mythology divided the living world from the world of the dead?

He hoped it was some interior designer's twisted imagination.

"Up the stairs and to your right," she said, as if she believed he hesitated because he was lost, not because his stomach had knotted to the point he felt queasy.

He gave her an insincere smile, then went up the flat wooden stairs and turned left. The hallway opened into a maze of rooms, but he could see the River Room at the very end, not because of the large sign above the door (he had initially missed that) but because people milled inside.

He probably should have ducked into his room first, brushed his hair, and checked his shirt for lint. But he had decided somewhere between River and River Styx that this job wasn't for him. So it didn't matter how he looked.

As he walked in the door, six people turned in his direction, including four women. Not the town fathers then, but the town parents. A woman walked over to him. She had her magnificent blonde hair gathered on top of her head in some kind of elaborate coiffure that he hadn't seen outside of a photo spread in a magazine.

"Chief Retsler," she said. "I'm Ron Bronly. Welcome to Marble Village."

Okay. He tried not to let his surprise show. One of the drawbacks of e-mail, apparently, were the assumptions. Retsler had imagined Ron Bronly as a comfortable middle-aged, middle-income man with a slightly round belly and a lack of hair.

He hadn't expected a woman as attractive as this one. In addition to her careful hairstyle, she wore just enough make-up to jazz up her Oregon-casual outfit of tan slacks and tailored blouse. The hand she extended to him was manicured.

He took her hand, shook, and repeated that insincere smile. Everyone else looked more like what he expected. Three somewhat tired-looking women in jeans and jackets, two middle-aged men whom he would have taken for Ron Bronly if Ron Bronly hadn't introduced herself.

"Thank you for coming all this way," Bronly said. Her voice was smooth, buttery, but it had a bit of an accent. Bryn Mawr, unless he missed his guess. Very Katharine Hepburn.

"I was curious," he said. "I hadn't been to the Chalet before. I've only been here a few minutes, but it looks like the restore was lovingly done."

He could afford to be nice. It didn't hurt that, in this case, nice was also honest.

"We're proud of it," she said. "It's the jewel of our little community."

"Have you had a chance to drive around?" one of the men asked. He wore one of those stick-on name badges that read "Martin." Everyone else had a name badge as well, including Bronly. Hers read "Rhonda."

No one offered Retsler a name badge. Of course, he was the only stranger here. Apparently, they were trying to make him feel at home.

The spread on the back table also should have made him at home. Pastries, coffee, all kinds of non-alcoholic beverages. He glanced at them, saw that the group had already partaken of some of it. He wasn't really hungry, more tired. And he wanted to get this over with.

"I came directly here," Retsler said.

"Pity," Martin said. "You'd be surprised at Marble Village. Most Oregonians expect some place like Sisters, when really, it's a lot more like Monterey, California."

"Without the ocean," said the other man whose nametag read "Stanley."

Retsler trotted out his insincere smile for the third time. "I've done my stint around oceans."

"Yes," said one of the women. Her name tag read "Anna," which somehow suited her serious mien. "We spoke to the folks at Whale Rock. They would love you back."

"I'm sure the new chief is doing just fine," he said.

"Why did you leave?" Bronly asked.

He looked at her. Direct. To the point. Usually he liked that in a person. Here, though, it made him uncomfortable. How could he explain that the world he thought existed didn't? Whale Rock wasn't so much a place he disliked as a place that confused him and made him question everything about himself.

"I was ready to move on," he said, and it sounded true. It *was* true on some level, but not quite true in the way he wanted it to be.

She nodded, as if the answer didn't satisfy her. "And what's wrong with Montana?"

He smiled—and this time the smile was real. "Nothing really. In fact, as I drove up here, I realized I was probably wasting your time—"

"Excuse me." The woman from the front desk peered into the room. Her eyes were wide, and her tone seemed a bit panicked. "I'm sorry, but it's back."

"Dammit," Martin said and took off at a run. The others followed, leaving Retsler behind.

He hadn't thought such conservative people could run like that, especially Bronly who wore heels too high for anyone but an actress to move quickly in. Yet she had managed.

With just a few words, the entire group seemed to have forgotten him, and just as he was getting to the important stuff. Maybe he shouldn't feel so guilty.

But he couldn't help it. Nor could he help himself. He had to know what "it" was.

He walked quickly into the hallway, half expecting someone to stop him. But no one did. One of the side doors stood wide open, and he heard loud, panicked voices coming from that direction.

He looked in, saw a flight of stairs that had probably been designed for employees but now modern regulations made it a mandatory exit from this floor.

He took the steps down—wooden also, and not as well reinforced as those in the lobby—and found himself on the ground level on the far side, with a door that opened toward the Caves (or so the hand-lettered sign said).

It felt like he had entered the 1930s. More Old Growth wood, expertly carved and polished to a sheen, and through an interior door made of a single pane of glass, a diner the likes of which he hadn't seen since he was a kid.

No one manned the counters made of that same Old Growth wood, but voices echoed from the back. Voices he recognized on such short acquaintance.

"…should do."

"…not like it sees us."

"…the mess, though."

He followed the sound to a swinging door, and pushed it open.

The six town parents, a man in a chef's uniform, and two waitresses stood in front of a back door. Beside them, steel tables had fallen on their sides, and the floor was covered in flour.

They all peered out the back door, and it wasn't until Retsler got close that he saw why. Prints from a pair of bare feet led down the path toward a rock outcropping.

"Problem?" he asked.

Everyone jumped. Everyone. He'd never seen that before.

Bronly turned around, and it was her turn to give him an insincere smile. "Nothing we can't handle," she said.

"Tourists? Vandals? Is this the kind of crime I'd be handling if I came here?" he asked. Not that he was planning to come here, but he hated it when people deliberately hid information from him. Perhaps that was one of the reasons he became a cop.

"It's not really a crime," Martin started to say as the chef said, "It's my fault. If I hadn't moved the table…"

"But you like the table there," one of the waitresses said. "It makes for a more efficient kitchen."

"A more efficient kitchen is one you can cook in," the chef said, and sighed. He was older—that indeterminate age some men got, where it was impossible to say if they were 35 or 75. If Retsler had to guess, he'd say the chef was closer to the upper limit than the lower one, but only because of the man's calm. "I just shouldn't mess with it."

"We're going to have to mess with it," Stanley said. "That grill has to come out. We can't keep repairing it. And then what'll happen? Will the new one get trashed?"

"Someone want to tell me what's going on?" Retsler asked.

"Nothing important," Martin said, giving him an insincere smile.

"It was important enough to interrupt our meeting at a run," Retsler said.

They all looked uncomfortable, the kind of uncomfortable that people often got with outsiders whom they felt would not understand. Retsler's heart sank. He didn't like the feeling he had, but he was a cop and a damned good one, and it looked like they needed something, so he pushed, even though his instincts warned him against it.

"Let me take a look," he said, and before anyone could argue, he followed the flour footprints out of the kitchen. They padded beside the newly installed stone path, which he thought odd, considering the owner of those feet had been barefoot. The stone should have felt better against naked skin than the sandy rocks beside the path.

"Chief Retsler, please."

He could hear Bronly behind him, but he also knew that she wouldn't be able to keep up with him, not in those heels on this incline.

The path wound into the trees and away from the parking lot, toward the mountain itself.

The footprints remained visible, even though the flour should have dispersed after a few yards. He felt a tingling he hadn't experienced since his last years on the Coast.

He wasn't going to like this. He really should have heeded their advice and turned around.

A six-foot-high mesh fence covered the path and disappeared behind boulders that had clearly fallen off the mountainside. Behind the mesh fence, grass grew summer tall, nearly up to Retsler's chest. The grass blocked part of a well-worn dirt path that led to a boarded off opening into the mountainside.

That denied entrance into the Oregon Caves. The Park Service had actually boarded it all off.

There was no easy access through the mesh fence either. A large sign posted to the right stated that the entrance to the Oregon Caves was a half mile away, with a map provided in case the wanderer forgot about all the signs he'd seen coming up to the Chalet.

The footprints continued on the other side of the mesh. They followed the path all the way to the boarded opening of the Caves. From this distance, it looked like the footprints went into the Caves itself.

Retsler swallowed hard, that knot in his stomach so twisted that he felt vaguely ill. He forced himself to look at the ground underneath the mesh fence.

Sure enough, one of the footprints went under the mesh, half inside the fence and half out, as if the fence wasn't even there.

He closed his eyes for half a minute. What he saw was impossible. He knew it was impossible, he hated that it was impossible, and yet it was there in front of him, which meant that what he saw was very possible indeed. Retsler just had to figure out what actually happened.

He opened his eyes. The footprint remained. Dammit. He grabbed the fence with his right hand. The mesh was cool against his palm. He shook the metal and it rattled, but it didn't give. He'd hoped that it was rusted, broken off somewhere that he couldn't quite see, and easy to move and replace. But of course, the simplest and most logical explanation wasn't the one that faced him at the moment.

"Chief Retsler, really." Ron's voice came from behind him, a bit breathless and a little exasperated. "You don't need to investigate this."

He turned without letting go of the fence.

Her perfectly coiffed hair had slipped its bun, half of it trailing down the side of her now-red face. Beads of sweat had formed on her collarbone, and sweat stained the area around her armpits. Brambles and leaves clung to the hem of her pants. She no longer looked like a society matron, but like a woman who would have been a lot more comfortable in sweats and blue jeans, a glass of water in her left hand.

"I don't have to investigate," he said, "because you know what this is."

Her mouth thinned. "I told you. It's nothing, really. Not what we wanted to talk with you about."

"Nothing?" he asked. "Something did about one-hundred dollars damage to that kitchen, maybe more considering the cleanup time. Then there's the problem of the grill and the fact that your chef doesn't feel like he can put anything in his kitchen the way he wants it. Now, unless I miss my guess, the Chalet is already operating at a loss. You want to tell me that you can write off an expense, even a small one, that seems to occur on a regular basis?"

"I didn't say this had happened before," she said.

"No, your receptionist did when she came into our meeting room," Retsler said. "She said that she was sorry but that 'it' was back."

Ron's eyes widened. She glanced over her shoulders, but the remaining town parents hadn't followed her, or if they had, they were moving at an incredibly glacial pace.

Since she clearly wasn't going to say anything else, Retsler continued. "It's also notable that your receptionist didn't give the vandal a gender. I thought maybe an animal when I saw the over-turned table, before I saw the footprints. After all, we don't call other people 'it' very often, now do we?"

Bronly brought a hand to her destroyed bun, realized that it was falling apart, and pulled out the pins. She shook her head, letting her hair fall. The hair wasn't blond like he'd thought, but silver. With her hair at shoulder length, she looked younger than she had a moment ago.

She still didn't seem willing to answer him.

"Why don't you be upfront with me?" he said, trying to keep his tone even. "When you set up this job, you didn't want an Oregonian. You didn't even want an average chief of police. You could have done just fine with some local hire, maybe a disgruntled park service worker or someone who had retired up here and just needed the extra money for a few hours of his time every day. That is, that would be all you needed if things were normal around Marble Village, which they're not, right, *Ron*?"

He couldn't help himself: he had to emphasize her odd misleading nickname, maybe to keep the other anger in check, the one that rose whenever he felt both embarrassed and betrayed.

She held up a hand, as if her palm could block his words. "We were doing a legitimate hire."

Were. He wondered if she even knew she had used the past tense.

"No one could understand why we needed someone full-time. And most people, they don't like how remote it is up here," she said. "You're perfect. You've been chief of police in two remote towns, one here in Oregon. That's all we're looking at."

Yet her gaze didn't meet his.

"Uh-huh," he said in the back of his throat, that Oregon acknowledgement that was both dismissive and somewhat rude, something he hadn't done since he moved to Montana. "You've had Hamilton Denne up here, haven't you?"

Retsler had worked with Denne in Whale Rock. Denne was the Seavy County Coroner, and a local who first introduced Retsler to the idea of the supernatural. That discovery had strained their friendship. Retsler's move might have broken it entirely. He hadn't tried to find out.

Bronly blinked, then took a deep breath. "We had a mysterious death a few months ago. The Oregon Crime Lab recommended Doctor Denne."

Retsler hadn't heard Hamilton called Doctor, maybe ever. "A mysterious death. What did Hamilton tell you that you had? A fairy? A troll? Maybe some kind of orc?"

She shook her head. "No, no, the victim was human."

"Really?" Retsler asked. "Then why was Hamilton here? He likes things that resemble space aliens."

That wasn't exactly fair. Denne had saved Retsler's butt those last few years in Whale Rock, and had somehow kept him sane. But Denne did like the stranger things in the world. He found them fascinating.

Retsler just wanted them to go away.

"We had a desiccated corpse," she said softly.

"Which, given the dry conditions, the caves, and the heat in the summer, shouldn't be that unusual up here," Retsler said.

"Except that he was fine a few hours before. Alive, laughing, and fat as a man can be and still be considered strong and tough."

She had known the corpse, and Retsler had been rude. He felt a flush build around his ears. He willed it away.

"I'm sorry," he said in his formal voice. "I didn't realize you had known the deceased."

She shrugged, blinked again, and he realized she was fighting tears.

"We lost a few others like that," she said, deliberately ignoring his sympathy. "Tourists, it turned out. Hikers, two of them. When we found those bodies, we thought like you just did, that they had mummified because of the heat and the dry conditions, and the alkaline nature of some of the stone up here—God, we had a thousand explanations."

"And none of them right," Retsler said, making it a statement instead of a question. Statements kept people talking; questions made them stop.

"It was a *thing*." She shuddered. Apparently, she'd seen that *thing*, whatever it was. She held up her hands. "Long story. Not appropriate at the moment."

"But Hamilton helped you identify that thing," Retsler said.

"Oh, yes, after Chief Davis's death," she said.

Retsler's fingers tightened on the mesh. The metal cut into his skin but he didn't let go. "The chief was the desiccated corpse?"

She nodded. "He was heading up Mount Elijah to investigate a cougar sighting last we heard. Just two hours before someone found him on the road. Like that."

Tears welled again. The chief had meant something to her.

Retsler shook his head. This was going to be one of those stories he didn't want to hear. Something supernatural, something no one would believe until they saw the thing kill something else, and even then they'd find it hard.

"I take it you all solved whatever it was causing the deaths," he said in the most clinical voice he had. If Denne had been up here, he would have known just how angry and trapped Retsler felt. He was back in Oregon, and he was back in hell.

"Yes," she said in a somewhat strangled tone. "Yes, we figured it out."

She straightened her shoulders, ran a hand through her hair, then gave him a watery smile.

"I'm sorry I didn't tell you that the previous chief had died suspiciously," she said.

He shrugged. "We barely got through the introductions."

She glanced at his hand, still wrapped around that mesh. "I feel like I'm not being fair to you. Doctor Denne told me a lot about you, about the strange things that happened in Whale Rock, and

then I Googled you. We did do an open hire, we did. It was just—
Marble Village isn't a normal place. People want normal, they go
to Cave Junction. Or Medford. Not here. And all of the applicants,
they were either too old or too practical or too expensive. And so,
I was complaining to Doctor Denne over the phone, and he told
me about you. That's when I e-mailed you. That's when I hoped
you would come home."

This isn't home, he almost said, but didn't. Oregon was closer
to home than Montana, that much was true. But this part of Oregon was very different from the coast, different enough to have its
own weather, its own customs, and, apparently, its own monsters.

He didn't want to know. Better to return to Montana, where
the monsters were humans prone to domestic quarrels fueled by
too much alcohol and an easy access to firearms.

Still, he couldn't just walk away. Not with his fingers wrapped
around this mesh fence, and that footprint below. He'd always
wonder.

He saw that as both a personal failing and as a curse.

"All right," he said. "Time to tell me what's going on here."

She swallowed, blinked, sighed, clearly steeling herself. Then
her gaze met his.

"This one really isn't important. We weren't going to mention
it. No one's been hurt, nothing has gone wrong—"

"Except the damage," he said.

"Which we can limit if we don't move anything in the kitch-
en," she said. "The problem is that the new chef—and it's really
not fair to call him new, since he's been here five years—he wants
to make the kitchen more efficient. And the grill is dying. We can't
keep repairing it. It's from the 1930s. They don't even make parts
any more and we can't find any others."

Retsler was still focusing on how she started. "What do you
mean you can limit it if you don't move anything in the kitchen?"

She gave him a small smile. "I feel so stupid discussing this."

"Believe me," he said with more feeling than he had intended. "I understand."

Her smile widened just a little. "We thought we had a little girl. It's not. It's something else—"

"A poltergeist?" He'd read up on the supernatural after he moved away from Whale Rock. And as he did, that always made him speculate if he had let go after all.

"Yeah, that's what someone called it," she said. "But that's not really true. We didn't have a little girl ghost. It's a thin young woman, I think, or a feminine boyish man, someone to whom that kitchen meant a lot. When things are running smoothly, in fact, when the hotel is full and so is the restaurant, you can see her—him—it—sitting near the door, a smile on his—her—its face as if it liked the bustle. Sometimes, it would even help one of the morning cooks. Our previous cook—a matronly woman whom everyone loved—would occasionally let it help her pick ingredients. She wrote the recipes down; they're spectacular."

"A cooking ghost that lives in the Caves?"

Her smile disappeared as if it had never been. Her dark eyes flashed, and her chin set. "Go ahead. Make fun."

Retsler had used the same tone with her that he used to use with Denne. It was a reflex, a way of pushing back at information he really didn't want to hear.

"Sorry," Retsler said. "I didn't mean to make fun."

She took a deep breath. Clearly she had to overcome his tone so that she could continue. She expected him to make fun of her, and it almost shut her down.

He wondered who else had made fun, and what had changed.

"Whatever it is," she said with a little less enthusiasm, "it loves the kitchen just the way it's always been. We got new dishware and fortunately, it wasn't china, because the whatever it is tossed the dishware around the kitchen for weeks, trying to get rid of it. A few pieces chipped, finally, but we replaced them."

"When did that stop?" he asked.

"After a few months. But we can't wait this one out. We don't want it to trash a new grill, and you saw what it did with the flour."

"Yes," he said, and looked down. The footprint was fading. Had there been a wind? He hadn't noticed. "Did you know that this creature lives in the Caves?"

"I'm still not sure it does," she said. "But whenever it gets angry, it leaves footprints, coming to this site. We've actually sent people into the Caves to follow the prints, but they disappear just inside the opening."

"So this isn't flour." Retsler let go of the fence and crouched down. He touched the print. It was ice cold.

"Are you sure you should do that?" she asked.

"I'm not sure about anything," he said. He checked his fingertip just to make sure the white whatever it was didn't transfer onto his skin. So far as he could tell, it hadn't. "Has anyone else tried to figure out what these prints are made of?"

"By the time we get experts here, the footprints have faded," she said. "You can understand why we're reluctant to call folks in."

He nodded, then stood. "You have worse problems than this ghost?"

She bit her lower lip. "Apparently—and we didn't know this during the boom of the 1990s—but Marble Village was built on the site of one of the first settlements ever on Mount Elijah. There's water near here—"

"Don't tell me," he said. "The River Styx."

She smiled. "No. Well, yes. But no. The River Styx runs through the Caves, and that really is its name. Outside of the Caves, it's called Cave Creek. There are tributaries all over the mountainside. One of the largest is here, although it does dry up during summers like this one."

"And floods in spring," he said.

She nodded. "See why we want an Oregonian?"

"Anyone who lives around mountains knows how winter run-off works," he said. He still wasn't convinced about the Oregonian part. "But you were telling me about the water."

"The initial settlers thought they had a great water supply," she said, "so they built here instead of at Cave Junction. Then they abandoned the town."

"That's not unusual in the West," he said. "There's a million ghost towns just like it, places that people tried, figured wouldn't work, and moved on."

"Yeah." She glanced around him at the Caves, as if she saw something. He hoped she would trust him enough to tell him if she did. "But they didn't leave because the creek dried up or because of a wild fire or anything. They just disappeared one night. Half the town fled and the other half was never heard from again."

"I don't remember reading that," he said. Then he smiled at her. "You're not the only one who knows how to use Google."

"Tourist town," she said. "Resorts. We didn't put some of the old history on any website, and fortunately, the initial stories of Marble Village, which was called Limestone Creek back then, weren't published in any guidebooks."

"You think this history is important," he said.

"I didn't at the time," she said, "but I do now."

He brushed off his hands and stood. The footprints were nearly gone now, but he saw where they disappeared, and made a mental note of it.

"Why do you think so now?" he asked.

"Because we're under assault, Chief Retsler," she said. "That's why we want you. Someone we don't have to convince that this is important, that it could be an emergency. Someone who *knows.*"

He sighed. Back in Oregon, having the same old discussions. "Didn't Hamilton tell you? I left Whale Rock because of the supernatural."

"He did," she said. "He also said he didn't think you'd take the job, but he said I should push."

Retsler nodded, sighed. "So, you've done your duty. You've pushed."

The wind toyed with her hair. She grabbed some loose strands and tucked them behind her ears. "You're going to say no, aren't you?"

"Yeah," he said, and almost added, *I ran away from all this.* But he didn't.

"Well." Businesslike again. She stuck out her hand. "I'm sorry we wasted your time."

He glanced over his shoulder. "Let's make sure it's not wasted completely, all right?"

Then, without waiting for an answer, he shook the fence. It rattled, warning whatever was behind it that he was coming. He wasn't sure if he had done that deliberately. He liked to think he hadn't.

"How do I get through this?"

"You don't need to," she said.

"I'd like to," he said.

She hesitated, then pointed to an overgrown blackberry bush near one of the boulders. "Through that."

He'd tried to go through blackberry bushes before. They were stubborn, and sometimes hid things with thorns.

"I guess I'll climb," he said, and gripped the mesh. The diamonds were big enough for the toes of his somewhat dressy shoes. He hauled himself up, and carefully eased over, landing in the dirt on the other side.

At least she wouldn't follow him here.

"I'll get someone to open the gate," she said.

He nodded absently, not caring if she did or not. "I'd rather have an expert on the hotel's history, preferably not a scholarly type, but someone who's been around for a few generations."

"Um, but—"

He didn't listen to her answer. Instead, he followed the fading footprints down the incline to the mouth of the Caves.

The prints stopped just outside the opening. He touched them again. Cold, but damp, as if they were made of ice and the ice had started to melt. Water, again. Dammit.

He sniffed his fingers, wondering if the dampness had an odor. It didn't, or at least, it wasn't an odor that he could smell over the pines and the dirt and the fresh Oregon air.

He stood. The boards over the cave entrance were old and rotted. They hadn't been replaced in years. Some had broken along the sides. He touched them, and two boards fell down, leaving a space just large enough for a young adult woman or a slender young man who hadn't reached his full growth to slide through.

Retsler peered inside. No lights, but a chill against his skin. The Caves had an ambient temperature of 41 degrees, a fact he remembered from his childhood. As a boy, he had wondered why the settlers hadn't built their homes inside the Caves—they would stay relatively warm in the frigid mountain winters and remain cool in the summer. He had mentioned it to his father, who had laughed.

Boy, forty-one is too cold for comfortable living, no matter what the season.

It was also too warm to keep ice frozen, so the water inside the Caves—that damned River Styx—would continue to flow.

Retsler wondered if he should break the wood and go inside. Then he decided against it. He didn't have the equipment for one thing. Just his cell phone, which could double as a flashlight, but wouldn't have service deep inside. And this was a part of the Caves that the Park Service had deliberately blocked off, so finding him wouldn't be easy if he got lost or turned around.

Or attacked.

He picked up the wood. He would wait until he had permission, or even knew if he had to go inside.

Voices echoed along the path. He decided not to wait for someone to cut the brambles away from the gate opening so he could get out. He climbed the mesh for a second time, his fingers complaining as the metal dug into his skin.

He landed on the path just as Bronly returned with one of the town parents. The curled name badge reminded Retsler that the man was named Stanley. Stanley didn't look as winded by the walk as Bronly did. Despite the extra weight he carried around his middle, Stanley was surprisingly fit.

He held up hedge trimmers. "Was gonna help you get out."

"Thank you," Retsler said.

"Guess you didn't need it."

"I figured climbing was easier."

Stanley looked at him through narrowed eyes. Then he said, "Bronly here says you want to know about our ghost."

He sounded calm about it, calmer than Bronly had. She glanced at him, then at Retsler.

"I did," Retsler said, matching Stanley's calm tone, "but I would rather have heard from someone who maybe lived here in the 1930s."

"Ain't got many of those folks left and what we do are down to the Village. I could give you some names of folks in a home in Medford." Stanley wasn't looking at Retsler. He was peering over Retsler's shoulder at the Caves.

"See something?" Retsler asked.

"Naw," Stanley said. "Just like to be watchful, is all. This ain't the best side of the mountain to be on."

"Why not?"

"Creepies, crawlies, things that go bump in the night. They like the shadow side best."

"And this is the shadow side?"

Stanley nodded. His gaze moved from the Caves to Retsler's face. "Let's go to the diner," he said. "I bet you could use you some pie."

"You don't have to ask me twice," Retsler said. He glanced over his shoulder at the Caves behind him. The white footprints were gone, but his remained. His and Ron's and Stanley's, tromping all over each other, showing their confusion and indecision. The only odd thing he noted was that on the other side of the fence, no footprints showed at all, not even where he had jumped.

Retsler frowned. That felt important, but he wasn't sure why. Or, at least, he wasn't sure why—yet.

* * *

Half a dozen patrons sat in the W-shaped counters lining the diner. None of the patrons were the town parents, many of whom nursed coffee near the kitchen door.

Bronly led Retsler to the farthest side of the W, facing the windows that overlooked the small manmade pond and beyond it, the Siskiyou National Forest.

This part of Oregon was pretty, he had to admit that, and pretty in a different way from Montana. Maybe it was the color of the dirt, or the narrowness of the sky or maybe it was just the smell in the outdoor air, which he shouldn't have been able to smell in here.

That faint scent of fried hamburgers grew stronger now, particularly since one of his burgers was on that grill. The waitress, wearing a blue-and-white checkered uniform and a little protective hat that made her look like something out of the 1930s, had already given him ketchup and mustard in red and yellow plastic squirt containers, without any labels. Nothing had labels, trying to maintain the illusion of history. He wondered what he would get if he asked for artificial sugar to go with his iced tea, then decided not to ask.

He didn't want to spoil the illusion either.

Bronly also ordered a burger, which surprised him. He would have thought that a woman like her would order a salad. Although he hadn't seen any salads prominently displayed on the old-fashioned menu.

Stanley had ordered a piece of apple pie a la mode, and the waitress had already given it to him, along with a cup of diner coffee—nothing fancy at all, no half-caf lattes or sprinkles allowed.

"We're talking over here," Stanley said as he turned his plate so that the point of the wedge-shaped piece of pie faced him, "because the others think this's all crazy, that some kids're doing pranks."

"You don't?" Retsler asked. His stomach growled again. That piece of pie looked like something out of a magazine, perfect crust, glistening apples covered in a lovely brown sauce.

Then Stanley ruined the perfection by slicing off the tip. "You seen it. You want to tell me how them footprints got where they are? And icy to boot."

"You've touched the prints, then," Retsler said.

"First time I saw them. Windy day, but the prints stayed the same. Ice shocked me. It was strange, and back then, I didn't like strange." Stanley shoveled the pie into his mouth.

"You do now?" Retsler asked.

"Let's just say I'm used to it," Stanley said around the pie in his mouth.

Bronly glanced at the town parents, still talking near the kitchen door. Her glance seemed almost furtive, as if she didn't want them to overhear—which they couldn't, given how far away the door was.

"So this has been going on for a long time," Retsler said.

"This, that, and the other thing. The killings, though, those were new." Stanley cut another piece of pie, shoving the side of his fork so hard into the surface that the plate moved.

"And Hamilton Denne helped you with those," Retsler said, wanting to make sure.

"Theoretically. He said, though, things're changing. He was seeing more weird things, and he blamed all kinds of nutty stuff— global warming, some kind of creature rebellion, pollution, you know. All that liberal conspiracy crap."

Bronly leaned back just enough to catch Retsler's eye behind Stanley's back. She shook her head just a little, warning him off this part of the topic.

Retsler already knew to move away. He'd met this Oregon type before. They were prevalent in the mountains, guys who had their own beliefs about the world and who believed that anyone who disagreed with them was crazy or nutty or worse. Retsler had always thought of them as the precursors to the survivalists who had moved up here in the 1980s. When he was in Montana, which had a slightly different version of the same type, he realized that many of these folks *were* the survivalists who had moved to the "wilderness" in the 1980s. They had integrated back into society, kinda, but hadn't lost their strong opinions about the way the world worked or about the people who disagreed with them.

"You don't think this thing that's visiting your kitchen is a killer, do you?" Retsler asked.

"Naw. It's been coming here since we reopened. It gets mad, but it don't hurt anyone."

"But it causes damage," Retsler said.

"Some," Stanley said. "Don't think we need to waste your time catching it."

"I wasn't thinking about catching it." Retsler tried not to shudder. He'd actually touched some of the supernatural creatures he'd seen on the coast, and he didn't want to touch any of them again. "However, if it is a ghost, we might be able to put it to rest. I've helped with that before."

"I don't think it's a ghost," Stanley said. He looked pointedly at Ron. "I know some of the others think it's one of them poltergeists, but I don't. I can't find nothing about anyone what died in that kitchen."

"What about on the land before the kitchen was built?" Bronly asked, with enough force in her tone to make Retsler realize she had asked this before.

"Naw, nothing," Stanley said. "Not even a worker died while putting this thing up, and considering all the problems the WPA guys had sometimes, and the fact that nobody thought anybody what worked up here was worth much, that's kinda surprising. They had to snowshoe out, you know."

"What?" Retsler asked.

"Freak September blizzard. We're high enough to get that kinda thing once in a blue moon." Stanley cut more pie.

The waitress came by with both burgers. She set them down with a flourish. Retsler's looked fat and juicy and damn near perfect, like burgers he'd had as a kid.

"They ran out of supplies," Stanley said as the waitress walked away, "and no one could get to 'em. So they had to snowshoe out. All of them come back, though. Brought supplies up with a sled. Finished the job. "

"Back in the days when men were men and sheep were nervous," Bronly muttered so softly that only Retsler could hear her. He was glad he hadn't taken a bite of burger. He would have choked on it as he stifled his laugh.

"So," he said to Stanley, "no one died here that you know of."

"That's right," Stanley said.

Retsler picked up the burger. Juice dripped along his fingers. He took a bite. The burger was better than he expected, marinated in something before it was placed on that grill.

"What about in the Caves?" Retsler asked. "Anyone die in there that fits the description of this guy—or whatever?"

"Cook's kid or a cook?" Stanley asked.

"Or someone who wanted to be chef, or maybe a tourist?"

"Hell," Stanley said, "lots of people have died in those Caves, more than the Park Service wants us to admit."

"All before the Park Service took over," Bronly said primly. She clearly didn't want Retsler to think something bad could happen in the Caves. Or maybe she was still protecting the area's reputation.

"Most of 'em did die before anyone kept records," Stanley said. "And the ones we know about got written up in the papers. But I figure lots of folks got killed and left wherever. You know, they died deep inside, got stuck or something, couldn't get out, never was heard from again."

"The Caves still haven't all been mapped, even now," Bronly said. "Although I've never heard of anyone finding a skeleton inside one."

"But if there are other creatures living in the Cave...?" Retsler let his voice trail off.

Both Stanley and Bronly looked at him. He immediately regretted the choice of the word "creatures."

"I mean," he said, "you know, cougars, raccoons, rats, anything going in and out that might feast on a carcass. Something like that might mess with the bones as well. You wouldn't find any then."

"Well." Stanley ostentatiously ate the last piece of pie, chewing and talking at the same time. "Things get ate all the time up there. And we do find bones, just not human bones, so far as I know."

Retsler ate some of his burger, thinking.

"So," he said after a moment, "what you're telling me is that we have no idea if someone died in those Caves who had a connection to this hotel or this land, and we have no way of finding out."

"I don't think it's a ghost," Stanley repeated.

"Why not?" Retsler asked.

"Don't act like a ghost," Stanley said.

"A stereotypical ghost," Bronly corrected.

"No," Stanley said. "A ghost. We got 'em all over the hotel. You know, folks die in their rooms or whatever. We got ghosts, we got stories, and this one, it don't repeat actions like ghosts do, and it don't seem stuck in the past like ghosts are. It interacts. That's why I don't think it's harmful. I just think it's young."

Retsler looked at Stanley. "Young? What do you mean young?"

"It acts like a kid. It tosses stuff around that it doesn't like. It gets angry when you tell it no. But it watches, like it's learning."

Retsler set down the last part of his burger. "When you were looking at the Caves this afternoon, when you were talking to me, what did you see?"

"I told you. I didn't see nothing."

"The area looked normal, then," Retsler said.

"I didn't say that neither."

Bronly leaned around Retsler. "If you saw something, Stanley, tell us about it."

"I didn't see nothing," Stanley said with the same emphasis as before.

Retsler frowned. The key to talking with people, he had always thought, was listening. And he hadn't been listening.

"What kind of nothing?" he asked.

"You know," Stanley said. "Like fog. Like a cloud rolled in over the mountain, but just for a minute. Then everything was clear again. It wasn't nothing."

That's right, Retsler thought. *It wasn't nothing. It was something.* But he didn't speak out loud. He didn't want to derail Stanley.

"Where was this fog?" Retsler asked.

"Right near the gate." Stanley gave Bronly a perplexed look. "You know what I mean. We get that kind a thing all the time up here."

"Not in the summer," she said. "Fog's for fall."

"Or spring," Stanley said. "We got lots of ground fog in the spring."

Ground fog. Retsler mulled that over for a moment. Oregon had all kinds of fog that he hadn't encountered since he'd left. Montana didn't have nearly as much fog because it didn't have as much moisture in the atmosphere.

Fog, ground fog, light fog, freezing fog.

Freezing fog.

Something that should have been impossible up here in these temperatures. Like ice cold footprints. Like a childish figure that overturned tables and handed cooking ingredients to a chef.

He went back to ground fog for just a moment. He hadn't seen any in years, but he remembered it clearly. It always looked like it was seeping out of the ground, not forming in the air around the ground. He'd always thought ground fog spooky and Halloween-ish, like something out of a Vincent Price movie or out of a Scottish ghost story.

Covering the ground. *Brushing* the ground.

Hiding footprints—his and the ice prints. Covering. Brushing. Hiding.

"Dammit," he said softly.

"What?" Bronly asked.

"Do you have a book of local legends?" Retsler asked.

"Upstairs," Stanley said as if he'd been waiting for Retsler to ask. "Gift shop."

"All right then. I'll go check those books out." But Retsler didn't leave immediately. He had to finish that spectacular hamburger first.

* * *

The gift shop was in a room just off the registration desk. The room had beautiful wood walls, so lovely that no one dared hang anything on them except photographs and single t-shirts on hangers. The rest of the merchandise stood on freestanding displays. Snacks, sundries, and local jams covered one display. A large art portfolio filled the area farthest from the window, and the clothing hung on racks in the middle of the room.

It took Retsler a moment to see the books. They were on built-in shelves behind the cash register.

The woman behind the register gave him a friendly smile. "Go ahead," she said in a tone that told him other customers had hesitated to go back there as well.

He did. The store carried some mass market paperbacks, some used books, and a whole bunch of local color. Books on the Oregon Caves, books on the Park Service, books on Southern Oregon, and books on the great lodges of the Northwest dominated. He saw a few books on the WPA plus a film of the building of the hotel. Then he saw the books that Stanley had mentioned, huddled together like forgotten children on the bottom shelf.

Retsler crouched, then sighed.

Ghosts of the Northwest, Oregon Folklore, Monsters of the Mountains—he'd seen all of these before. He hadn't really looked at them with Marble Village or the Chalet in mind, but he didn't trust the authors of these tomes as far as he could throw them.

But Stanley had recommended them, so maybe there was a kernel of truth in them.

"You're the new police chief?" the woman asked.

Retsler grabbed the *Monsters* book. It was covered with dust.

"We haven't gotten that far yet," he said, knowing it was a lie. He'd already told Bronly he wouldn't take the job, but he didn't feel he should confide in this woman.

"I'll bet you Stanley sent you here, didn't he?" the woman said. "He thinks those books have truths in them."

"You don't?" Retsler opened the *Monster* book. Just like he remembered: hand-drawn images and tiny type. He had tried to read this thing once and hadn't been able to.

"Oh, they have little bits in them," she said, "but nothing like what really goes on up here."

Retsler set the book down, wiped his hands on his pants, and stood. He hadn't expected her to say anything like that. He had expected her to tell him that Stanley was a bit nuts, that he imagined all kinds of things.

"What goes on up here?" Retsler asked, looking at the woman carefully.

She was middle-aged, carrying just enough weight to make her seem matronly. Her hair was going gray but hadn't gotten there yet. When it did, someone would describe the color as gun-metal gray. Right now, it dulled her red-brown hair. She'd spent too much time in the sun, judging by the faint wrinkles on her skin, and her current tan. But she had spectacular green eyes. She hadn't been a beauty in her day, but she had turned heads.

She said, "You're asking about the child in the kitchens, aren't you?"

"You think it's a child?" Retsler asked.

"I certainly hope so," she said.

She sounded certain, as if an adult would be a bad thing. Retsler frowned. "Why?"

"Because we live on the shadow side," she said.

He leaned against the counter. "That's the second time someone mentioned the shadow side to me, and frankly, I'm confused.

There is no shadow side to a mountain. The sun hits all parts eventually. I know there's a shadow side in different seasons—"

"The sun does not hit all parts," she said. "Some sections never see sunlight. They have overhangs or side croppings or there are trenches—"

"All mountains have that," he said.

"Yes," she said a little ominously. "Yes, they do."

He took a deep breath, trying to control the sarcasm that wanted to flow out of him. That sarcasm had almost gotten him in trouble with Bronly, and it was going to get him in trouble here, if he wasn't careful.

He extended his hand. "Dan Retsler."

"MariCate Webber."

They shook, and that gave him a moment to get himself under control. He remembered Denne once saying to him, *Either you accept this stuff or you don't, Dan. You're an evidence guy. How much evidence do you need to realize that strange things exist?*

"So," Retsler said, "what's wrong with the shadow side here?"

"Our shadow side isn't unique," she said. "But that child is."

"You're convinced it's a child."

"Aren't you?"

"I haven't seen it, but others seem to believe it." Then he winced. That "seem to" would have gotten Denne to jump all over him.

MariCate didn't seem to notice. Instead she offered what seemed like a nonsequiter. "My grandfather helped build this place."

And suddenly Retsler understood why Stanley had sent him up here. Not to see musty old books, but to talk to MariCate who, like most people in an area routinely flooded by tourists, wouldn't answer direct questions, but might talk to someone she trusted.

"You know they got snowed in," she said.

"Stanley told me they snowshoed out."

"They did, but not to escape or get supplies. That's the cover story."

"What's the real story?" Retsler asked.

She smiled. "It was a rescue."

He didn't follow. "Leaving was a rescue?"

"No, no," she said. "Stanley must've also told you no one died building this place."

"Yes, he did," Retsler said.

"Which is true. You, as a policeman, probably know that truth hides in the words you choose."

Somewhere in this conversation, he had stopped leaning. He placed his hands on the polished wood countertop.

"People did die then," he said after a moment. "Just not building the place. They died during the blizzard...?"

"No," she said. "They died in the Caves. Where they went for shelter. Most of a family died. The cook, his wife, and his adult son."

"Most?" Retsler's palms felt damp. He removed them from the wood, saw the prints he left, then shoved his hands in his pockets.

"The twelve-year-old daughter, she got out. They rescued her and four other children."

"What were children doing up here?" Retsler asked. "I thought this was a WPA project."

"It was," MariCate said, "but a lot of families, you know, were homeless then. And when the man got work, sometimes the whole family came along. They weren't supposed to, but they camped nearby, on Cave Creek, and probably got sheltered in the buildings the men made for themselves."

"Probably?" Retsler asked. "You don't know?"

"There's a lot I don't know," she said. "My grandfather didn't like talking about this. He was 81 when I divorced and moved up here. He tried to talk me out of it. He didn't want me on this side of the mountain."

"The shadow side," Retsler said.

"You didn't notice, did you, when you drove in that this is a kind of high valley? Marble Village is actually in a box valley, at 4,000 feet, mind you, but a box valley just the same. Only one real way in. At least there's light there."

"And not here? I seem to see quite a bit of sunlight around this place."

"Around parts of it. But there's never sunlight from the kitchen to the Caves. You didn't notice that, did you?"

He hadn't noticed it. He would check out what she said later. "Why didn't your grandfather want you here?"

"He said it was dangerous. He especially warned me out of those Caves. The access here isn't used at all by the Park Service. It's mapped, but it's blocked inside and out, except for a tributary of the River Styx that they couldn't block without hurting the rest of the Caves."

"Why is it blocked?"

"Oh," she said with that smile. It was impish, and he rather liked it. So far today, he'd found two women his age attractive. Maybe he had been alone too long. "They'll never say why. They'll say it's too dangerous for tourists, which is true, and they'll tell you that there's nothing to see, which isn't, and then they'll tell you that it hasn't been mapped, which is an out-and-out lie."

"They won't tell me," Retsler said, "but you will."

Her smile widened into a grin. "As my grandfather spins in his grave, certainly. The reason is that people die in this part of the Caves, and not normal dying either. They freeze to death, sometimes in a matter of minutes and sometimes over days."

"I thought the Caves were forty-one degrees," Retsler said.

"They are," she said.

"The people just get chilled then," he said.

"If exposure can turn you into a block of ice, then yeah, they just get chilled," she said.

"Block of ice." He wasn't even trending toward sarcasm now, not with that icy footprint. "So you think the child is an ice-ghost? One of the children that died in there while this hotel was being built?"

"Children didn't die in there," she said. "That's what I was telling you. One got out—a girl. She came back to the men huddled in their cabins during the storm. How she found them, well, that's subject to conjecture, because you know how hard it is to find anything in white-out conditions."

He hadn't known that until his sojourn in Montana. The scariest day he'd had as chief there had been during a severe and sudden snowstorm, one that had stranded him beside the highway. Fortunately, he'd pulled off, or his jeep would've been totaled by the idiots trying to drive blind.

He nodded. "Yeah, I know."

"Well, she told them that the cook's family was in there, and a few of the kids, who'd been playing near the River Styx, and asked them to get the family out. The men waited until the snow had eased, thinking the family would be safer in the Caves. By the time they got there, there was a snow barrier, or so it seemed, covering the entrance. Avalanche, they thought, or something. Anyway, as they tried to dig out, they kept hitting rock. They were using their hands and some shovels that broke. They needed more equipment."

"What kind of equipment?" Retsler asked. "They couldn't use dynamite and there wasn't anything that would have made it up the mountain in a storm, no grader or anything."

"I don't know," she said. "I never asked. My grandfather and his friends snowshoed down with the girl, got help, came back up with supplies. A handful of guys remained. They managed to make a small opening, found the frozen adults, but the children were still missing. So they did a search."

"The adults froze near the entrance then," Retsler said. Of course. That made sense. Nothing supernatural at all. He felt a thread of relief.

"No," she said. "They were nearly a mile into the cave, in a room appropriately called 'The Ice Palace.' My grandfather said after this whole thing, there was talk of digging out that room to see if the stalagmites were actually people, frozen in place, but that idea got scrapped. It haunted my grandfather, though, I tell you."

It couldn't be that easy. It never was. Not here, not in Oregon. Retsler sighed. "And the children?"

"They left on their own, while the men were trying to get the bodies out of the Ice Palace. The kids said they were playing with their friends, and hadn't even known there was a storm, had no idea they'd been there for days, weren't even hungry, and certainly didn't look like they'd been trapped in a cave."

"Denial," Retsler said.

She gave him an appraising look, then shrugged. "They didn't use that word back then, but a lot thought it might be something like that."

"Your grandfather didn't."

"He finished the winter here, and never came back. He kept moving south, away from snow or snow-capped mountain peaks. Died in Los Angeles, in a house where he couldn't see any mountains at all." She was clearly waiting for Retsler to ask a question, and this time, he knew what the question was.

"Why was he afraid of snow?"

"Said there were things in it. He could see them. Creatures. Said Hans Christian Andersen's Snow Queen wasn't a story after all."

"I never read it," Retsler said.

"Think of a winter queen. She had an army made of snowflakes, and commanded the ice. She could steal a man's soul with a single kiss."

"Sounds like a fable to me," Retsler said. "And there are no mountains in Denmark, so Andersen wouldn't have been writing about the shadow side."

"He was writing about snow, and ice, and what some call ice fairies."

"Is that what you think this is?" Retsler added.

"I think the word 'fairy' gets used for all kinds of magical beasts," she said. "But the children lost time, like people do in fairy kingdoms. Washington Irving wrote about that in 'Rip Van Winkle.'"

"Which was a metaphor for the changes that occurred during the Revolutionary War," Retsler said.

Her expression cooled. "I didn't expect a skeptic. They said you knew about these things."

He sighed. "Not snow creatures."

Although snow was water. Frozen water. Ice crystals.

"You said the children were playing with their friends," he said, hoping to get back on track.

She nodded. "That's why my grandfather never let me up here. The children had always talked about their imaginary friends in the Caves. After the incident, he decided those friends were real. He says he saw them."

"Children," Retsler said.

"Yes," she said. "He said they loved coming into the camp kitchen to get warm."

* * *

Retsler didn't know if he believed any of it. He didn't know if he disbelieved any of it either. He poked a bit more, discovered that others had died in the Caves, but that the deaths were ruled exposure, which could happen to anyone in prolonged forty-one degree temperatures.

Plus, he never trusted death analysis from the previous century—at least, not before 1950 or so, when the practice of forensic medicine, like the practice of medicine itself, became more science-based and less reliant on the skill of the practitioner.

By the account that MariCate had given, these men had pulled bodies out of that cave that were "frozen to death," but that phrase got used for everything from exposure to being too cold to actually freezing in a snow bank.

Retsler could imagine what Denne would say. Retsler was using supposition just like everyone else was. Only Retsler's reinforced his own bent to the practical, to the real world, not a willingness to believe in fairies and poltergeists and things that go bump in the night.

Even though he had seen those things, more than once.

He took the proffered hotel room, which was beautiful. It had clearly been redesigned in recent years, with a modern bathroom added, and the most comfortable mattress he'd ever encountered. The hotel had internet access and more television channels than he had in Montana. Even so, the place still felt rustic. Maybe it was the rough hewn walls, or the ancient bed frame. Maybe it was the photographs on the walls, black-and-whites of former guides and mountain men and the men who built this place.

Or maybe it was the remoteness. Even with all the connectivity, he still felt far away from civilization. If he closed his eyes, he could imagine himself back an entire century, learning about the real-world magic of the Oregon mountains, the pines, the caves, the breath-taking views.

To Retsler, that kind of beauty had fairy dust sprinkled all over it, and not the kind that made a man lose ten years, but the kind that made him realize there was no other place on Earth like this one.

At a very good dinner in the fancy dining room, the town parents regaled him with stories about Marble Village, true-to-life stories about the town drunk and the occasional domestic and the one real murder the town had had in the past five years.

He'd had a conversation just like this one in Montana before his hire there, and back then, it had sounded like heaven to him. Dealing with everyday problems, with families and bar fights and the occasional true crime.

But this time, he couldn't make himself focus. He had already told Bronly that he wasn't interested in the job, and no matter what kind of stories the town parents told him, he wasn't going to change his mind.

He didn't even change his mind when they offered him nearly double his current salary, plus a house at the edge of town. He had never been in this business for the money. He wasn't about to start now.

No one mentioned the supernatural at all. No one talked about the event in the kitchen or the strange things he'd seen just since he got here, and he didn't blame them.

After talking with MariCate, some of the interest had left him. The others had been right: this wasn't something that a police chief would deal with, even if he did work up here. The vandalism wasn't really vandalism, the intruder was known to everyone.

It was one of those things that people put up with. Had the intruder been an actual person and not something magical, everyone would make excuses, telling Retsler about the kid's bad home life or his poor upbringing or his limited intelligence. No one would ask the chief to intervene, especially since it seemed that no one got hurt.

That was what had cooled him, if "cool" was the right word. So far as he could tell, these creatures hadn't ever killed anyone. In fact, if the story MariCate had told could be believed, the creatures had saved the life of the children during that snowstorm, and got them out untraumatized.

All of the stories were relatively benevolent. There was no evidence that the creatures were what killed the adults, they might have simply died in a colder part of the cave, thinking they were safe. The creature that invaded the kitchen had never harmed a soul, not even when that cook years ago had let the creature choose ingredients for meals. In fact, the meals had to be good because the recipes were still in use.

So, aside from the occasional angry outburst, the kind he'd seen from a variety of humans in a variety of circumstances, the creature seemed somewhat normal.

If such things could be called normal.

After a few bottles of Blackberry Porter from Wild River Brewing (something he couldn't get in Montana and missed, the summertime microbrews from his home state), Retsler planned his drive back to Montana. He decided he wouldn't even go to Whale Rock. He still didn't want to see anyone there, still didn't want to revisit the place.

He was still, despite his momentary lapse, running away from all things unworldly.

And, he told himself, he always would.

* * *

Sunlight woke him, which he found ironic since everyone talked about living on the shadow side. Apparently, his east-facing hotel room avoided that shadow altogether.

He supposed he could close the curtains, but they were gauzy and white and wouldn't make a lot of difference. He checked his watch, saw that it wasn't even six yet, which was when the diner opened. He had checked the night before, knowing he would be leaving as early as he could. He could make it back to Montana in one long day, but he preferred to drive sensibly. No reason the chief of police of any town should get caught weaving all over an empty highway due to exhaustion.

Even with a leisurely shower, he got downstairs ten minutes before the diner opened. He found himself wandering outside, to the path. It was dark here, shadowy, the pond itself looking a bit grim and more algae-covered than he remembered.

It was also cold, the kind of cold he loved about the West. Yeah, it would heat up to maybe ninety-five later in the day, but right now, it was fifty and he wasn't wearing a coat.

He looked at the mountain, rising up before him. He couldn't see the peak here because he was too close. The mountain didn't look formidable when you were on it, only as you drove up to it from sea level. Then it seemed impossible to cross.

A chill breeze touched him, the kind he hadn't yet gotten used to in the Montana winters. Some of the locals there called it a prairie breeze because it came from the East, bringing Midwestern or Canadian cold onto the part of Montana that passed for flatland. The weather guys called it an arctic wind, but that suggested gales filled with snow particles. This felt only like the precursor.

And he shouldn't feel it, not in summer. He looked over his shoulder, realized that he was standing near the kitchen door.

He should have been warmer standing here, but he wasn't.

He turned slowly, holding his hands up like a man with a gun trained on him.

The creature stood behind him, just like he had expected from that chill. All of the descriptions were right: childlike, young, maybe male, maybe female. The eyes looked older than a child's ever could, but the slender build reminded Retsler of some paintings he had seen of androgynous figures looming out of the mists.

He didn't know how to talk to it. If he asked it questions, it would probably leave.

So he said, "Beautiful morning, isn't it?"

Its mouth opened, as if it were going to answer him, revealing a slightly pink interior. As he watched, the creature gained a bit of pinkness all over, as if it were trying to mimic his flesh color.

"They think you come down here to get warm," he said. "I don't. I think you come down here for company."

It tilted its head. Its eyes were now blue, the blue of the Montana sky. Its face had no more definition than before, but it seemed to relax a little.

"You like cooking, you like listening to conversation, and you miss your friends. When the Park Service blocked off the interiors of the Caves, did you lose your own people or access to ours?"

It nodded toward him, just once, and his heart leapt. It was answering him.

"I thought so," he said. "Your people, they're not fond of us. The rest of them hide, don't they?"

It raised its shoulders slightly, then let them drop. A small shrug. It had been around humans long enough to learn gestures. He wondered if it could talk. He suspected that it couldn't or it would have spoken before now—not to him, but to the others.

"They call this the shadow side," Retsler said. "You can't travel outside of it, can you? You can't look for your friends anywhere else."

Water dripped off its chin. He didn't know if it was melting in the relative heat or if those were tears.

He didn't know if this thing could cry.

Denne would want him to photograph it. Denne would want him to ask all kinds of procedural questions.

But Retsler wasn't interested in procedure. This creature had done nothing wrong. It was just lonely.

He understood that.

He nodded, glanced at the kitchen door, then back at the creature. "They need to talk to you," he said. "They want to make some changes."

Its head snapped back, its hand came out, and for a moment, Retsler thought it might hit him. He could actually feel the anger coming off the creature.

His heart pounded. He kept his hands up. "They don't want to get rid of the kitchen," he said, keeping his voice calm. "But out here, outside the Caves, our equipment decays. Falls apart."

More water dripped off its chin.

"We repair that damage," he said. "But sometimes we have to replace things. Like the dishes. Remember how we replaced the dishes?"

It watched him. He had no idea how old this thing was, but he would wager it was decades older than he was. And he would wager that it was one of the younger members of its species.

He had no idea if it understood. He hoped it did. Because he finally figured out its anger.

The interior of the Caves had remained the same for hundreds of years. The early deaths might have been caused when humans wandered in, interfered with something important. He would wager that the Ice Palace meant something to this creature's people.

But he didn't know, and obviously, it couldn't tell him. Not easily, anyway.

"Let us make the changes," he said. "Then we'll stay. The kitchen will stay. The path will stay. You can still observe, and maybe even help again."

It wiped a hand along its chin, a very human gesture. Then it closed its fingers around the water it had collected.

When it opened its hand again, it was holding what looked like tiny diamonds. It extended that hand to Retsler.

His heart pounded. He'd learned not to accept magical items from any creature. He'd once lost a friend to centuries-old wine. All of the fairytales cautioned against eating anything offered by the supernatural.

But the creature didn't want him to eat the diamonds, at least so far as Retsler could tell.

He brought his right hand down and extended it, palm up. The creature touched the tips of its fingers to the tips of his, its skin sending an icy shock through him.

Then the creature closed its hand again, and smiled.

The smile was a surprise. The face warmed, and the creature looked almost human.

Retsler smiled back.

The creature nodded, then walked around Retsler, heading down the path toward the Caves.

Retsler watched it until it disappeared around a small corner. The chill slowly left the air. He could feel the warmth of the day wrap itself around him.

No wonder the creature left so early. It would melt faster in the heat of a mountain summer.

His stomach growled. He ate too much up here, and he still wasn't getting full. He glanced at his watch to see how long the interaction took and was startled to see that three hours had gone by.

He had lost time. A few minutes conversation, to him, and he had lost time.

No wonder those children had lost days. He wondered what they had done in the Caves as the snow fell, as their parents died in the Ice Palace.

Then he shook his head slightly. He was intrigued. Dammit. He hadn't been intrigued in years. Frightened, yes. Overwhelmed, most definitely. And then he had run away to a place that hadn't challenged him at all.

He had never been intrigued in his Montana job, although learning the job had occupied him for a while. It had brought him a feeling close to intrigue. But he had never quite achieved it.

He stared at the path down the center of the shadow side, leading to a blocked off part of the Caves. Home, but not home. Water creatures, but no great body of water. A history, but not the history he had grown up with.

A new start, again.

"Dammit," he repeated.

And then he turned, and walked into the kitchen. He didn't run, and he certainly wasn't running away.

In fact, he had some information to give to the chef and the entire staff, maybe to the town parents, and certainly to Stanley and MariCate. He knew how they should treat their visitor, and how to keep that visitor calm.

He also knew he was signing on for a ride. They were, as Bronly had told him, under some kind of assault. But so was Whale Rock. He didn't want to go back there.

But he didn't want to return to Montana either, where he faced domestic quarrels fueled by too much alcohol and an easy access to firearms.

Retsler suspected he would find enough of those up here. It was a rural village after all, despite the obvious wealth backing the hotel. Wealth didn't prevent people from getting angry or drinking too much or losing sight of the things they loved.

Hell, nothing did.

Humans reserved the right to be stupid.

And they deserved the right to change their mind.

Leah Cutter loves diverse settings. Her first three novels, Paper Mage, Caves of Buda, *and* The Jaguar and the Wolf, *take place in Tang Dynasty China, World War II Budapest, and the Viking Era. Lately, she has focused on contemporary fantasy in such novels as* Zydeco Queen and the Creole Fairy Courts. *She also writes a lot of short fiction, with stories upcoming in anthologies and* Alfred Hitchcock's Mystery Magazine.

Her work has received starred reviews and a lot of deserved acclaim. She should receive even more acclaim after people read "Sisters."

Sisters

Leah Cutter

Lin Han still knelt in the courtyard, as still as the towering rock *steele* behind her that the names of her family's ancestors were carved into. The bleak early morning light washed everything gray: the hard brick she knelt on, the black iron brazier in front of her, the twisted pine in front of the double wall that stood guard before the door leaving the family courtyard. The sacred smoke from the brazier had long since disappeared, but the heavy smell of burnt wood and paint still hung in the air.

Double-hour bells rang in the distance, muffled by Lin Han's fog. She felt herself stirring, as if she were waking, though she hadn't slept all night. She blinked dry eyes and stiffness poured through her body, as if she were suddenly no longer young. Her knees started to ache. Her shoulders felt weighed down, as if a yoke with buckets filled with water lay across them, like the laborers she saw in the street. She took a deep breath, the taste of smoke mingling with the tears still gathered at the back of her throat.

Lin Han curled her fingers into fists on her thighs, realizing how cold the tops of her hands were when they touched the warm silk. She pushed herself forward, trying to rise, and ended up catching herself with her hands, the cold hard brick pushing back at her. Her legs were filled with sand, leaden, hard to move.

Slowly Lin Han rose. She swayed like young bamboo in a storm trying to gain her feet.

As if that was a signal, Old Cook scurried out.

"Please, Miss, you must go to bed now," he whispered urgently.

"No. I will not leave my sister," Lin Han said.

Old Cook didn't have to say it. She heard it echoing again against the hard bricks of the courtyard, the proclamation by her mother, her father.

You no longer have a sister.

"Enough of that," Lin Han said, banishing those ghosts of memory. "I must take her with me." Sometime in the night a plan had come to her.

Old Cook opened his mouth, then closed it and gestured at the huge brazier. It had *Fu* dog heads on the sides, each bigger than Lin Han's head. Ornate legs curved down to splayed toes. It had taken six men to haul it into the courtyard.

Lin Han had grown the last year, and so it merely came up to her chest now. However, she would never grow big enough to carry it away.

"Fine," she said. "I need, I need..."

The chill of the morning finally entered her bones. She shivered abruptly and swayed again. But she refused to give in to the horror of it, what she needed to do.

"I need something to hold her in."

"Right away, Miss." Old Cook bowed low before racing away.

The long shadows of the courtyard wall to Lin Han's right began defining as the sun rose. The twisted pine took on long needles and distinct branches. The brilliant red tile on the rooftops beyond the courtyard sprang to life. All around the quiet courtyard the city of Yen Tu woke up. Already the street venders with their buckets of millet porridge and clear chicken broth called out their wares. People walked in the street, snatches of conversation floating up over the wall.

Lin Han just waited.

Old Cook came back out with an ornate, porcelain, red-and-white vase. It was skinny at the bottom and blossomed out at the top. Hard nubs of white stuck out from the body in curling lines.

Dao Ming would have wanted to put tall lilies in it, something graceful and overflowing.

Lin Han accepted the weight of the vase, cradling it in her arms for a moment before taking the cold metal scoop that Old Cook also handed her. She stood on her toes and looked into the brazier.

The pile of ash was so small, like Dao Ming had been.

Mama would kill Lin Han for handling ashes. She'd insist on a cleansing ceremony from the stinky Taoist priest with the dark robes who never smiled as well as a second one from the Buddhist priest in his bright orange robes who was more sour still.

Tears gathered behind Lin Han's eyes again. This was all she had left of her younger sister. A burnt spirit tablet, taken from their ancestors' altar in the front greeting room.

A hard spike of hurt pierced her chest as she remembered how her parents were going to deny Dao Ming's birth, just like they'd denied her death. They claimed now that there had only ever been two children: Lin Han and her older brother. Dao Ming had been written out of the family records. Father had talked of bribing the census takers to cross out her name. All her clothes had been given away or burned. Her favorite straw-stuff doll destroyed.

Last night, Mama and Father hadn't even held a funeral, barely said a single prayer before they'd placed Dao Ming's spirit tablet in the brazier.

Someone had to do something for Dao Ming. There was nothing to anchor her spirit. She would become a red-faced angry ghost, stealing food and paper ghost money meant for others.

Lin Han's tears fell as she stuck the shovel in the ashes. The mound crumbled, the fine ash sliding away like sand. When she lifted the first scoop, the early morning breeze puffed away some of the soot, sending it dancing across the courtyard.

She carefully tipped the scoop into the vase so no more of the ash escaped. Moving slowly, she completed her task, though some of it had spilled onto her fine dark-blue robes. Mama would be mad, but Lin Han didn't care.

Finally, Lin Han stepped back. With a bow, she solemnly handed the small scoop to Old Cook, who just as solemnly took it.

"I will bury this," Old Cook assured her.

Lin Han swallowed around a dry mouth. "Thank you," she whispered, touched that he was treating Dao Ming's burnt spirit tablet like a body, as if they were actually handling the dead.

"You take care of Little Miss," Old Cook instructed. "We will hide you as well as we can today, me and the gardener and your mother's dressing maid."

"Thank you," Lin Han said again, bowing low.

Though her family might deny Dao Ming, Lin Han was still going to see that at least in the afterlife, her sister would be taken care of.

* * *

Lin Han stood on one side of the dusty street, looking at the Taoist priest's shop on the other. The tiny wooden shack sat nestled between two larger stone buildings, almost as if he'd blocked off an alley to make his home. No paint decorated the walls, no mystic symbols were carved into the wood. Just a hand painted sign, weathered gray wood with bright red paint promising suitable mates for all.

The mid-morning bells had already rung. A few laborers remained in the street, squatting under the eaves of one of the stone buildings, rolling dice and drinking strong pear wine. They hadn't seemed to notice her—no one had. Lin Han knew her fine blue robes didn't belong in this part of Yen Tu, knew that the vase she carried was worth more than a few *cash*.

Either Dao Ming protected her, or Lin Han had also turned into a ghost.

Finally, the old man she'd watched go into the Taoist's shop came out. He clutched a brown leather bag tightly to his chest as he hurried off. Maybe the old Taoist was also an apothecary, though he didn't have a sign for that.

Feeling great daring, Lin Han stepped out of the shadows and into the brightly lit street. She rushed across though there was no traffic, no people or palanquins to avoid this far from the city center. She fumbled with the latch and had to use her elbow to push on it so she wouldn't have to put down the vase.

The dark of the shop made Lin Han stop and blink her eyes for a moment. Spicy medicine smells, the scent of burnt *jing* sticks and incense all came to her, as well as long boiled tea and sweet chrysanthemum. The Taoist sat silent and still behind the counter against the far wall. Rough wooden floorboards snagged her sandals as she walked forward.

Jars bigger than her vase filled with bulbous white roots in yellow liquid hung from ropes from the ceiling. A long dried snake skin marked with a black diamond pattern stretched from one side of the room to the other and swayed in the slightest breeze. Eggs cooked in tea sat in another jar on the counter. The back wall held row after row of sealed porcelain jars, all meticulously labeled with either red or black characters.

The Taoist rose from his seat. His long face ended with a hanging jowl and his forehead lifted up to a bald skull. Fringes of greasy white hair curled down from just above his ears, over his shoulders. His nose hung like a foreigner's and his ears stood out like long handles.

"Good day," he said, giving her a small bow. His voice belied his skeletal stature, ringing from him like a deep bell.

"Good day," Lin Han said. She hugged the vase closer to her, the hard nubs pressing into her chest. "I need to find a mate."

At his raised eyebrow, she made her voice stronger. "For my sister."

She carefully lifted the vase out to show him, missing its hard pressure against her chest. "The ashes...the ashes of her spirit tablet are in here."

"Ah, a *minghu*," the Taoist priest said, nodding. "A spirit wedding."

"You must find someone who will look after her. She was, she was a good girl. She will work hard. But she should also be respected. Honored."

"Thank you for honoring me with your request," the Taoist said gravely, giving Lin Han another bow.

Relief made Lin Han sag where she stood. She'd done the right thing gathering up the ashes.

"Tell me," the Taoist said over steepled fingers, looking down at her from his tall height. "How old was your sister?"

"She was eight. Her name was Dao Ming."

The Taoist came around his counter and stood in front of Lin Han. He bowed very low to her, then knelt down so he was closer in height to her. "I'm so sorry," he said. "But Dao Ming was born in the year of the Ox."

"She was," Lin Han said.

The lump was back in her throat.

"I cannot find a mate for her," the priest said simply.

Surprise took away some of the sting.

A grown up, speaking so plainly?

"Why not?" Lin Han said.

"She's too young. She can't even have a funeral. Veneration is only right from the young to the old. The other way, from someone older to someone so young—it isn't the natural order of things. And brides, as you know, are very honored."

"Please," Lin Han whispered. The room had suddenly grown very dark, and the medicine smells clogged the back of her throat.

"I'm sorry. But I can't help."

The Taoist reached across and turned her gently toward the door.

Lin Han felt as light as a leaf blown by the wind, no weight to push back.

Before she could think she found herself outside in the bright sunshine.

A group of boisterous students were walking by in the street, causing Lin Han to shrink back under the eaves. She stood blinking, her breath heaving.

Of course the adults couldn't help. They hadn't been able to help after the accident, when Dao Ming had been hurt.

A wailing sound startled Lin Han. She pressed her back against the rough wood of the Taoist's shop. Where was it coming from? The sound of clashing cymbals and drums rolled out next, meant to scare away any bad spirits.

From down the street she saw a group of men carrying something on sticks over their shoulders, a palanquin she assumed. Someone very important. As they drew closer, she saw she'd been wrong.

They carried a paper-wrapped wooden coffin.

On top of the coffin was a painting of the dead: a young man with stiff black hair, a sharp nose, and kind eyes.

Lin Han carefully watched the funeral procession, picking out his mother and father, his younger brothers, and the other relatives.

No wife.

As if sleep walking, Lin Han found herself drawn out of the shadows, following the procession.

She would find a mate for Dao Ming, one way or another.

* * *

White grave stones embraced the hill outside of Yen Tu. Lin Han followed at the tail of the funeral, still clutching her vase. Her head felt light, like a feather fluttering across the road, while sand chained her body to the earth, heavy and slow with exhaustion.

Wailing mourners shrieked at the front of the procession, followed by the musicians banging cymbals and drums to chase away any evil spirits attracted to the dead body.

The graves nearest the entrance hadn't been cleaned in several months—probably since the last *qingming* festival that spring: leaves littered the curving white stone and bright grass marred the smooth lines.

Lin Han vowed to come out and clean her sister's memorial place every month, not to wait for the annual tomb sweeping celebration.

As Lin Han followed the procession up the hill her heart lightened. Only those with a proper rank were buried up on top of the hill. This meant the family not only had money, but power and placement.

It wouldn't matter if the family found another bride for their dead son: Lin Han would make sure he married Dao Ming first. Any other brides would be second or third wives. Not first.

The clanging cymbals and drums started to get louder, the pace, faster. Lin Han hurried, catching up to the stragglers in the procession, then pushing her way forward. No one stopped her. She didn't wear the proper white mourning clothes over her robe, but her face was still streaked with ashes and tears, so she must belong.

A Buddhist priest in bright orange robes stood at the head of the grave. He was a tall, pompous man, the kind who smiled at children but then treated them as if they couldn't understand even the simplest words.

Lin Han knew she wouldn't get any help from him.

The parents of the boy stood beside the priest. The mother wept loudly while her husband and sons consoled her. Lin Han looked at them closely.

Would they be kind to her sister?

They were kind with each other. Maybe they would welcome Dao Ming, too, if their son visited one of them in a dream and told them about his wife.

The paper-wrapped coffin sat poised over the grave, balanced on the long poles used to carry it from the town. Alongside each pole was strung a strong rope.

When the priest finished his prayers and blessings, the laborers came forward. They slid the poles away while holding onto the ropes.

Lin Han stood poised, right beside the grave, the ashes of her sister's spirit tablet still clenched tightly to her chest.

As was custom, everyone in the funeral procession turned their back as the coffin started to disappear into the earth.

Lin Han didn't care if the laborers saw her: they wouldn't say anything, not to the family. It wasn't their place.

So she tipped the vase and scattered the ashes on top of the coffin.

Dao Ming and her intended would be buried together. Their funerals would be held together, because now all the prayers said for him would be for her as well.

It was as good an introduction between the families as any.

* * *

Lin Han waited for the priest to finish the funeral under the fragrant pine trees in the graveyard. The family was still wailing, and they were burning incense. She'd learned her sister's future-husband's name—Tu Shr. The empty vase sat beside her. She was so tired. She just wanted to sleep. But Dao Ming must be married, first.

The early afternoon breezes tugged at Lin Han's hair. She gathered twigs to her, stripped the bark down and used it to tie the sticks together, making little figures. The one with the sprig of long soft needles from a yew tree was Dao Ming. It didn't really look like a skirt but it was the best Lin Han could do. Tu Shr's had a knotty twig across the top, like big strong shoulders.

Lin Han hid behind the tree as the procession started back down the hill. She didn't want anyone to ask her any questions. There she found the cap of an acorn that she also gathered up.

As soon as the last person had reached the bottom of the hill, Lin Han raced back up. The laborers wouldn't fill in the grave until later, closer to twilight, when light ran away from the world. In three days time, the younger son would return and take a cup of the dirt back to the family that they would use to represent their dead son on their ancestors' altar, replacing the spirit tablet which was buried with the body.

At the edge of the grave, Lin Han found three trampled pieces of paper ghost money that hadn't been thrown into the grave, money the dead could spend in the afterlife. She wished she had more, but she couldn't climb into the grave and ever hope to get back out.

The three pieces would have to do for the bride price, what the groom's family gave the bride's.

Lin Hand made a small pile of dirt on the left side of the grave and placed the figure of Dao Ming there. She formally presented the bride price to her, wishing she had a red envelope for the money. She tucked the money in under the little figure. On the right side, she created a second pile, and placed the figure of Tu Shr there.

When everything was set, Lin Han picked up Tu Shr. Carrying him well above her head to honor him, she did a couple of dancing steps as she walked around the top of the grave to the other side.

"Look Dao Ming! The wedding procession has arrived!"

Lin Han kept Dao Ming in one hand while she hid Tu Shr in the other. It wasn't proper for the couple to see each other yet. Then she danced back to the other side.

"Dao Ming! You've arrived at your husband's house now. It's so big!"

From the top of the hill, it almost seemed that way. Tu Shr didn't control all of the graveyard and ghosts from his high point, but she could pretend.

Finally, Lin Han brought the two stick figures together on the mound of dirt. She didn't know the words the priests would say, so she sang a hymn to Xi Wang Hu, asking her for blessings on the couple: May they never grow hungry, may they have many children, and may they always be honored.

Lin Han placed the acorn cap next to Dao Ming, telling her, "Drink up! Drink your wedding cup!"

Then she placed it next to Tu Shr, telling him, "This is your bridal cup. Drink and be together forever."

Lin Han stepped back, bowed her head and closed her eyes to give the happy couple a moment of privacy.

Exhaustion slammed down on her and she swayed. The wind played with her hair, stronger now. Maybe a storm was blowing up.

When she opened her eyes, Tu Shr had slid down on the dirt mound so his head was now close to Dao Ming's.

Lin Han clapped her hands. Tu Shr had surely accepted Dao Ming as a bride! Her sister had a husband, someone who would look after her and treat her with respect.

Lin Han bowed low to the happy couple.

Normally, what followed would be the wedding feast. But there wasn't anyone else to celebrate.

"I will eat for both of you later," Lin Han promised as she picked up the figures, holding them together in the palms of her hands.

"The goddess will look out for you and bless you always," she promised as she opened her hands over the edge of the grave and let the figures tumble onto the paper coffin below.

They landed on a bit of clean paper, not where every member of the family had dropped a handful of dirt.

Lin Han gave them the acorn cup, and the ghost money as well.

She didn't know what to do with the vase. It didn't belong in the grave. She couldn't take it home: it was just one more thing of her sister's that her family would deny.

Instead, she planted it firmly at the head of the grave. Maybe when the younger son came back to get the dirt for the ancestors' altar, he'd see the vase and use it instead. That way, both Dao Ming and Tu Shr would be venerated.

After one last low bow, Lin Han turned away from the grave and started down the hill. She was too tired to skip or dance, though she knew she should—she was still part of a wedding procession.

But her feet dragged on the earth and her tears started again. No one else would ever know what she'd done, how she'd taken care of her sister.

Still. She'd finally managed to find her peace.

In 2013, multiple World Fantasy Award winner Richard Bowes will pub-
lish two short story collections. A new novel, Dust Devil on a Quiet Street, *will*
also appear, along with a reissue of his Lambda Award winning novel, Minions
of the Moon.

As he assembled the collection The Queen, the Cambion, and Seven Others, *he received the invitation for* Unnatural Worlds. *The Queen, the Cambion, and Seven Others collects his modern Fairytales. He had finished a story*
for the Datlow/Windling dystopian anthology After. *He writes, "When Kris*
Rusch invited me to contribute a story to Fiction River, combining these two
themes seemed perfectly logical to me."

The result is a memorable story impossible to characterize.

The Witch's House

Richard Bowes

First Month

All I know is I'm in a forest, staring past trees at this dirt road. I know
I'm here forever waiting for travelers on the road to Avalon. They come
by and I challenge them, ask for a password and when they don't give it
I go in their brains and kill them: simple as that. I can't move, can't think
except about this and I've been here for fucking ever.

Someone comes down the road and I recognize a kid called
Nice from my old crew back in the city. The AK47 he carries won't
do any good against me. I go into his mind, look through his eyes
and see him seeing me. I'm massive and metal, like a robot or a
giant warrior in armor. I ask for a password, one we both know
from back there.

Nice and me were like brother and sister but now he doesn't
recognize me, is too scared to think. Twenty seconds ticks away

without a response so I reach in and crush his heartbeat, rip the breath out of his lungs and watch him fall dead with blood running out of his mouth and nose.

Before I can realize I'm a fifteen-year-old girl, a Mortal here in Fairyland, not a metal monster, another mind goes into my head like I went inside Nice's in the dream.

'*The Soldier's Malady*,' I get told mind to mind by the Witch of Avalon. Then I understand I had a nightmare, past horrors working their way into my dreams, making my brain run scams on me.

The Witch being in my skull scares me. It means I let my guard down and that it's possible she could have killed me just like I killed Nice in my dream. I remember how Nice actually died; have a heart crushing memory of him cut in two on the bank of the Hudson. It happened months ago in the wrecked city where I spent all my life until last month. I guess I still feel I should have been able to save him.

But before I can even open my eyes, the Witch tells me '*Rest easy. Sleep will follow.*' She rules here in the Forest of Avalon and I'm asleep before I know it.

When I do wake up and open my eyes it's dark, with dawn light just starting. My mattress is on a hardwood floor. Looking around, I make out the bark that's one whole side of the room. The Oak of Ware is part of the Witch's house. Or the house is part of the Oak.

Almost a month ago Kailen and Evalyn, two Fey officers escorted me here through worlds full of wrecked war machinery and down forest paths guarded by things like a giant with eight eyes so he could see in all four directions. The giant stood with a club and asked who went there. When I asked the Fey how far I was from New York, I got told, '*Many spells and more miles than you can imagine.*'

In the predawn I find myself automatically inhaling and exhaling in a rhythm the Witch taught me. The six senses: smell, touch, taste, hearing, sight, telepathy each get exercised. With every breath I feel the shield I've built around my mind. Anyone trying to bust into my head sees an image: a brick wall like the ones in my wrecked city and they bounce off it.

In the same way, crazy stuff inside my head like the Soldier's Malady should stay inside. Last night, obviously, all this broke down. The Witch entered my mind without my even knowing she was going to do it. And before that the horrors my mind produced got out.

Here in the forest, there's no one but the Witch to notice. Back in the city it would have spread terror in friend and enemy, adult and child. Back in the city I was the only telepath. Fairyland, though, is full of us.

All I can hope is that keeping my shield in place pleases the Witch, makes up a little for my guard coming down last night. Making her happy is my only ticket back to New York as far as I know. I'm here for three months training. What happens if she's not pleased I don't want to think about.

Minerva the owl flies in one window and out the other. The Witch's familiar is going to roost. At the same moment I sense the Witch of Avalon reaching out and catch her question on my shield, '*Are you awake, my dear Real?*' And I tell her I am.

The owl needs to sleep, I need to sleep but the Witch never seems to. Getting up, I catch the smell of tea down in the kitchen. I wash myself and put on this long T-shirt they call a shift. That's pretty much all I get to wear these days. My clothes and everything else got taken away the night I arrived. They gave me sandals but they're out on the porch.

On the sideboard in the kitchen, there's a slab of bread and jam and a pot of the Witch's tea. No sign of her. The Witch of Avalon is everywhere and nowhere and makes sure I never forget it.

When they brought me here almost four weeks ago I was in bad shape. The only thing I knew how to do with my telepathy was to kill people. Back then I didn't know how to block an enemy from my mind or communicate mentally with anyone else except by force. The Witch told me I was a danger to myself and others, though she smiled as she did.

Now I've developed this mental shield that mostly keeps others out and keeps what I don't want anyone to know I'm thinking inside. Before she taught me all that, the Witch found out every last thing I had inside me. Maybe some of that makes her kind of distant and unsure about me now. Or maybe that's just how she is.

But she controls my fate and I make sure she doesn't catch just how much I hate the touch of her mind first thing in the morning like this. Because maybe that would mean I don't get back to my city, bad as it is, to my girlfriend Dare and to my life.

The Fey who found me, crazed and exhausted, fighting to save my crew, my people, said they'd take care of things while I was gone. But they told me I had to get fixed up. There was no choice involved.

So I eat the bread, swallow the tea which I always want to drink and walk barefoot onto the big wooden porch with its roof and tables and chairs. Birds sing and dart through the air. A rabbit runs across the grass. I look around for Phil, this baby faun the Witch has as a pet. I wanted to kill him at first. Now I kind of miss him when he's not around.

Tall trees surround the house. A breeze makes their leaves shimmer and catch the light. And suddenly there's this mutilated body on the grass. A woman, caught and butchered, her breasts cut off, her crotch slashed open. She was someone I was supposed to protect back in my city.

Automatically I reach out to find the one who did it, wanting to get in his head, grab his heart and brain and tear them apart. Birds screech in the trees, fly away. Small animals run in the bushes.

When I look at the grass again, there's no body. It's the Soldier's Malady, a twisted memory of home. I want to scream but

I take some deep breaths and don't. This time the dream stayed inside my head.

I go over to the table on the porch where there's a viaculum. It's this device they have in the Fairy Kingdom where you control a story with your thoughts. This is how the Fey teach their children. And some of them feel I must be a long lost relative.

Nothing can distract me while I'm using the viaculum. The first couple of weeks I took part in stories about Fairy princes, and princesses and witches. I was supposed to learn some moral but the real point was learning how to use all six senses.

I got frustrated, lost my temper all the time, tried to tear the heads off characters I hated, kept having to stop and start over when I lost track of what I was doing. Now the stories are more adult, more complicated but I've learned stuff.

So I stand as tall as I get, which isn't very, on the porch. I'm aware of the growing morning light, the noise of the birds, the smell of the woods, the tea I can still taste and the feel of the floorboards on my feet.

It's taken many hours of patience and practice to get all my senses working like this. But that's how you make the game go forward. When the usual five senses are engaged, I let my mind scan around me; touch the flitter brains of birds, the deep throb of old trees, the way a hive of bees is kind of like one brain. I don't encounter the Witch. But I think she's got ways of concealing herself from me.

I say the spell I was taught and move my hands like I should. It seems stupid but if I don't do it just right nothing happens. This morning I do the ritual and a voice in my head says, 'Lady Enigma in Dragon Country.'

That's the game and I'm Lady Enigma, an advisor/ operative sent by the Queen beneath the Hill to investigate goings on in Claysmoran, a province way-gone in the backwoods of Fairyland.

For the first week or so, I had trouble operating this story, keeping all my senses alert, watching for clues from the characters. And I'd had trouble controlling my temper.

The story picks up where I left off. The nobility of the province are celebrating our hunt for the Giant White Wolf and her pups. Back home in my lawless, wrecked America I saw lots of people die and some of them were kids closer to me than brothers or sisters could ever have been. I myself have killed quite a few individuals and all of them deserved it as far as I know.

All that and having the viaculum repeatedly close down as I lost touch with various senses made me impatient and anxious to finish things off.

We finally cornered the huge fiendish beast, whose mind was hard to get hold of, after I'd seen her snap our dogs' spines and cripple horses. And I tore into her as she ran at me, whipped her head back and broke her neck. She was defending her pups, which would have grown to be red-eyed monsters but were still big innocent beasts who whimpered in terror as we snuffed the life out of them. I figured I needed to show I can handle stuff like this if I'm going to get out of here and back home

The celebration takes place in the High Sheriff's castle. I taste the wine, feel the warmth of the fire, smell the perfume, listen to the stupid conversation around me and catch sight of myself in a mirror. Lady Enigma, emissary of the Queen, is tall, fair, maybe twenty-five, instead of small, dark and turning sixteen this fall the way I actually am. She flickers because of all the Glamour she uses.

Trying to keep my mental probe gentle so it doesn't get noticed, I slide among these backwoods half-breed Fey aristocrats, dressed up in ratty old uniforms and hunting outfits. They're all red faced with wine and Fairy Dust. I pick up mental images of the pups as they died and wonder if maybe it was a mistake.

The Sheriff's big ass is stuck in front of the fireplace with tiny fire sprite faces peeking out of the flames behind him. Magic's so common here that you hardly notice it.

Speaking aloud because some of this gang's telepathy's not so good, he says, "Well Lady Enigma, I hope your report to the Palace will be favorable."

Before I can say anything a no-tune whistling back on the Witch's porch makes my concentration wobble and starts to pull me out of the viaculum. A quick glance to the side shows me Phil the Faun, half-goat, half-human kid blowing on a pipe and dancing on the porch with his little hooves, looking for my attention.

Phil is part pet, part pest and I need to get rid of him and stay focused on Lady Enigma. If I really go into his mind I'll find myself blocked by an image of the Witch and her grey wand.

But I can plant in his empty little head the sight of this great hairy, winged monster swooping down. Phil sees it and runs away bleating and crying. The figures in the viaculum waver but I run through my six senses and they stabilize. I don't have to start over again.

It takes a lot of patience and concentration to get everything inside my head working right. Only the fact I've got to learn how to do this if I'm going to get back to my own world makes me hang in.

When it feels like I've done enough with *Lady Enigma in Dragon Country* for the morning, I perform the ritual that stops it. And I step away from the viaculum wondering if the way I'd handled the pups had been as wise as it seemed.

Phil is snuffling and I see him standing a ways off glaring at me. He's figured out I sent the black, hairy thing. A couple of weeks ago I'd have been happy to kill him; now he seems like the only friend I have in this place.

He can't be let indoors because he's not housebroken.

RICHARD BOWES

Since the Witch isn't around I go in the kitchen and get him a couple of these ginger cookies he goes for and grab one for myself.

First he won't take them, backs away from me rolling his eyes and stamping his hooves. But I hold them out and he grabs them with his human hands. Once he's shoving them in his mouth he lets me scratch his head between his horns, which he likes.

Pretty soon he forgets how I scared him and he's skipping on his animal legs with his little boy parts bouncing around, pretending to butt me with his tiny horns. This maybe is what it's like to have a kid, a thing I'm not going to do, or a baby brother which my mother didn't do. I realize he's probably the nearest thing to that I'll ever know.

I'm thinking about this when out of nowhere there's a sheet of flames and voices inside it screaming with laughter. Except Phil doesn't notice and nothing's burning. It's something from the Witch's mind and she uses it to smash the brick wall defense I built in my head, gets inside me and I have to try and throw her out. Maybe she's doing this to teach me. But half the time I feel inches away from death.

* * *

Second Month

After weeks of being Lady Enigma it seems like I've got a certain feel for the rhythms of the game. I'm not in control but as I travel in the service of the Queen I know there will always be times when I'm in a crowd with dozens of other minds around me and things happening at the sides of my vision. I've cut way down on the violence. I notice if I stay calm the story does too.

This one morning I'm standing on the porch, patting Phil's furry head, remembering the taste of the Witch's tea, smelling blossoms, seeing the light, hearing birds, feeling this hum which I realize is somehow the mind of the trees.

At the same time Lady Enigma is using her senses in the grand salon in the Palace of Prince Oberon. I have to stay aware of the room, overhear the servants whispering gossip, sip the wine and recognize something bitter there.

I smell a dozen different perfumes, catch the glances of women and men above their decorated fans. Thoughts, messages fly through the air: most of them pretty stupid.

"Bouquets of kisses for one so angry!"

"The Chancellor of Dreams will hear of this!"

Once in a while one catches my attention.

"A Queen has reasons and her reasons have reasons."

"Not an enigma so much as an empty vessel."

Was that last about me? Was the first? Was I intended to catch the thought?

Images fly too: A male Fey in full silken court dress but with the head of a cat. Clouds part and a chariot bearing a naked child and pulled by three winged horses flies toward a tower made of roses.

Then I catch for a second, someone in the room seeing a pair of eyes so old and smart and cruel that they chill me. Those eyes scan the salon of this ornate palace in this rich province.

I've learned to probe minds lightly. Around here even some of the servants have a bit of telepathy. I notice a butler who, like me, obviously caught a glimpse of the eyes. I watch as he turns slightly and steals a glance at a slender, young noble. This man, whose name is Lord Robin, stares at a mural. I follow the gaze and see a floor-to-ceiling portrait of a dragon with glittering blue and gold scales, wings furled, head raised.

The eyes move but Lord Robin does not react. My guess is that the first time he saw them move he was surprised enough not to conceal his reaction. This time he looks then turns away. But it has got to be important—dragons are in this adventure's title after all.

I've done enough for one morning. As I run through the rituals to disconnect from the viaculum, Phil looks up, offers me a crumpled, grimy piece of cookie. I refuse and he stuffs it in his mouth.

When I was brought here, I was basically under arrest. The two Fey who brought me, Kailen and Evalyn, were all flickering Glamour and polished gold. But they were tough and one or both of them always had their minds trained on me.

The idea I got was if I didn't shape up I'd get abandoned and end up about like the eight-eyed giant. The Fey had discovered me, crazed and killing anything that moved, holding onto a few ruined blocks of New York. My crew, even Dare my girlfriend, were scared of me. But the Fey decided I'd make a useful ally in some war they've had forever with the Elves if they could fix me up.

So they took me to the Forest of Avalon and the Oak of Ware and introduced me to the Witch. Her specialty is patching up damaged warriors for the Fey.

She's tall, seems far away even standing next to me. She welcomed us, smiled a smile I found scary. All of a sudden, behind her in the bushes around the Oak of Ware I saw some kind of animal and then saw it was a naked kid. He grabbed hold of the Witch's dress, hid behind her staring at me. I tried to go into his mind and found the image of the Witch with her grey wand blocking me.

The Fey chuckled, the witch was almost amused; patted his head which was human except for a couple of little horns. I saw furry legs, hooves and eyes and ears like an animal's but the rest is maybe a six year old boy. *"Philippe's a Faun,"* the Witch explained, *"orphaned. He's shy around strangers."*

The Witch dismissed the Fey. She and I sat on the porch one late spring evening and she served dinner, explained to me that as part of a treaty with the Fey King she sometimes teaches untrained or damaged telepaths, ones with the Soldier's Malady. She brings us back, allows us to return to duty.

Birds sang in the trees. I was angry, lonely, and ready to kill. I looked up and the faun was staring at me wide-eyed. I unleashed every bit of hate in me, imagined a flaming face with eyes spouting fire and hurled it at him.

Phil ran away crying, hid in the bushes which was stupid because I knew just where he was. I started to go after him again then was aware of the Witch gazing at me, hard; felt her in my mind seeing any and everything there.

A couple of months later, on the same morning when Lady Enigma discovered the dragon eyes, I notice Phil is sucking his thumb and make him stop. I remember my mother doing that when I was little. She'd tell me it would spoil my smile when I grew up. I do it for Phil even though I'm not sure what difference it will make in a boy/goat.

We walk down a path to a lake. I hold out my hand and Phil comes skipping over and grabs it. With the sun starting to come through the leaves I take in the sounds, the breeze on my skin, the smell of leaves and some musky urine, a bite of ginger cookie. I scan in the way I'm learning to, not busting into minds, just touching them.

I close my eyes and look through the eyes around me, ones that just see black and grey, ones where light is like a knife blade. I see twigs that look like tree branches and leaves big as tents. I feel life under the dirt and in the air.

A weasel, startled by me, loses a rabbit she had in her sites; a jay spots me as an intruder and starts to scream. Phil puts his head down, rushes at the jay, chases it off and comes back looking happy and proud.

Then a tree seems to shift and turn and takes the shape of a woman in green and brown robes carrying a twisted grey stick. The Witch of Avalon smiles and looks as pleasant as she ever does.

Knowing one of our sessions is about to begin, I gird my senses for what's to come. As we walk Phil trots in circles around us, stopping every once in a while to piss on a favorite tree.

Out of nowhere a huge red bat spouting flames suddenly rushes at my face. That was a nightmare I had as a little kid. When I first came here months ago with no control over my telepathy the Witch had free access to all my memories. She doesn't hesitate to use what she found in these duels.

But I feel the path through the soles of my feet, concentrate on touch and summon the memory of a broken brick wall. This time there's a poster on it with me looking tough and the words, "SHE FIGHTS FOR US!" I take the bat image and smash its head into the bricks.

The flavor of her tea's still in my mouth. Before the Witch does anything, I concentrate on the taste; take the memory of a 'copter flying low, spitting bullets right above me and try to shove it into her head.

She shows me a dark passage, torch lights on the walls and a huge dog with five heads and each head has eyes big as plates. I know this is something she actually saw. The heads are at my throat, I feel their breath.

Then I catch a hint of smoke in the air from some chimney far away. I twist that into my memory of the Hudson River on fire, boats burning, people screaming. And I hurl the smoke and flames into the mouths of the dogs. Their saucer eyes go out like lights.

I take the murmur of the trees and the sun coming through the leaves. I want to lift the forest and everything in it, smash them down on the Witch and crush her. And I start to do that.

But I see a woman, half bald with cheeks sucked into her skull and her empty eyes staring through me. It's an image of my mother dying in a plague started by some terrorist militia. It's something I never want to remember and the Witch uses it to beat me.

She's inside me. It's like she gets her hand on my heart before I shake her off. And I'm down on my knees on the path, gasping out tears with Phil holding my arm and crying because I am.

So the Witch wins like she does every day. But this time she says, "*You have learned*" and sounds thoughtful. We both know only that memory of my mother stopped me. And the Witch is the only one besides me in this world or any other who's seen it.

* * *

Third Month

The trees are like giants. My first days in Avalon, I felt them glaring down at me and blocking the sun and sky when I looked up. I told this to the Witch and she shook her head like she was sorry that I was so wrong.

Yesterday I heard the trees mutter a name they've given me. When I mentioned that to her, she nodded and looked pleased that I'd finally noticed.

Today I'm aware of flowers like a whisper in the background. The sound changes when a breeze passes through. The wind is like a living thing.

That's still on my mind when I go into *Lady Enigma*.

Seeing the dragon's eyes move was a key; and so was getting to know Lord Robin. Over the next few weeks we tracked the biggest and most beautiful of dragons.

This morning we see her in all her glory and I know we can't beat her or outsmart her. Cassese's tail is as long as railroad trains I've seen in pictures. When her wings flap the wind almost blows Robin and me off our horses. She breathes fire into the ground to spook our winged mounts so we rise into the air. Robin flies to the right I fly to the left and our minds go into Cassese's. She spins her head like she's shaking away flies and almost knocks us off our horses.

We can't beat her but I think we can amuse her. When it becomes obvious she can't get rid of us and we can't harm her she sits down and we do the same. Cassese sends her greetings to our Queen; gives us a formula for turning turnips into gold, predicts the birth of a royal heir and promises to leave the local folk alone though I know she's lying. Suddenly she rises, shimmers in our eyes like sunlight on a mirror and slips away.

Lord Robin and I mount our horses all ready for another quest. I've pretty much gotten this story down just like I did with the fairytales.

I'm even able to manipulate the system. Robin is meant to be some kind of romantic guy, young with long hair and a nice smile. He's not my type being a guy and he's an aristocrat, a Fey lord which doesn't work for me.

Just after we met, I found myself looking at his hairless face, the long lashes on the eyes. Now, maybe because I'm so lonely, Lord Robin reminds me of Dare. They get tangled in my mind. I can't look at him and not think of her.

It turns out he's actually a woman in disguise. And Lady Robin and I share a bed and get it on and I'm pretty sure I'm bending the game and making up my own story. What worries me is whether this is what I'm supposed to be doing. Or is this and talking to the dragon instead of trying to kill her, a big mistake that means I'll never get home again.

And that worry is with me deep in the night when the dragon Cassese returns and I'm trying to grab and twist her brain. And I can't because it shimmers like glass and slips away from me. And instead of the dragon it's Lady Robin I'm wrestling with.

Then instead of Robin it's Dare and she's screaming because she's afraid I'm going to kill her. This is what happened with us before I ended up here.

But as I remember Dare and me, I know what I'm seeing is all in my mind. I'm awake in the Witch's house. I feel the sheet, smell the night woods, scents so strong I can taste them; hear bugs bouncing off the shades. See the outlines of a quarter moon.

I know the nightmare stayed inside me and I disarmed it myself. The Witch won't even know this happened. The Soldier's Malady is still there but I recognize it faster now. I've worked out a kind of treaty with it. At times I want to yell and scream at the top of my lungs but I know that won't get me back home.

When I go downstairs the tea and bread are there. Out on the porch, though, the viaculum is gone. I hope what I did with *Lady Enigma* makes the Witch happy. A three-month stay was what was talked about when I arrived here. I'm down to my last couple of days.

Later Phil and I walk on a forest path. A bunch of kids from the nearest town are heading the other way with baskets to gather berries. Phil doesn't like it when there are lots of people around, and wants to take my hand. When I let him he looks up like I'm the greatest thing in the world. I wonder if they'll let me take him with me if I go.

Around here kids my age are all woodcutters' daughters and millers' sons like in the fairytales. A lot of them are barefoot and they're all dressed simple like me. Everyone knows I'm staying with the Witch who is a much respected figure and that I have some kind of magic. They step aside for Phil and me and kind of bow which I don't like.

Instead of just busting into their heads like I'd have done when I got here, I do a gentle scan which I've been taught. Through their eyes I see myself walking around with this magic creature holding onto me.

First in one then in half a dozen minds I find their memories of ones who stayed here before me. One is a big bruiser with a beard and a missing arm, another is a Sprite with blank eyes and wings, and there's a woman with a sad face and an Amazon's body. Each has Phil. The woman leads him on a leash, the bruiser carries him over his shoulder like a small sack. Phil trails behind the Sprite who doesn't seem to notice him, hurries to keep up. Phil is never any bigger or smaller, older or younger than he is now.

He continues to hold my hand and to look up and I scratch his head. I managed never to think about why he was around. But this is school and he was a test.

When a tree turns into the Witch I'm in no way surprised. Over my time here she sent images of knives slashing my eyes, made me feel like the ground crumbled under me. I showed her the Oak of Ware burned to the ground and made her see her stomach blown open with a grenade.

The Witch holds out her hand and Phil immediately runs over and takes it. "*I watched you with him very carefully, saw you change,*" she tells me, nods and gives an actual smile. "*It tipped the balance.*"

She shows me her regrets about taking young warriors, smashed and maddened by what's happened to them and what they've done, piecing them together and sending them back to maybe get smashed again. But it's doing this that makes the Fey protect these woods and her people from their enemies.

I understand that I'll be going back to a place where even the ones who knew me before I developed my powers came to be afraid of me. Like The Witch I'll serve the Fey to keep my people alive. She takes my hand for a moment.

It's late summer now, almost fall and clouds form as we walk toward the Oak of Ware. After hating this place and this woman I don't want to leave.

Hearing Dare scream; being shown her cut in two doesn't stop me now. But as we approach the Oak, a figure, tall, thin with curly hair stands and all I can think is that this image is one more of the Witch's tests. Dare was afraid to be near me; everyone was. Now she's running towards me with her arms out smiling and crying. And the Oak and the Witch, the satyr and the forest slip behind me like a dream.

Newsweek *calls Jane Yolen "the Hans Christian Andersen of America." She is that and more. Her 300 books range from picture books to novels for adults. She has won two Nebulas, a World Fantasy Award, the Golden Kite Award, three Mythopoeic Awards, two Christopher Medals, and has had many more nominations, including one for the National Book Award.*

"Dog Boy Remembers," she writes, "explores the birth/creation of one of the characters in Except the Queen, *a novel that Midori Snyder and I wrote together. As Dog Boy was my creation, Midori gave me permission to write more about him."*

Good thing she did; what follows is one of the most powerful original stories we've ever read.

————————

Dog Boy Remembers

Jane Yolen

The Dog Boy was just a year old and newly walking when his father returned to take him into Central Park. It was summer and the moon was full over green trees.

The only scents he'd loved till then were the sweet milk smells his mother made, the fust of the sofa cushions, the prickly up-your-nose of the feathers in his pillow, the pure spume of water from the tap, and the primal stink of his own shit before it was washed down into the white bowl.

When his father came to fetch him that first time, his mother wept. Still in her teens, she'd not had a lot of knowledge of the world before Red Cap had taken her up. But the baby, he was all hers. *The only thing,* she often thought, *that truly was.*

"Don't take him," she cried, "I've done everything you asked. I promise to be even more careful of him." Her tears slipped silently down her cheeks, small globules, smelling slightly salty, like soup.

His father hit her with his fist for crying, and red blood gushed from her nose. He hated crying, something Dog Boy was soon to find out.

But Dog Boy had never smelled blood like that before, only his mother's monthly flow which had a nasty pong to it. His head jerked up at the sharpness, a scent he would later know as iron. He practically wet himself with delight.

His father watched him and smiled. It was a slow smile and not at all comforting, but it was all Dog Boy would ever get from him.

"Come Boy," his father said, adjusting the red cap he always wore, a cap that was the first thing Dog Boy recognized about his father, even before his smell, that odd compound of old blood and something meaty, something nasty, that both repelled and excited him. Without more of an invitation, his father reached into his pocket and pulled out a leather leash, winding it expertly about the Dog Boy's chest and shoulders, tugging him toward the door. And not knowing why, only that it would surely be something new and interesting, Dog Boy toddled after him, never looking back at his mother who still simpered behind them.

* * *

Off they went into the city, that big, noisy, sprawling place so full of sound and movement and smells, Dog Boy always shuddered when the door opened.

Oh, he'd been out with his mother before, but always held in her arms, smothered by the milk-mother smell. This time he was walking out on his own. Well, walking might be a slight exaggeration. It was more like falling forward, only to be caught up again and again by the leather leash.

Their first stop was at a spindly ginko right outside the door

of the house, the tree just leafing out. Dog Boy stood by it and inhaled the green, soft and sharp at the same time. He reached over
and touched the bark. That was the soft smell, and it was not—he
realized in surprise—the bark itself but the mallow he could sense
inside, though of course then he hadn't the words *mallow* or *bark*.
The leaves were what smelled sharp and new and somewhat pep-
pery. The other smell was clearly much older. Old and new had
different scents. It was a revelation.

Next, he and his father walked along a stone walk that was
filled with other interesting scents. People smells, lingering leather smells, the sweat of feet, plus the sweet cloy of dropped paper
wrappers, and some smallish tangs of tobacco in a white cover.
Then Dog Boy found three overflowing garbage cans, overflowing with smells.

Suddenly, there were far too many odors, most of them much
too strong for his childish senses, and Dog Boy ended up swoon-
ing onto the pavement, his legs and arms making quick running
motions, like a dog does when it dreams.

With great disgust, Red Cap slung him over his shoulder like
some dead thing, and took him right back home.

Once upstairs, he flung Dog Boy onto the sofa, saying in his
growl of a voice, "I have kept you in comfort all this time and you
raise up this. . .this wimpish thing. I need a sniffer-out, an off-
spring who can track and trail. Not this puling, fainting. . ."

"He's only a baby," his mother said quickly, picking Dog Boy
up and unwrapping the leather leash from his body which—
strangely—burned her hands. Dog Boy smelled the burning right
before she cradled him against her milk-full breasts, before that
familiar scent comforted him and made him forget everything
else. "And I have kept him in this room, as you demanded. . ."
his mother murmured above him, neglecting to mention the bi-
weekly runs to the bodega when she was so lonely for an adult to

speak to, she couldn't stay in and didn't dare leave the child in the room alone.

For her outburst, she was hit again, this time on the cheek, which rocked her back and made Dog Boy whimper for her, though she made no sound at all. But her cheek came up quickly into a purplish bruise that his little, plump fingers explored gently, though by then Red Cap was already gone, the door slamming behind him. He didn't return for a month, on the next moon.

* * *

During that month, Dog Boy's mother wept, fussed, petted and spoiled him outrageously, thought about running off with him, hiding out somewhere.

"Just the two of us," she'd whisper before the tears pooled again in her eyes. "Anywhere." But she couldn't think of a single place that would be safe. Red Cap could come and go to anywhere on earth, seemingly at will. He'd told her so when they'd first met, and she believed him. His fists had made her into a believer.

Red Cap was the only name she had for him. He said it was the only name he had. She'd tried calling him Red once, and he hit her so hard, she lost consciousness and never tried again. Even her father had never hit her so hard. But after that, she had trouble calling him anything and spent stuttering moments whenever she had to address him directly. She thought if she could only call him by his right name, he'd forgive her, but the words never seemed to come out right.

He wore that disgusting cap everywhere, even in bed. The only time she'd ever seen him take it off was when they were first seeing one another. It was a pearly evening, and they'd come upon a dying squirrel run over in the park, it's insides squashed onto the pavement, made even more horrible by the moon overhead and the shadows it cast. She'd started to turn away from the sight. But when Red Cap took off his hat and dipped it into the squirrel's blood, she'd been mesmerized and couldn't stop watching. For a moment, the hat had seemed to glisten and glow, red as a sunset, though she knew that couldn't really have happened. Then the squirrel's eyes glazed over; so, in a way, had the hat.

After the moment in the park, she shrank away from him, which seemed to make him even more ardent. He showered her with money. Especially when he found out she was pregnant. He didn't ask her to marry him, but by then marriage was the last thing on her mind. Escape was foremost. That and getting rid of the child in her womb. But Red Cap stayed with her, imprisoned her really, in that little house in Brooklyn, with its view of the backside of another building. Threatened her. Hit her a couple of times a week just to remind her he could. He knew how to draw blood and how to bring bruises. He did not mistake them. It was as if he knew her body better than she did. And her soul.

He stayed just long enough for the child to be born. Childbirth tore her up so badly inside, the doctor warned she'd never have another child, though she didn't want another. Certainly not with Red Cap.

When she was well enough to take care of the child on her own, he showed her what to do, and then left, warning her not to run away.

"I can find you wherever you go," he'd said. "I'll be back when he is walking." She believed him.

The money he paid her with—it came in brown envelopes stuffed under the door—was generous and arrived mysteriously after she was asleep. But it had to be given to a bank first thing in the morning because by midnight it turned into leaves or ashes or bits of colored paper. So he'd warned her, and she knew that to be true because once she'd kept an envelope a second night, first checking that it was full of the promised money. When she opened the envelope the next morning, it was filled with red and gold autumn leaves instead. And so she'd nothing for almost a month and had to go back to tricking to keep the baby and herself alive.

Predictably, Red Cap had beaten her when he returned. Somehow he'd known what she'd done without having to ask.

"It's written on your stupid cow face," he told her and flung another envelope at her. He never asked about the child.

After that, she went early to the bank, the baby bound up tightly to her breast so that he didn't smell anything but her and the milk, just as Red Cap had demanded. Of course, every few months she had to change banks, but since Red Cap continued his generosity that made it only a small burden.

Of course she grew to love the child who looked nothing like either one of them but had a dark feral beauty and a brilliant smile. He seemed content being in the little apartment, entranced by the television Red Cap's money had purchased, and absolutely stunned by the music he heard there. She bought him a little pipe that he tootled on incessantly, and soon was able to mimic bird songs, and so she named him Robin after her favorite bird. His father refused to use that name, continuing to call him Dog Boy, which she hated.

One time she shorted herself on food and bought Robin a small tape CD player along with a variety of CDs: Battlefield Band, Janis Ian, Steeleye Span, the Silly Sisters—all favorites of hers. None of this new stuff. Except for Amanda Palmer and the Dixie Chicks. He begged then for a fiddle, and she went on short rations for several months till she had enough to buy it for him, a quarter-size fiddle that he taught himself to play.

And she talked to the child constantly. Well, she had to, didn't she? There was no one else to talk to except when they went quickly to the bank or to the local bodega at the end of the road. She kept herself busy during the day with the boy—playing with him, singing to him, washing his clothes, teaching him numbers, nursery rhymes, dreaming of escape.

But Red Cap came back as she knew he would. As he'd warned he would.

He put a stupid strap around the boy's shoulders and chest. Then off they went, her little boy trotting along in that new, funny, rolling sailor walk behind him and Red Cap yanking on the leash as if Robin had been a dog and not a human boy.

* * *

Of course Robin was a disappointment to his father. So he worked harder at trying to please him. He learned the smells of the city as if they were his ABCs. Graduating from milk and mother to finger foods and distinguishing ginko from maple. Learned the difference between sandals, shoes, and sneakers. Then the differences between Nikes, Pumas, Reeboks; between Birkinstocks, Kurt Giegers, and Crocs; between Doc Martin's, Jimmy Choos, Manolo Blahnik, Mephisto, and Birkenstocks. Though it would be years before he had names for the shoes, just the smells.

By the time he was four, he was able to follow a woman down a street an hour after she'd walked by without ever seeing her, simply by the smell of her Jimmy Choos and the waft of perfume.

By the time he was six, he could track two men at the same time, and when they parted, he could find one, mark that territory with his own personal scent (a piece of chewing gum, a wipe of his hand over his hair which was now long and shaggy as a dog's, or even by peeing around the spot if no one was watching). Then he'd go back to the place of parting, and track the second.

The praise he got from his father was little enough.

It felt enormous.

* * *

"It's time," Red Cap told the boy on his tenth birthday.

Dog Boy knew what he meant without having to be told. He was well-trained. He was old enough. He'd long been off the leash. This day he would be in at a kill. *A blooding*, his father called it. He couldn't wait.

His father handed him a small child's cap. It was a school cap, blue with an insignia, a red pine tree and the numbers 1907. He sniffed it. He would know that scent anywhere.

They walked to a small park, a kind of grove. It was filled with lovely smells that made Dog Boy shiver with delight. The sharp, new growing things, both white-rooted and green. Little mealy-smelling worms. The deep musk of the old oak's serpentine roots that lay halfway above ground.

There were many sneaker smells, too, mostly the rubbery scent that made his nose itch. But there was a familiar odor, faint but clear enough for him to follow.

He lifted his right hand and pointed at a place where the path forked. Eager to be off, he was stopped by his father's rough grasp on his shirt collar.

"Now is when we must take care," Red Cap told him. "Be subtle. Act like everyday humankind. An ordinary father and his ordinary son on an outing. Not a hunter and his dog." Though there was nothing ordinary about the pair.

Dog Boy nodded, he could scarcely contain his excitement. His father had spoken quietly, not in his usual sharp trainer's voice, nor in his dangerous growl. Dog Boy liked this new, quiet, unexpected sound. It soothed him. It calmed him down.

"Steady, steady now, show me the way." Red Cap took his son's hand. This was so unusual, Dog Boy almost stopped to say something, then thought better of it and went on.

They walked along, almost companionably, and any onlooker

would have no reason to think they were not a happy pair out for a Sunday stroll. When they reached the fork, the smell drew Dog Boy to the left. And then another left. And because his father still had hold of his hand, he was drawn along as well. They came into a small, hidden, grassy place where dark trees bent nearly double.

A boy, younger than Dog Boy, was standing, his back to them. By the way he stood, Dog Boy knew he'd come into this out-of-the-way place to pee.

"Let him finish," whispered his father. "We have time." As an afterthought, almost as if laughing at the child, he added, "Though he does not."

Dog Boy wondered: *Time for what?* But deep inside he knew, had always known, had tried to keep himself from knowing. For him, it was the seeking, the finding that mattered. But not for his father. Never for his father. He shuddered.

They moved closer to the boy who, turning, looked a bit alarmed, then relieved, then frightened, then terrified.

Then silent.

Dog Boy couldn't stop staring. There was blood everywhere. The sharp iron tang got up his nose as if it had painted itself there. He wondered if he would ever smell anything else.

Watching his father dip the red cap in the boy's blood, he tried to weep. He tried to turn away. He could do neither.

* * *

They walked in silence back to the house. A tall black boy his age ran by, his legs scissoring. A smaller kid, maybe a brother, cried after him, "Chim, Chim, wait for me."

The bigger boy stopped, turned, caught the little one up in his arms, swung him onto his shoulders. "Hold tight!" he said. "Don't want you to fall." Then off he trotted, the little one's legs wrapped around his arms, his small hands in his brother's afro. Their gales of laughter floated back to Dog Boy who shrugged himself further into his own shoulders, as if he might disappear there. Had he ever laughed that way? Maybe with his mother, once or twice, certainly never with his father. He pictured himself swinging a small child up on his shoulders, the weight of the child, the laughter. He imagined trotting along the park path, the wind blowing the scent of lilac and azalea, the smell sweet, not cloying. Both child and laughter were light in his reverie.

At that moment, Dog Boy had forgotten what his father looked like dipping his cap in the slaughtered boy's blood. How his face had changed into some sort of. . . creature. *An orc, maybe. Or a troll*, he'd thought at the time, pulling monsters from his reading. A smiling monster. But in the wake of the two laughing boys, he couldn't retain the horror of the child's blood. The memory of Chim and his brother—Dog Boy was suddenly sure it was a brother—that memory was even stronger than the memory of the dead child. He couldn't think why.

* * *

Once home, the image of the murdered boy returned to him, as well as the smell of it so he went immediately into the bathroom where he washed his face and hands obsessively for what seemed like hours though in fact it was just ten minutes. Then he took out the NettiPot his father made him use whenever they were about to go out on a practice run. The warm water through his nose and nasal passages flushed away the lingering blood scent and the last of the memory of the dead boy. He would remember the day as the one where he saw the black boys and their joy with one another.

When he joined his father in the living room, Red Cap was standing awkwardly, staring at the sofa where Dog Boy's mother sprawled. Neither one of them was moving.

Something in the room was strange. It smelled off. Muted. Cold.

Dog Boy ran over to the sofa and looked down at his mother's face. All the lines in it had been oddly smoothed out. She looked almost happy. She smelled. . . For a moment he had no name for it. And then he had it.

Peaceful.

Then realizing what that meant, he threw himself across her body and began to weep.

When the weeping was over and he had no more tears to cry, he picked her up in his arms as if she were a child, and the bottle of pills she'd been clutching in one hand shook loose.

He turned to look up at his father, to ask him what had happened. Why it had happened.

Red Cap was smiling. It was—Dog Boy thought—the same smile he'd stretched across his mouth when sopping up the murdered child's blood.

"Now I can take you to the Greenwood," Red Cap said. "Nothing holds you here any more."

Dog Boy opened his mouth. For a minute no sound came out. Finally, as if it was a truth that needed telling, he said quietly, "*She* holds me here."

"*She* is dead," Red Cap said as if the boy hadn't the sense to realize it on his own. "And not even blood for the dipping."

That was when Dog Boy first understood how much he hated his father. How much he hated being his father's dog. He set his mother's body down on the couch again, carefully, as if afraid he might bring her back from her final escape. Taking the small crocheted quilt that hung on the sofa's arm, he covered her with it. She looked tiny, small, and—suddenly—safe.

"I'm staying."

"You cannot."

Dog Boy made his hands into fists. More tears began to roll down his face. He expected to be beaten. It would not be the first time. Probably not the last. He was prepared for it.

What he was not prepared for, though, was his father reaching into a pocket and taking out the leash which Dog Boy hadn't seen in years. Quickly Red Cap bound him as easily and as tightly as he'd ever done when Dog Boy had been a child.

For the first time Dog Boy could actually feel the leash's power. Perhaps he felt it because he didn't want to go where it willed him, where his father willed him. Always before he'd been eager to go outside, to smell the city scents, to do what his father would have him do. When he'd been little, he thought that the leash was only to keep him safe. He'd been proud the day he was old enough to go outside with Red Cap leashless. He believed he and his father had forged a team; two hunters, leaning on one another. He had the nose, his father kept him safe. *Equals.* He'd reveled in that.

But now he understood the truth. The leash was not just a piece of leather to keep him from getting lost, to keep him out of harm's way. There was something else about it. Something that glimmered on the inside. Something fierce. Something old that he was powerless to resist.

Red Cap pulled on the leash and it drew Dog Boy relentlessly toward the door.

"I want my fiddle and pipe." His voice was high, but not pleading. He would not make his mother's mistake. Pleading just gave his father some kind of strange pleasure.

"You'll not need it where we're going."

"Where is that?"

"Under the Hill."

For a moment he thought his father meant *underground.* It was something he'd watched on a TV show: a family on the run from the mafia had to go underground to escape certain death. His father had killed someone, maybe the child of a mafia chieftain, maybe the child of a policeman. Or the FBI.

Underground. They'd be on the run. Together.

But then he remembered the smile, the dipped hat, the blood, the obvious pleasure that his father had taken in the stalking, the killing of an innocent child. And he remembered something else. His father—for all that he was a bloodthirsty, vicious murderer—never lied. They were going *Under the Hill*, whatever that meant.

Looking back at his mother's body on the sofa wrapped in the red and green coverlet, at the silver pipe on the table, at the fiddle in its case resting against the wall, Dog Boy told himself: *Some day I will kill him for this.* Once more the murdered boy was all but forgotten. By *this* he meant his mother's suicide.

When I am old enough and big enough and strong enough, he will pay for this. Then I will take the red cap and dip it in his *blood.*

He wondered if this was just a boy's wish or whether it was a promise.

"A pledge," he whispered.

Like his father, he did not lie.

New York Times *bestseller David Farland keeps busy. In addition to his bestselling Runelords series, Dave produces a daily newsletter on writing and acts as coordinating judge for the Writers of the Future contest. He has published more than fifty books that range from picture books to novels to anthologies. He holds the* Guinness Book of World Records *for the largest book signing. He's also won a lot of awards for his short fiction.*

About "Barbarians," he writes, "For several years, I have thought about writing a prequel to my bestselling Runelords fantasy series. I'm currently finishing the last book in the series, and so I thought I might write a little tale set a thousand years earlier than the current series. As I began it, this tale just came tumbling out pretty quickly. I guess that happens when you've thought about writing something for ten years."

Barbarians

David Farland

The smell of dust and guts and horseflesh told the tale: running steeds at dusk, a tight corner on a narrow mountain road, a carriage rolling over the cliff.

Dval stepped to the margin of the rutted dirt road and stood beneath a sprawling live oak. In the gloaming darkness he spotted wreckage a hundred yards downslope: a fine black carriage rested on its side without a door, so that it opened like the nest of a weaver bird. The carriage was of barbaric make—Mystarrian. They were a clever people, but did not understand the ways of true humans.

Instantly Dval crouched low, lest any survivors spot him, and pulled his dagger from its hip sheath. The handle of his obsidian blade felt good in his hand.

Near the carriage, trunks had tumbled open, spilling dresses and undergarments, while a pair of mangled horses lay broken

229

over boulders. One animal struggled to breathe, while the other had given up the fight.

The driver had been thrown far downhill and lay wrapped around a tree, preternaturally still. Dval wondered what treasure they might have left behind. He knew that he should run and tell his uncle what had happened. His uncle was the leader of their tribe.

But the lure of treasure called. Dval bounded down the hillside, his leather moccasins whispering through dry grasses. The only sounds were the songs of cicadas among the scrub oak, and the distant screech of a burrow owl. Overhead, stars glimmered dully in a smoke-filled sky.

The smell of smoke worried him.

On the plains in the distance, crimson flames burned in a crescent, as if Fire itself had shaped a scythe to harvest the fields to the Mystarrians. Winds from the sea swept the scythe steadily westward.

The sight of flames filled Dval with foreboding. He had not yet heard of the "grey fleet" that had been sighted near the Courts of Tide. He had not heard of the inhuman "toth" and their strange ways. Yet all the events that would shape his destiny had been set in motion.

When he reached the wagon, Dval checked on the live horse; its cavernous breaths thundered in and out. Its back was broken, and it could barely lift its head, but it smelled him and stirred, a whinny that was part scream, then turned enough to see him. Dval rested one hand on the horse's chest, to calm the poor creature. As its breathing eased, he peered about.

Dval studied the fine carriage—black lacquered wood without any markings. He found a door on the ground. Silver inlay in the black lacquer outlined a man's face with a beard and hair made of oak leaves. He recognized instantly the symbol of Mystarria.

He found a guardsman near the wreck—a young knight in fishmail and helm. The fine steel would be worth a fortune, he knew, and the soldier wore a gold ring. Dval worked the ring free from the man's fingers, put it on.

Farther downhill lay another woman, a young matron, with glazed eyes peering up into the stars, as if to ponder eternity.

Dval smiled. *Keep pondering, woman.*

The wounded horse cried. Dval loved horses, so he drew the knight's bastard sword from its sheath. The blade was made of strange metal—a dull silver, neither northern steel nor brass. It was extraordinarily light. Runes inlaid along its length were like nothing made by men. The strange geometric shapes gleamed like silver fire in the starlight. This was a duskin blade, at least four thousand years old. He tested the blade's edge with a thumb. It pricked like a wasp sting. Blood throbbed out.

Dval wondered where the blade had come from. Duskin blades were usually found at least a mile underground, in ancient tunnels.

He addressed the dead knight. "You're a lucky man to have such a fine blade." Then he saw how the man's tongue hung out between his teeth. "Well, not *that* lucky."

He strode to the horse, plunged the blade in its neck.

The horse lay down its head wearily, as if in relief, and the scent of copper filled the woods as it bled out.

He imagined its spirit galloping away in fields of dreams.

Hoping for more treasure, Dval went to the overturned carriage, climbed the axletree, and peered inside.

At the bottom lay a girl, cradling an injured arm. She looked up and gasped. Deep-red hair framed a heart-shaped face, cheeks stained with tears. Like some northerners of legend, she had brown speckles on her face. He'd never seen freckles before. Her large green eyes engulfed him, pupils wide and black, filled with terror. She was a daylighter—one who could not see in the dark. She could not have been more than nine, two years his junior, perhaps three. Her left leg lay askew, badly bruised, possibly broken.

"Weir bisth dua?" she asked, trembling. Dval did not speak the uncouth tongue of Mystarria, but guessed at the question.

"Dval," he said, pointing at his chest.

She tried to repeat it, using one of her own words. "Val?" Close enough. He nodded.

She pointed to her own chest: "Avahn."

If I crush her skull, he realized, *they will think she died in the wreck. I can take their treasure. . . .*

He peered around for witnesses. Everyone else from the wreck seemed to be dead. He did not see any reason why she shouldn't die, too. Their people had been at war since before either of them had been born.

But he felt guilty. He was in their territory. One of his uncle's blood mares had been high on the mountain slopes, grazing in the lush alpine grass, but had "wandered" down into the hills, as they did to give birth.

When he'd told his uncle that the horse was gone, he'd said. "Are we not poor enough? Go find the mare, you fool." Always that sneer in his voice.

Dval hadn't expected the horse to wander far from camp, but moccasin prints suggested that his cousin had actually driven the mare away as a prank.

He was trespassing in this land; the penalty for getting caught was death.

A cool wind blew down from the icecaps above, whispering over him, raising goose pimples on his arms.

A mournful howl arose from the woods downhill—a low moaning sound that ululated, then tapered off. It was the hunting cry of a dire wolf. The wolves in the Alcair Mountains were as large as ponies, each weighing as much as three hundred pounds.

In winter they followed herds of shaggy elephants that roamed the Kakolar Plains, but in the summers they often foraged into the hills to hunt for elk.

Sometimes their cries were filled only with ravening hunger, but this wolf was telling others that it tasted the scent of blood.

Dval crouched, frozen in indecision. If he left the girl and kept searching for his uncle's lost blood mount, the wolves would finish her. He could simply come back and plunder the wreck later.

A deep growl sounded nearby in the oak forest, not more than a hundred yards away. There was no time to climb a tree.

Dval scrambled for safety into the carriage. The girl shrieked and shrank away. He was Inkarran after all, with skin and hair whiter than ice, and green-white eyes that could see in the night.

He knew few words in her tongue. "Gud," he said, pointing at himself. "I gud."

She nodded, and tried to rise, but startled at a low growl outside.

They froze, trapped inside the carriage, while wolves began racing outside, panting, heavy paws mincing dry grass. A wolf howled, high and eager, inviting others to the feast.

Dval raised a finger to his lips, begging the girl to keep silent. She nodded, then gently lay back down on the floor. Though she stiffened when her arm moved, she did not cry out.

There was only one entrance into the carriage—the broken door above. Dval stood with sword raised upward, prepared to thrust.

For long minutes dire wolves growled and ripped at the dead outside, sometimes snarling at one another. He could hear padded feet circling the carriage. Dozens of them.

Let there be enough to feed them all, Dval silently prayed to his ancestors.

He gripped the hilt of the unfamiliar sword so tightly that it felt as if his muscles melded with it. Long after he ached with fatigue, he stood peering up.

To relax vigilance is to die, he heard his uncle's warning.

The girl hardly breathed.

Suddenly heavy paws scrabbled against the frame of the carriage above, and Dval was unprepared for the wolf that leapt through—a large black one, with grizzled hair turned to mist by starlight.

Dval stabbed upward blindly.

The girl shrieked. The dire wolf yelped in pain, scrabbled backward, and blood rained down. The girl kept screaming.

Did I kill it? he wondered. But the blow had not been deep. The beast would probably only be wounded.

An injured dire wolf will attack again, he knew, if only to prove its fierceness.

Outside, other wolves growled and yipped excitedly. Some sniffed at the carriage while others raced around it.

A second wolf put its paws up on the carriage and whined, sniffing at the opening. Dval jumped and stabbed hard, taking it beneath the throat. It leapt away.

Wolves danced about the carriage and snarled in a frenzy. The girl shrieked some more.

"Shut up!" he shouted. "Fear draws them!" But the girl did not understand.

He slapped her face, shocking her into silence. "A rabbit screams like that when it wants to die." He explained, but she did not know the ways of the forest.

Sometimes, when one faces a bear, the best thing to do is to sing. It confuses the animal and shows that one is not afraid. So Dval shoved the girl and sang now, an old battle dirge.

> *"I was born to blood and war,*
> *Like my fathers were a thousand years before.*
> *Sound the horn. Strike a blow.*
> *Down to death or glory go!"*

Wolves whimpered. One barked at the carriage.

Faster than a serpent, a wolf leapt up into the doorframe. Dval lunged with his blade; the wolf bit it. Blood spattered, but the blade twisted in Dval's hand. He lunged, struck the wolf's shoulder, but the beast growled and snapped. Fangs sank into Dval's shoulder, close to the neck, crushing more than piercing.

Dval shoved the blade up with all his might, driving the creature away. His vision blanked; he stood blinking, blood in his eyes.

At his side, the little girl began to sing in her own crude tongue. Her voice caught with fear at first. It was not a battle song, but a lullaby, such as a mother might sing to a child to frighten away imaginary wights, and as she sang, her voice grew in strength.

Sometimes, a song does not just show courage, it lends it, Dval realized.

He wiped spatter from his eyes. His shoulder was running thick with blood. He feared that it would only attract wolves, or that he would pass out.

The girl continued to sing, and struggled to her feet. She put her right hand around his, as if to hold hands.

In his land, when a woman took a man's hand, it was a proposal of marriage. Was it the same among her people?

They were both too young, only children.

There was terror in her eyes still, and fierce intelligence. Her lower jaw quivered with determination.

She only seeks comfort, he thought.

She pulled up her skirt, drew an ornate dagger, its silver hilt crusted in gems. It was a pretty weapon, such as a wealthy merchant might carry. She peered up at the roof, as if to do battle.

* * *

Avahn waited for the wolves and wondered at her situation.

On sighting the gray fleet, her father had sent Avahn and her mother to safety in the mountains. But safety is an illusion.

Avahn's mother had been thrown out the door during the wreck, and the silence of the woods spoke eloquently of her fate. Avahn didn't want to look outside, see the inevitable. Avahn's grief was a tremendous weight.

She didn't know where she was, how to get home.

She wished that she were a runelord, that she had an endowment of strength. Her father had suggested that she get one.

Avahn knew little about wolves. The Wizard Goren said that a dire wolf is not afraid of a man. A lone man makes good prey. But he'd once said, "The smell of metal frightens them, especially if more than one man is near."

Avahn and the boy were vastly outnumbered, but she determined to show no fear, even though her heart pounded as if it might break. Perhaps someday, if she grew to become a powerful runelord, she wouldn't be so swayed by fear. Today was not that day.

The boy was bleeding badly. She knew that he might not be able to protect her much longer. There was nowhere for her to hide in the carriage.

She studied him. Dval was not huge. Like most Inkarrans, he was lanky and pale in the starlight. Only his calves were dark, for they had been tattooed with a tree, one that bore totems giving the names of his ancestors. He wore little besides his moccasins—a summer kilt, a necklace of wood beads, earrings made of dyed cotton.

Another wolf leapt up on the carriage and peered in; Dval lunged, but it leapt away so fast, it seemed a creature of mist and dreams.

Once, from her mother's castle at Coorm, Avahn had watched a silver fox out in a field on a green morning. There were mice in the field, and the fox danced about tufts of dry grass. Any mouse that stuck its head outside its burrow risked getting eaten.

Their only hope was to stay inside. She thought about the Master of the Hounds, Sir Gwilliam. When given a new litter of wolfhound pups, he'd spanked the largest and explained, "Every pack of dogs has a leader. To control the pack, you must control their leader."

She tried to warn the boy: "Val, we must kill their leader." She jutted her chin up toward the opening. He shook his head, not understanding.

We only have to make it until morning, she thought. *My father will send soldiers to look for us.*

But no one at Castle Coorm knew she was on her way.

Her right arm and leg were so badly bruised, they were nearly worthless. She did the only thing she could. She sang.

* * *

Five more times that night, wolves attacked, and Dval managed to strike deeply and drive them away, but with each hour his strength waned, and Avahn didn't know how long he could continue.

Near dawn a crescent moon climbed overhead, spilling silver light down so that it glistened like a spiderweb.

Avahn worried. The grey ships had come, and she'd seen fires in the valley shortly before dark. She did not know who set them.

All that she could do was keep singing.

When the sky began to brighten and the smell of morning dew filled the air, the leader of the pack came. It was a great wolf, larger than the others. It lunged through the doorframe without preamble, snarling and snapping. So quick was the attack that Dval struggled to repel it, thrusting his blade awkwardly.

Avahn was thrown backward, and the wolf made it halfway into the carriage, shoving Dval to the ground. It focused on the boy, bit him on the head.

Without thought, Avahn lurched forward and plunged her blade deep into the wolf's neck. Its fur was so thick, she wasn't sure how deep the wound was, but hot blood spurted from a vein at its throat, and the wolf yelped and snapped at her, and Dval scrambled away.

The wolf's strength was so great, it whipped its head sideways to bite her and slammed her into the wall of the carriage. She heard wooden struts crack from the impact, even as her ears began to ring.

Unconsciousness came so swiftly and completely, it was like falling into a deep dark bottomless pool. She struggled to remain conscious, but struggling was no use.

* * *

Dval stabbed at the monster wolf, though he was crushed against the floor. The light blade flickered up, and entered the beast's torso as cleanly as if it were a sheath.

The wolf growled and twisted its head away from Avahn, and he struck thrice more, slashing now.

The wolf growled and backed away, leaving the entrance open to the starlight.

Outside, the creature jumped about and growled ferociously, like a hart struck by an arrow.

Other wolves yapped at it, and Dval waited for it to come back, for a wounded wolf was more dangerous than a bear.

But it raced about erratically, then gave a lonely howl just outside the carriage, a howl that made the wood paneling shiver. The beast couldn't have been ten feet away. Dval could hear it panting louder and louder, as if it were growing more fatigued by the moment.

Dval's head was bleeding now, along with his shoulder, and he could hardly stand, but he remained on his feet, fixed his eyes on the opening overhead.

The pack leader is dying, he thought. But that seemed too . . . hopeful.

He waited for it to leap into the carriage again, but instead heard it get up, panting heavily, and wander toward the woods.

For many long minutes Dval stood waiting.

He felt he could stand no longer and began to float in and out of consciousness.

If they come for me, he thought, *I will be standing still.*

So he held his striking pose, as morning came. Nuthatches chirruped outside in the forest, and mourning doves called. Flies began to buzz inside the carriage, spinning, spinning, in lazy circles, and Dval's head spun with them.

He waited, a monument.

I am stone. He told himself. *I am stone.*

* * *

The final attack came in the later morning. Dval must have fallen asleep on his feet. He wasn't aware of a scuffle on the carriage or even a shadow filling the opening above him. All he felt was a tug as he was jerked from the carriage by his topknot.

He swatted with his sword in vain. A giant had grabbed him, and now held him dangling with one hand, while he wrested the sword away with the other. . . .

* * *

The giant hurled Dval to the ground. He rolled and struggled to rise, but the giant slammed one huge foot onto him, pinning Dval. "Stinkende theif!" the creature boomed in a voice more guttural than a bull's.

It was a hill giant, nearly nine feet tall, from the land of Toom. He had to weigh a thousand pounds, and no matter how Dval squirmed, he could not wrest free. Dval squinted up into the impossible sunlight. The giant's hair was as blue-black as ink, and he wore rat skulls braided into his bushy beard. He stank of rum and sweat and unnamable nastiness.

Dval would rather have faced more wolves. He closed his eyes, blinded by the sun. Other Mystarrians surrounded him, men with drawn swords, and runes of brawn and grace branded onto their necks. Dval smelled of woods and crisp mountain air. These men stank of ale and grease and cities.

Some shouted at him, and one ripped the stolen ring from Dval's finger while another man, with tears in his eyes, salvaged the damaged sword, taking the relic in both hands.

Dval did not understand all of the accusations leveled against him, but one man drew his sword and strode forward, intent on taking Dval's head.

Dval gritted his teeth and bared his neck. He stared into his executioner's eyes as befitted a man who was no coward. The soldier raised his tall sword high, brought the blade down.

"Stobben!" the girl shouted.

The sword veered and bit into the ground near Dval's head.

Dval looked up in time to see a knight in fishmail help the girl come limping from the carriage, while six others circled him, eager for the kill. They forced Dval to sit on the ground in the sunlight, where his skin would burn and his eyes could not see.

They pulled the bodies of the wolves that he'd slain together, and laid them side-by-side. The pelt of a dire wolf was valuable. Few men had ever killed five at a time.

* * *

Avahn found her mother's body downhill. Wolves had mauled it and pulled it into the shadows under the oaks. Only a bit of blue dress identified the corpse.

One of her father's soldiers covered it with a forest green cloak and tried to pull Avahn away, but she stayed rooted, let the tears flow long and hard while flies buzzed about.

The soldiers kept the Inkarran boy on his knees, in the sun. In the bright light, she could see his hair like braided silver, running down his neck. The wool earrings were as crimson as blood. Many bites and scratches marred his smooth skin.

She begged them to let him go, but Captain Adelheim said, "He's more than Inkarran. He's Woguld. They're all under a death sentence. Only your father can stay the boy's execution."

"He saved my life," she said.

"He was robbing corpses, and he would have killed you," Captain Adelheim said.

"But he didn't," she said vehemently.

Just then, one of Adelheim's men kicked the boy, knocking him over, and others jeered.

Avahn stared hard at Captain Adelheim. He was a fair man, with a red beard and piercing blue eyes. His frame and features were flawless. Silently she begged for compassion, but he just shrugged. Avahn whirled and slugged Dval's attacker in the gut.

The soldiers all roared in laughter. "Careful there, Pwyrthen, or the princess might drop her aim a bit."

The soldiers backed away then, leaving the boy to gasp on the ground, like a landed trout.

Avahn got one of her mother's riding cloaks and put it over him, then settled next to him, prepared to beg her father for the boy's life. She feared that it was in vain. For two hundred years they'd fought the Woguld.

She asked Captain Adelheim, "Did you see the men from the gray ships?"

"It wasn't men on those ships," Captain Adelheim said. "They were creatures with black exoskeletons, like reavers, and philia hanging like worms off of their head plates. Where they came from, we are not sure. But we think we know. Your father went searching for new territories. Now, we've been discovered. . . ."

Legend had said that there was a land far across the Carrol Sea, a vast continent where no man had set foot and returned. Three years back, her father had sent an expedition to that land, hoping to learn if men lived there. The expedition had never returned.

"So they landed? They set the fires?"

"Their ships never beached," Captain Adelheim said. "The creatures just stepped off them, into the water, and walked on the bottom of the sea until they reached the shore. Yes, they set fires. But none of them will ever return home." He paused. "We call them *toths*."

"Toths," Avahn repeated. *Fangs.*

Avahn had never seen a reaver, only their skulls. She could not imagine what a toth might look like.

There is a moment in every person's life where they recognize that they are going to have to survive through hard times. The night fighting wolves had seemed terrible, but Avahn knew in some deep part of her, that it was only the beginning.

* * *

At midday, the King of Mystarrians came—a plump man with sandy brown hair and a dark crown carved from oak, and robes of royal blue. He rode in with thirty men, circled Dval, studied him.

In the hills above them, Dval heard a woodpecker tapping. Peck peck. Peck, peck, peck, peck.

It was Woguld warrior speak, made by tapping sandstone against a tree. "We are here."

The king and his men did not seem to notice.

Instead, the Mystarrians argued.

* * *

King Harrill was filled with grief at the death of his wife, and he strode over the field of wreckage like an angry badger, like a storm in the brewing. His eyes were bloodshot and glazed from lack of sleep. He'd been fighting all night, and now he paced restlessly, moving one direction first, changing in an instant. Until that day, he had been called Harrill the Cunning, but many argue that on that day he became Harrill the Mad.

For a long time, he knelt above the body of his dead wife, silently grieving. Everyone fell silent, showing quiet respect.

Suddenly a growl sounded. Avahn whirled. The huge leader of the pack stood at the edge of the forest, beneath an oak, drenched in blood, crimson flowing over black fur. It lowered its head, peered at the king from yellow eyes, and snarled. It was making its last stand. By instinct, every man froze in fear.

It gathered its strength and lunged across the clearing, leapt, its fangs seeking her father's throat.

A lesser man would have cried out or fled in terror, but her father was a runelord, with runes of brawn and grace branded upon his neck. He merely leaned away from the attack, and brought up a mailed fist.

His blow sounded like a crack of lighting. It split hide and shattered bones, sent wolf teeth and blood flying in the air. The blow sounded like finality.

He stood, glaring down at the body of the wolf for a long minute, gasping, as the wolf's legs shivered and spasmed.

Finally he growled and whirled on Dval. "Why is that . . . creature still alive?" he shouted to his men.

"He saved my life," Avahn answered softly.

"More than likely," her father argued, "he's the one who caused the wreck. They do it all the time, spook our horses at sunset, steal our crops in the night, murder travelers in their sleep. They're barbarians, not even human."

He went to Dval, pulled his own battle axe, and raised it high.

The boy, dazed and forlorn, did not cry out in fear. Instead, he spit at the king's feet.

"No," Avahn called out to Dval, for she knew better than to test her father's wrath. The boy raised his chin and offered his neck, glaring.

"Oh, this one has spirit," the king mocked. "I like him, but I'm still going to kill him."

Avahn shouted at her father, "Da, I *trust* him. We can trust him."

"He's a barbarian," her father argued. He prepared to take the killing blow.

She stepped in front of the boy. "You train your knights for years, never knowing if their hearts will remain true in the depths of battle. This boy's heart is true."

The king jutted his chin toward her, and the giant Sir Bandolan grabbed Avahn's shoulder, pulled her out of the way.

In the moment, the world went quiet. King Harrill strained. Up in the forest above, a woodpecker pecked, and in the distance a squirrel called from an oak tree.

"Hear that?" the king asked his men. His eyes danced left and right, as if he were thinking faster than a water strider could dance above a pool. He whirled and looked uphill, to where green oaks spread over the dead grasses, casting deep shadows.

He shouted, "Come on, you bastards! I hear you up there. May you all taste my wrath this day!"

There was no answer from the silent woods for a long moment.

Suddenly a single archer stepped out from behind a tree. As a warlord of the Woguld, he wore a crimson breechcloth. A white silk cape flowed over his shoulders like a waterfall. A sunmask adorned his face, a silver imale like an elk with broad antlers, with black-glass covered eyes to guard against bright light. The blue tattoos of his family tree wound around his calves, naming his ancestors and their deeds. He was glorious to look upon, regal and perfect.

He stood with his great bow, its wings flaring wide, and nocked an arrow.

The king laughed and rubbed forefinger against thumb, the sign for "trade." He pointed to Dval.

Avahn did not know whether her father was offering to buy the boy, or to spare his life for a price.

* * *

To Dval, it was the worst of insults. The folk of the Woguld did not trade in slaves. Every man served his clan. The warlord up above them was his uncle, and Dval felt certain that his uncle would order his men to waylay these foreigners.

Instead, his uncle drew the bow and fired.

The arrow sped toward them, and Dval thought, "He plans to kill their king!"

Yet even as the thought came, he realized that the arrow was winging toward him.

A flash to his side, a heavy thud—and Dval went flying from harm's way, his face skidding into the leaves. The girl Avahn had shoved him, thrown him to the ground as the arrow whistled past. Avahn lay beside him, groaning in pain. Dval saw red on her bicep, and realized that she hurt from more than bruises. The arrow had kissed her.

Dval's uncle called out, "What kind of fool are you? Do we not have enough enemies? You must save one?" Always that tone. "The friend of my enemy," the uncle said, "*is* my enemy!"

His uncle spat, turned, and strode into the shadows under the trees.

For a second, Dval knew the sorrow of one who has been dispossessed.

Dval watched his uncle, and did not know who was more a barbarian—his uncle, the northerners around him, or Dval himself.

Perhaps we are all barbarians, Dval thought, *struggling to be human.*

Only one person here seemed truly human—the child Avahn.

After that, no one threatened to kill Dval. Apparently now that he was cast out from the Woguld, his death sentence was rescinded. By trying to kill him, his uncle had saved his life.

Avahn took Dval's hand. Together they rode down to the sprawling cities of Mystarria, to her home at the Courts of Tide, where the war fires of the Toth still burned.

Acknowledgements

This project wouldn't have gotten off the ground without the Kickstarter support from these wonderful people:

Karen Abrahamson	John Haines	Jeff Rutherford
Gerard M. Ackerman	Mark-Wayne Harris	Jeanette Sanders
Claire Alcock	Joel Horton	David Schibi
Susan Allen	Julie Hyzy	Ken Schneyer
JC Andrijeski	Jim Johnson	Risa Scranton
Michael Bellomo	Jane Kennedy	Janna Silverstein
Donald J. Bingle	Malachi Kenney	Kristine Smith
Robin Brande	Pierre L'Allier	Bob Sojka
Kirsten Brodbeck-Kenney	Rich Laux	Margaret St. John
AnneMarie Buhl	Stephen Lebans	Christopher Stout
Tom Carpenter	Christel Adina Loar	Robert E. Stutts
Brenda Cooper	John Lorentz	Lisa Sullivan
T. Thorn Coyle	Michael Lucas	Raphael Sutton
Leah Cutter	Big Ed Magusson	Randy Tatano
Ron Dionne	Lisa M. May	Melissa Taylor
Louis Doggett	Robert J. McCarter	Scott Tefoe
Marcelle Dubé	Sean Monaghan	Edd Vick
Eric Edstrom	Patricia Nagle	Ray Vukcevich
Lynda Foley	Carole Nelson Douglas	Leslie Walker
Karen Fonville	Shyam Nunley	Terry Weyna
Robbyn Foster	Alexei Pawlowski	Sarah Woodbury
Annaliese Furnas	Steve Perry	Stephanie Writt

Thank you!

FICTION RIVER: YEAR ONE